Praise for GOD'S DAUGHTER

"Vivid, powerful...triumphan
heart."
 ~ **Joanne Bischof**, award-winnin
series

"God's Daughter offers a brave, fresh look at a lost way of life
and the Vikings who left an indelible mark in history.
Author Heather Gilbert weaves a riveting novel with
unforgettable characters and circumstances, the first
installment in a series sure to resonate with historical fans.
The stunning cover is only the beginning!"
 ~ **Laura Frantz**, Christy finalist and author of *Love's Reckoning*

"As a lover of Vikings, I was hooked from the start, but what
drives this story is Gilbert's ability to somehow eliminate the
thousand years between the Viking age and modern day,
reminding us that our thoughts, our feelings, our struggles,
our goals are not dissimilar from what they were so long
ago. I identified with Gudrid every step of the way, and as I
learned about her story (both what was and what could have
been), I also learned about myself."
 ~ **Amanda Luedeke**, Literary Agent and author of *The Extroverted
Writer*

"Opening with the chaos of a pagan sacrifice, *God's Daughter*
will sweep you up into the intriguing world of the Vikings, a
people who lived with the same kind of passion and courage
and yearning that we do today. Heather Day Gilbert's voice
comes out raw and haunting through Gudrid, a real woman
struggling with real issues, in a time when survival meant
strapping your dagger to your thigh rather than wearing
your heart on your sleeve. A gorgeous novel about a
fascinating time in history."
 ~ **Becky Doughty**, author of *Elderberry Croft*

"A gripping and unique insight into the life and emotional turmoil of a Viking woman at the cusp of their adoption of Christianity."
~ **Graeme Ing**, author of *Ocean of Dust*

"*God's Daughter* by Heather Day Gilbert is a stirring tenth century saga of early Christianity, and one Viking woman's heroic struggle to sustain her faith and her marriage amidst a dangerous voyage to North America. Heather Day Gilbert's voice is strong and certain, her story world breathtakingly vivid, the character of Gudrid one I will never forget."
~ **Lori Benton**, author of *Burning Sky*

"Powerful. Moving. Gritty. *God's Daughter* is an action-packed adventure laden with Biblical truths. A hearty Viking war cry to author Heather Day Gilbert for penning a hard-hitting debut novel."
~ **Michelle Griep**, author of *A Heart Deceived* and *Undercurrent*

"*God's Daughter* was a fascinating read, with strong characters, complex relationships and a good dose of adventure. Most of all, I loved the intriguing glimpse into Viking history."
~ **Rachel Phifer**, author of *The Language of Sparrows*

GOD'S DAUGHTER

HEATHER DAY GILBERT

God's Daughter
By Heather Day Gilbert

Copyright 2013 Heather Day Gilbert

ISBN-13:978-1492880417
ISBN-10:1492880418

Cover Design & Illustrations by Jon Day

Published by Heather Day Gilbert

Author Information: http://www.heatherdaygilbert.com

To my husband David. Like Gudrid, I'd travel with you anywhere.

And to my three children, who prayed every day for many years

that Momma would get her book published. And to any who share

Viking blood—long may that indomitable spirit live.

"Gudrid was a woman of striking appearance and wise as well, who knew how to behave among strangers."

–*The Saga of the Greenlanders*

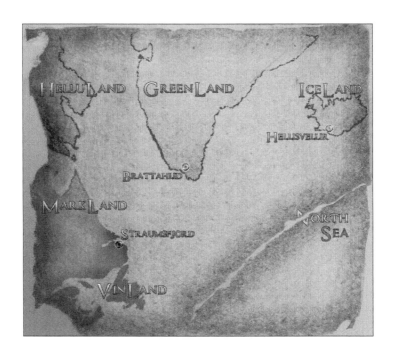

Prologue

Hellisvellir, Iceland

The gods only accept what is valuable.

Gudrid repeated this to herself as they hoisted her mother into the tree. Her beautiful mother with the long shining hair, like her own.

Her cousin, Yngvild, touched her hand. Not a word was spoken, from anyone. No one could believe a young mother would die for the required nine-year sacrifice, along with the expected slaves and animals. But the chieftain had ordered it. And the chieftain was her father.

Gudrid's aunt hunched over, sobbing into her sleeves. Uncle Thorgeir did not even look at the tree. He seemed happy to gain more control of her mother's family farm.

Gudrid clenched her fists on her shift, bunching it so tightly she felt she could rip it apart. She longed to fight the men who would drop the ladder, breaking her mother's neck. But interrupting a sacrifice to Thor was punishable by death—the immediate death of hanging.

The sprawling, twisted tree loomed like a giant against the gray Icelandic sky, its limbs clutching at the dangling dead animals and people. Gudrid imagined the tree held them back from dropping straight into Helheim. Truly, Mother should go straight to Valhalla for being a willing sacrifice. But only the men who died bravely in battle got to go there, to drink endless mead for eternity.

Her father blew the ram's horn, and a slave kicked the ladder out. For one second, Father's eyes glazed over, as if he was far away. Even though he was devoted to Mother, he believed the only way to restore the bounty of the farm, failing since he had charge of it, was to give up the one thing he really cared about.

Mother's face went slack and lost color. Gudrid was strangely thankful that she did not turn blue, with her eyes bulging, as some of the slaves had. It meant she died quickly, as a perfect sacrifice should.

Gudrid looked around, aware she needed a protector. Even at eleven years old, she understood this. Father had never wanted a girl. Her aunt was too grief-stricken—she would barely be able to care for her own children now, after watching her sister die.

Orm's sad gaze met her own. He was a neighbor from a nearby farm, on a cliff overlooking the shoreline. His wife, Halldis, was a *volva*, a seeress who knew magic. Gudrid refused to look at her. She did not want to see the eyes of the woman who had told Father he needed such a significant sacrifice this year.

The last body was hanged, and another volva led a chant with the drum. Since many slaves had been killed, their families began to sing quietly in their own languages.

As the words clashed, each group sang louder and louder. It was the only time they sang publicly.

Gudrid felt her insides burning, down to the core, like the volcanoes on this island. Anger and loneliness forced her from her seat. She hated Thor and anything to do with him. She groped for her knife before raising it to her throat. Then she charged straight for her father.

PART ONE

Straumsfjord
(upper North America)
Circa AD1000

Chapter One

Some bulls are just better off dead.

The beast huffs on the other side of the wooden fence. The fence has no permanence, like the rest of the makeshift houses in this camp at Straumsfjord. A stopping place, Finn said, just a place to live until we can search for Vinland. And now we have been here over two years. I hate this empty land as much as I hate this bull.

I grip my *seax*, its long blade tight against my thigh, and walk toward the bull. Deadly as my knife is, I would be lucky to sink it into the bull's side without being gored or trampled first.

"Get on with you." Usually my low-toned warning works, at least with the smaller bulls my father gave me. But this bull, his reddish hair dropping out in patches, his horns far too long, paws the ground and bellows.

I hold his gaze, stepping backward on the soft grass. We have two pastures here, and one is far too small. The four cows who survived the winter are crowded into the larger pasture, giving this bull his fill of summer grass in his own pen. Even so, he causes no end of trouble when he can't be with the cows to breed them.

"Don't move, Gudrid!" Freydis shouts from a tree on the other side of the fence, her red hair gleaming in the afternoon light.

Freydis acts more like a brother than a sister—always prying into my love life, practicing with knives, and climbing up trees. She knows no better, since her father, Eirik the Red, trained her with swords and bows from the time she could carry them. She's the only family I have here. Her brother, Thorstein the Red, was my second husband for such a short time. Yet even after his death, I remain part of Eirik's family.

What does Freydis have in mind? If I stand still, the bull might charge me. But I won't let her risk her own life for mine. She is with child, even though she forgets that fact most of the time.

Surely someone in the longhouse at the foot of the hill can hear this bellowing. Surely someone other than my overly confident sister-in-law will protect me.

The bull plods to the fence and rubs his head on it. Maybe he just needs to scratch. But the top board breaks as he pushes heavily against it.

Freydis inches down the tree, her pale legs sticking out beneath her skirts.

The bull charges. Turf rips and boards splinter close behind me. He's out of the fence. Freydis gives a distracting warrior shout as I race toward the closest maple and scramble up.

I catch my breath, hanging onto a limb. Freydis stands in the middle of the pasture, her bow drawn and ready. The arrow she releases penetrates the bull's rump. Our men finally approach from the bottom of the hill, axes and swords drawn.

Before anyone can move, the bull turns on Freydis. He struggles to gain speed, trying to run up the hill. Blood trickles out of the wound, but not enough to kill him. Freydis turns and runs, fast as any wild animal, toward the other side of the fence. She climbs toward her previous tree perch just as the bull collapses, sides heaving, in the middle of the grass.

Before the men reach the bull, Snorri Thorbrandsson positions himself beneath my tree. The man has an uncanny sense of where I am at all times. I tell myself this is only because he's my husband's trading partner, and not for a more personal reason. But it's hard to forget he once asked me to marry him.

He extends his arms, waiting for me to drop into them. Instead, I scoot down the tree, pinning down my rough linen skirts with my hands.

I could have died today in this foreign land, with practically no family to mourn me. Here, it makes no difference that I'm a chieftain's daughter. Here, I bring water to angry bulls, grind barley, and do countless other slaves' chores, making myself and everyone around me uncomfortable. For it is necessity, not loss of position, that has forced this work on me.

Perhaps sensing my dark thoughts, Snorri nods without a word, then walks over to help the men repair the fence. Someone pulled the arrow out of the bull, and though it's still panting and sweating, it's grounded for now. I'm glad Freydis didn't kill it, so the cows can keep calving and we'll continue to have milk. But I won't be the one to feed it again.

Freydis, short husband by her side, makes her way to me. Though he has a name, most of us call him "Freydis' husband," for he lives in her shadow. She tosses her red curls, proud of herself.

"Did you see that shot?"

I throw my arms around her to stop her bragging. "You foolish, foolish girl, what were you thinking?"

Her blue cat's eyes regard me slyly, as if I should know. "I told Leif I'd look after you over here."

"He wouldn't want you to do it at the expense of your own life!"

"Well, my fair Gudrid, wouldn't you be shocked to know what my brother would want me to do?" She glances at her silent husband. "Go, be of some use in this camp, Ref."

Her mention of Leif brings a picture to my mind—Leif, his soft beard the color of chicks, telling outlandish stories just to make me laugh. Leif, begging me earnestly not to leave his farm at Brattahlid to sail here. I didn't listen. And though I traveled across the ocean so Finn and I could be closer, it's still Leif I dream of every night.

Finn and I married two winters ago in Greenland, when I was only twenty-two but already twice widowed. He planned to sail for Vinland, legendary land of grapes, wood, and self-sown wheat, to seal his fame as a trader. Leif encouraged this, thinking Finn would leave me behind. But I was with child and didn't want to be alone again. So with a crew of nearly a hundred men and three of Leif's ships, we left Greenland, our baby boy coming soon after we set up camp at Straumsfjord.

"I'm not ready to die yet, you know." Freydis breaks my thoughts as she hitches her bow over her shoulder. "And the gods know it."

"But only one God controls these things, Freydis—the Christian God. Who knew the bull would charge the fence today?"

Freydis snorts. "Same as Thor, your God kills whoever he wants to. He's no different, really."

Sometimes I wonder at the depth of my love for this wild girl, so determined to fight with everyone she knows. Usually, I don't give her the satisfaction of seeing my anger. But, as the bull starts bellowing again, everything I've seen today builds in me, until my very arms shake.

"I served Thor for years, Freydis. I saw how he warps the mind, bringing nothing but death to women and babies alike. Death is nectar to Thor. The Christian God takes no delight in death, even of the wicked."

"Well, I won't serve either one; I don't care what you say." Freydis kicks a torn clod of turf at my leg.

A rough shout fills the air. "Go bother someone your own size, Freydis, like your scrawny husband." Hallstein lumbers up the hill, almost like a bull himself. The swarthy old man is a never-ending curse on this camp. He tries to win my favor now by interfering with Freydis. But I only despise him more for it.

"I told your husband I'd make sure you were safe." Hallstein's eyes rove over my body. "We wouldn't want that vexing bull of yours to hurt you, now would we?"

"Leave us, Hallstein," I say. I doubt Finn instructed this rogue to check on me.

His dark face wrinkles and his jaw tightens: he has no choice but to obey. Not only am I wife of the expedition leader, Thorfinn Karlsefni, but I am ward of Leif Eiriksson, his chieftain.

He mutters all the way back down the hill, his solid form finally vanishing into the longhouse.

"If he had just died on his last trip to Vinland, I wouldn't have to kill him over here." Freydis blows a curl off her face and shoots me her winning half-smile. Freydis came here to take lives—to avenge her older brother, Thorvald, who was killed in this land by a native arrow. But, like the goddess she was named for, she shows no discretion in her killing. She hates Hallstein, because he shows her no respect.

I will ignore her today. But I know the day will come when I can ignore both Freydis and Hallstein no longer.

Chapter Two

Mornings bring bands of color I've never seen before, with reds as vivid as the rooster's comb. Halldis used to grind roosters' combs, making salves to ease the pains in her father's hands. Her healing techniques, so carefully taught, have become part of who I am. It's strange that the volva who ordered my mother's death became a second mother to me. But she stopped me from stabbing my father during the hanging, and took me home as her own child, knowing my father was not concerned with my welfare.

I wake early to nurse my baby. There have been times, in this harsh land, when my milk has been the only thing keeping him alive. He is so thin, and even though he's taken a few steps, he seems too sleepy to keep trying. Sometimes I blame Finn for letting me join him on this expedition, though I was determined to travel here with him, even knowing I was with child.

These days, there's heat in the air from the men as they divide into groups. Hallstein stubbornly rallies men to go north with him, convinced he'll find wondrous treasure. He doesn't think of the price he'll pay if he brings Leif's ship back to Greenland empty.

Finn breathes deeply, sleeping sounder than the boy. His name fits his love of the ocean. I stroke his long, curly hair, the golden-brown color of oats. It seems as if baby Snorri will have his father's hair and my eyes, which Finn says are green as a cloud-filled jasper.

As Finn shoves his foot out, I slide off the blue blanket with Snorri, wrapping him tightly in his reindeer-skin hide and placing him slowly in his cradle. The beechwood cradle, a gift from Eirik's men in Greenland, is covered with carvings of dragons, ships, and Viking heroes long dead. I could look at it for hours. But I must grind barley and search for berries before anyone wakes.

I reach below my shift, making sure my seax is secure in its leather sheath. Then I put on my overdress, hoping it will be warm enough for the day. I fix it in place with the large amethyst brooches Finn gave me when we were married. "A man who could buy such brooches must surely be a good husband," Leif had said, laughing in his low, thunderous way. I had to seek Leif's blessing on the marriage, since he became my caretaker when Eirik died.

Outside the hut, the salty, heavy air presses on me. I turn sharply to the right, heading toward the forest, and away from the men's huts. We're lucky to have a private hut near the longhouse, since Finn is the leader. The rest of the men share the larger houses, and I stay away from them. They should still be sleeping this early in the morning. I quickly pray they will stay that way as I go about my errands. Men have followed me into the woods before, and I've successfully hidden from them every time. Finn does not know of this. It would only add to the strife in camp.

During my walks in the forest, I've discovered which berries we can eat by comparing their seeds with the ones in

Greenland and Iceland. Some of my favorites resemble cloudberries, only they are darkest ruby red instead of yellow, with small seeds. I've filled many pastries with these. Also, small trees near the forest's edge are laden with tiny black fruit in late summer. These are good for making juice and bread pies. We have found no grapes here yet. Summer has blessed us with bounty, but winter will eat up the excess, leaving us with little fresh food.

The still-green forest calls to me, so I plunge into it. The darkness mingles with heavy fog, and I can't see my own feet. I stumble onto the path our men have made. At its side lies another trail, almost covered with pine straw. We've all seen it, but no one will say it could be an abandoned trail of the native *Skraelings*. We make ourselves believe it's an old animal trail.

At a scuffling in the underbrush, I drop to the ground. I imagine myself a stone, slowing my breathing and heartbeat. This ability comes from placing Snorri, barely asleep, in his cradle at night, while I sit quietly behind it to wait for any cries. Finn says he's never known anyone with my patience.

Thrashing fills the air, and a small whining, like a dog's. The animal is not aware of me.

I raise up, bit by bit, until I can see the brush ahead. The animal sniffs at the air. It is larger than a dog, light-colored, with a dark stripe down its back. It looks exactly like the wolves we have in Greenland, except for its color. I start to lower myself, but the wolf has seen me.

Its great amber eyes fix on me, wooing me to help. The wolf's paw is caught in a snare of some kind, attached to a tree behind it—not one of our hunter's traps. He must have tightened it as he ran.

The wolf whines and raises its other paw toward me. I slowly put my hand under my shift and pull out my knife. We need food. This trapped wolf should be an easy kill. I'm not sure what wolf meat tastes like, but it is meat, and could be cured for winter.

I crawl through the brush. In this position, his side is exposed and I could drive the knife straight through. My long-knife seax is a bit unwieldy, since it belonged to my first husband.

As I come closer, the wolf does a strange thing. Instead of snarling its lip and bristling, as I expect it to do, it stays on the ground. It rolls over, fully exposing its stomach. So it trusts me.

And this wolf is a female. Her teats are somewhat full, as if she gave birth not long ago. Her stomach is small; not round with pups.

My strength of purpose fails me. I won't take her life, though the meat would make my milk stronger. She probably has pups somewhere. Who am I to take a mother from its baby?

I crawl so close I could touch her fur. It's shedding in clumps, as the days have become warmer. Using my knife, I slash at the rope in a quick move I usually reserve for gutting animals.

Squatting on the ground, I start to back away. She pulls her foot up and realizes that she's free. Instead of running, she puts her head down near my feet.

I've made a mistake—squatting to her level, like prey. I stand instead.

When I'm full height, she stands, too, then turns and lopes off into the forest, still lame on her back leg.

The fog has burned off: it is early no longer. I only have a few berries in my basket, and I haven't even ground the barley.

Snorri probably cries for my milk, for my shift is wet underneath. Finn must go out with the men, and he won't be happy with me for returning late.

As I come to the edge of the forest, the dove's song is muted by the men shouting outside their huts. Already they are up and fighting each other.

Deirdre comes out of our hut to meet me. She has been loyal to me, since the day Hallstein demanded that she and her husband, Magnus, be the first to scout the land here, because they're only Scottish slaves. I offered to join them, exposing Hallstein's cowardice. He finally went with them, taking the small ship's boat inland while the rest of us secured the *knarr*. Deirdre and Magnus have never forgotten that day, but neither has Hallstein.

Deirdre smiles, her black and white hair curling around her. For a woman twice my age, her face is young and fresh as a girl's. Only her hair tells of the hardships she's endured, before she was brought to Brattahlid. Leif and Finn have always treated their slaves fairly. Perhaps this is why she watches over the boy and me as a grandmother would.

"I've checked on young Snorri." With her thick accent, she tries to make her words sound more like mine. "He woke, and I've fed him. Karlsefni refuses to go out until you are back. He worries for you." She's always respectful when she speaks of Finn, almost reverent.

I nod and press her hand. "Many thanks, Deirdre." I pull back the deerskin flap, my eyes adjusting to the dim light from the fire. Finn hasn't even lit a lamp yet. He sits at our small table, drumming his fingers, while Snorri leans on his leg. When Snorri sees me, he tries to walk, but falls to the floor and crawls instead.

I pick him up and smell the smoke in his hair. It's cold here in the mornings, even with the straw we stuffed into the walls. I search for more clothing to layer on him, avoiding Finn's angry glares.

"Where have you been? I couldn't go out with the men, and Deirdre says they have already taken sides. Some will go with Hallstein, and some with me. I must be out there."

"I was in the forest." I drop my eyes, like a scolded child.

"Looking for berries?" He peers into the basket I brought in, nearly empty.

"Yes...and I saw a wolf."

His eyes focus on my face. "So close to camp?"

"She was in a trap...a Skraeling trap we hadn't seen."

The blue of his eyes darkens. The threat of these natives haunts him, since they killed Eirik's son, Thorvald, on the last expedition to this new land.

He takes my upper arms in his hands, though I'm still holding Snorri. His hands are wide, with shorter fingers. The skin inside them is tough—sailor's hands. He squeezes them so tightly, it makes Snorri squirm.

"Don't go out alone." His voice is low, masking the undercurrent of danger. I understand the meaning behind his words, behind those stormy eyes. He doesn't want me hurt.

"But who will gather berries?"

"From now on that will be the men's job. They'll disapprove, but we can't risk our women."

True, these Viking men couldn't survive without women for long, since we're responsible for all the household chores, from spinning wool and making clothing to preparing their every meal.

Without waiting for my response, Finn yanks on his boots, throws aside the deerskin flap, and charges out. Deirdre enters so soon after, I'm sure she was listening outside the door.

"You were long in coming back from the forest." Her voice is almost a whisper. It's not her way to ask a bold question. She takes Snorri from my arms and starts playing with him on the floor, her back to me.

Deirdre is the only woman I can tell about the Skraeling trap. I trust her as I would my own grandmother. Even though she likes to talk about others, she keeps her silence about Finn and me—frustrating Freydis to no end.

"I found a trap of the Skraelings, with a wolf in it."

"Ah." She nods slightly.

"I didn't kill the wolf."

She wipes the dust from Snorri's hands. "It must have been a special wolf."

I can't explain why I didn't kill it—why I didn't act like a *skorungur*, as Finn calls me. A woman who stirs up the fire. A courageous Viking woman should have killed that wolf. But Deirdre explains it for me.

"You do not enjoy killing as Freydis does, for you are a healer." She claps Snorri's hands together and smiles at him.

With this, she'll doubtless begin to gossip about Freydis. She can't understand how an illegitimate forest child should be treated with any respect. Even if she's daughter of Eirik the Red, she's just as surely the daughter of his mistress.

I don't enjoy gossip, but it has a purpose. In this way, Deirdre keeps me aware of what's going on in the camp.

Deirdre lowers her voice. "Freydis attacked Ref and called him a coward to his face last night."

No Viking husband should put up with this behavior in his wife. But Ref is fearful of Eirik's family and friends. He knows there will be retaliation if he treats Freydis badly. Besides, he's loved her for a long time, regardless of her fiery words.

"She runs all over him," Deirdre says. "She is always—"

Freydis charges in the door, her red curls flying like flames. Both Eirik the Red and her brother Thorstein shared her hair color. "Uncanny" is what Deirdre calls it, declaring it comes from the otherworld.

"Aha, I heard you, you old hag." Freydis' hands rest on her narrow hips.

Deirdre carries Snorri to the table, where she slowly and deliberately turns her back on Freydis.

"Pouring out lies about me, as usual. You know me better than that, Gudrid." Freydis' eyes cut through me like steel, waiting for my response.

I ask her a question to change her thoughts, using my talent for bringing peace to angry situations.

"And how are you feeling? You're now six months with child, aren't you?"

"Yes, and I feel wonderful." She smiles. "I'm not groaning around with my weight as most Viking women do at this point! I'm healthy and strong. I know my child will be a great warrior."

"Of course, Eirik's grandchild could be nothing *but* a warrior." I know she's flattered at this thought.

"Ah, how he loved you, Gudrid! That old man would've married you, if he could have!"

Her wide blue eyes sparkle like gems. Freydis doesn't shock me with the way she speaks of her father. He would have done no such thing. But I understand she's trying, in her own way, to compliment me.

"Well, Thjodhild was more than enough woman for him." We laugh at my joke. Freydis hates her stepmother. We've both seen how Thjodhild spent most of Eirik's life discovering new ways to drive him mad with rage.

"My Ref wastes time arguing with the men this morning." Freydis drops her full lower lip. "That old troll Hallstein wants to go north in a week's time."

"Are you following Hallstein or Finn?" I know Freydis will decide, and not her husband.

"Of course we'll be with Thorfinn." She's intentionally disrespectful, using his given name, instead of his surname, Karlsefni. "He is such a *good* leader." Her lips curl upward.

Freydis has been enamored with Finn since the first time he came to Brattahlid. She was only a child then, easily impressed with the fine wares he showed her father. Thankfully, Finn has no time for Freydis. "She doesn't listen," he's told me. "And her hair's so red. She's too thin and tall. She has no curves, as you do."

"I must go and talk to Ref." Freydis sighs as if the weight of the camp's strife rests on her shoulders. "I will come back to do the weaving later."

She nods to me and ignores Deirdre as she sweeps out, her small stomach sticking straight out with her child. It hasn't dropped yet.

Snorri drifts to sleep again as Deirdre balances him on her hip. I motion toward the door and go out. The men have scattered. Several practice with weapons near their huts. Snorri Thorbrandsson bashes Hallstein's sword to the ground, with only an axe. The way he brings his axe up to Hallstein's face, with no hint of a smile, says more than any threatening words.

I pray silently that my child won't have to grow up in this land. The ground is easy to work, true, and there are plenty of fish. We haven't seen any Skraelings yet. But there is no peace here for me, and no family. Only Freydis—a sister who isn't really my sister.

I stop abruptly, feeling someone watching me from the woods. I've always had a sense about spiritual things, things no one else sees. Deirdre calls it "the sight"—high praise in Scotland.

I sweep my gaze along the forest. The wolf stands toward the outer edge, head aloft, eyes focused. I feel the strangest urge to name her, like a child. She looks toward me again, then out to sea. I follow her line of vision, and my heart stops. Skraeling skin boats glide straight toward our shore—too many to count.

Chapter Three

Before I can think, I throw my skirts over my arm and push through the door covering. Deirdre takes one look at me and thrusts Snorri into my arms. The boats slide up on the sand. Our men rush past us, gripping axes. We run the other direction, toward the forest.

We stumble toward a brush hedge in the forest's border and lie down. I place Snorri beneath my skirt, his head barely uncovered. Deirdre keeps watch, since her hair blends with the forest better than mine.

"Karlsefni talks with Snorri. Our men are putting down their axes." She strips the leaves off a branch as we wait. "The leader is tall—he waves his hands about." More leaves fall to the ground beneath her. "Now Snorri holds the white shield." Only Snorri Thorbrandsson can hold the shield, as Finn's trading partner and second in command.

Do they really believe the Skraelings mean no harm?

"They have such large, dark eyes. Their hair is so ugly and uncombed." Deirdre speaks under her breath, but I fear they will hear.

She says nothing for several minutes. Her skin is white as alabaster, and she doesn't sweat. I lie completely still over my son, trying to quiet my breathing. The trees rustle deeper in the forest, where someone else hides.

Finally, she sighs. "They're leaving...taking their boats around the point. Stay down."

We curl in the leaves, waiting for what seems like hours. I pull Snorri closer, putting my finger in his mouth so he can suck it.

"Gudrid!" Finn's voice reaches us, and I struggle to get up. Snorri begins to cry.

Deirdre motions him to us. Finn cocks his eyebrow at me. "You hid in the forest? I said to stay away from the wolf."

"The wolf won't hurt me. You choose to scold me now?" I challenge his look with one of my own. This is no time for arguing.

Finn returns my stare, but says no more. He embraces us, thanking Deirdre for her help. She half-nods at Finn before running to find Magnus.

All the men huddle near the shore. I hear Hallstein before I see him, his harsh voice filling the air.

"I ship out in two days," he says. "This isn't the Viking way. We don't sit and wait to be attacked—we attack first! Every raider among us knows this!"

Finn leaves my side, striding into the group. "No, it's not the Viking way. But I have been on the seas all my life. Going north is too dangerous, with winter only five moons away. We will leave in two days, but to go south, toward Vinland."

A large, very yellow-haired man in the middle shouts, "How do we even know this Vinland exists? What if Leif was lying? His father certainly did."

My heart speeds up, blood throbbing in my hands. Before I can speak up to vouch for Eirik's good name, Finn speaks again.

"Leif is no liar. He lost his own brother on these shores. That was no fool's imagining. And *some* of you saw that arrow fly into Thorvald's chest." He points to Hallstein.

No one can contest this, for Hallstein himself was on that trip.

"Leif gave me the larger ship." Hallstein loves to brag of this. "I'll take this ship and go north, where I'm sure we'll find Vinland. We can camp in the houses Leif built there. No longer will we sit in this cove, waiting for trouble, with no women of our own to comfort us!"

Several men shout their approval. "Then let's choose now," Finn says. I wonder if I'm the only one who sees his hand resting on his sword hilt. Finn is fast with his weapon, but not as fast as Hallstein, who cut a man down in Greenland before he could turn around.

Freydis shoves Ref. Her hair looks like a bird's nest, with leaves scattered through it. She hid from the Skraelings in a tree.

Ref shouts, "We're with Karlsefni! And if you have any hope of surviving, you'll join us."

Hallstein draws his brows together and his heavy jaw clamps shut. He walks over to Ref, so he can tower over him. The spit comes out of his mouth as he talks.

"Coward, you let your own wife rule you. You—"

Freydis draws her husband's sword from its sheath, pointing its tip under Hallstein's chin before anyone could notice the movement.

"One more word, *coward*, and I will show you what fear is." Her voice is low as a man's. The fire in her eyes matches her hair.

Even Hallstein isn't such a fool as to harm Leif's sister. He wheels back to the men. "If you join me, you join Thor! He alone will save us!"

Slowly, a group of twenty-two men join Hallstein. The women leave to prepare the mid-morning meal, and I trail after them to the longhouse. The rosemary, mint, and lavender drying in the beams lend a comforting smell to the room. Its constant bright fires and rough-hewn long tables remind me of Brattahlid.

Deirdre talks with the brown-haired Norwegian slave girl named Inger, while Freydis chops clumsily at her herbs. She's a poor cook, since all her skills lie in using weapons.

I beat pieces of dried cod, to start a broth. I'm deeply pleased that most of the men chose to stay with Finn.

Freydis stops chopping and approaches me noiselessly, like a cat. She touches my shoulder and whispers, "He'll regret what he said about Eirik."

So she's been thinking of the yellow-haired man. I try to make light of it. "No one believed him."

Her eyes widen with hatred. I wish again that Thorvald could be here. He was the only one who could reach her mind when it was so set on something.

Freydis' gaze softens, as if she knows my thoughts. "I miss my middle brother. You know, even though Thorvald only knew you a short while, he told me you were the finest woman in Greenland."

I continue adding cod to the broth. I know full well Thorvald loved his wife, Stena, and no one else.

"He even said he'd fight his own little brother for you, if he could. But of course he was already married." She gives me a sly half-smile.

"Sometimes I think you hear too much, little sister." I soften my tone, despite my irritation.

"But Thorstein was so different. He was always too concerned about himself." Freydis rubs her stomach. "He took you on his fool's errand, when he couldn't even sail."

True, when my red-haired husband of only a few months told me he must avenge his brother's death, I couldn't believe it. It seemed a most un-Christian thing to do, although Thorstein never fully owned Christianity like his older brother, Leif. His mother wouldn't stop dripping the words on him to take vengeance on the Skraelings, since his father was dead.

"And then he got so off-course, he arrived back in northern Greenland." Bitterness sours Freydis' laugh. "He met his death because he didn't listen to good sense, Gudrid. *Your* good sense."

So...the family is aware I had begged Thorstein to stay. I couldn't support him, since everything we needed was at Brattahlid, and revenge was pointless.

"In fact, he never listened to anyone but himself." She fishes leaves out of her hair. My laugh bubbles up and out, surprising her. She and her youngest brother were the same. Freydis always believes *she* is right. This is why she and Thorstein always clashed.

Deirdre and Inger edge closer to the fire, pouring milk into the soup. Inger gives me a hunted look. I switch to Scottish, asking Deirdre what's wrong with the girl.

Freydis glares at me, since she knows no other languages. She returns to the herbs, green stems dropping to the floor with her careless chops.

"Inger is afraid," Deirdre says. She comes closer. "She overheard Hallstein's men, when she washed their clothes in the creek. They were bathing. One shouted at her to come over, and she refused. But she could hear them saying they would take what they wanted, soon enough."

"Finn must know this." I collect Freydis' mangled herbs and drop them in the pot. "We have to protect the few women we have."

"Make no mistake, *you* will be the prize, Gudrid. That old man would love to spite Karlsefni by taking his wife." Sometimes Deirdre's insight alarms me.

Freydis no longer pretends to chop, but watches us out of the sides of her eyes. She moves toward the bench in the wall.

Finn and the men arrive for the meal. As they eat, I watch them from my spot near the fire. Some stare at the women openly. Finn talks intently with Snorri Thorbrandsson and doesn't notice. Thoughts creep into my mind. He married me only for my beauty and my position. He cares nothing for my safety. I push these doubts out; perhaps my first husband was this way, but not Finn.

Hallstein motions to me. I approach the table, so he won't think I fear him.

He slams his spoon down. "This broth is too thin, *blaudur*." His lips curve at his insult, meaning that I am soft, weak, and womanly. I glance at Finn. He still doesn't look my way.

Hallstein puts his arm around my waist, whispering. "Even so, blaudur, I enjoy a soft woman as much as the next man."

I make myself small and slippery as an eel, spinning out from his grasp. As I walk back toward the fire, holding my green overdress tightly, he gives a low whistle.

"Mark my words, she has more fire than the redhead." He pokes the yellow-haired man at his side. His friend has a section of hair missing from his beard, with a huge scar in it, no doubt won from fighting.

Freydis sits on the bench in the corner. Her eyes are shadowed, but she cradles her knife. It's lightweight, and curved especially for skinning animals. It has a metal loop that fits over her smallest finger. Although it looks harmless, I've seen her slash seals' throats with it faster than I can blink.

Deirdre comes to me quickly. "You must have time to talk with Karlsefni. Magnus will sit outside your hut tonight, if you wish." Blindness has given Magnus uncanny powers of hearing and smell.

"I am not the only woman in danger." I turn from the men, ignoring a crude hand movement from the yellow-haired giant.

"Perhaps we all must gather in one hut?"

"Hallstein's men would like us to be together, so they could take us easily, like fish in a barrel. No. We'll sleep in our own huts, with our own husbands guarding us," I whisper.

"You there, woman—more soup!" A man shouts to Deirdre from the table.

She takes his bowl, ladling up the thin white broth as she whispers. "One husband will not be enough to protect his wife, if they come in a group."

I turn slightly toward the table, watching the men. Hallstein must feel my glance, for he looks up from his bowl and loudly smacks his lips.

"Then we'll be Vikings tonight," I say. "Tell every woman and her husband. Tell every slave girl. If there's to be bloodshed, it won't be ours."

Deirdre nods and returns the full bowl to the man at the table. Stirring the soup, I glance at Finn. He seems unaware of our guarded talk. But Freydis has missed nothing.

She walks over and squats next to the fire, extending her long, white fingers to the warmth. Her palm bears a mark from her hard grip on the knife.

"I know it all." She leans toward me. "I may not understand Deirdre, but between her looks and Hallstein's boldness with you, I can see what's to pass. Tell me your plan."

Her face is slightly fuller now from the pregnancy. In her cold blue eyes, there's a hatred that can never be quenched.

"Just make sure Ref is armed every night until Hallstein leaves." I hold her gaze.

Freydis nods and walks purposefully out the door. The men stare. It is uncustomary for a woman to leave until the men are finished eating. Whether she will even ask Ref for protection, I don't know. But any man who tries to enter her hut is as good as dead.

Finn seems to wake and stands from his chair at the head of the table. He bangs his mug down—a sign for quiet.

"We have many preparations to make before we leave. Our men will go south next week, for Vinland. Hallstein sails to the north in two days. But what if the Skraelings return first?"

Magnus speaks first, dark hair hiding his useless eyes. "They came peacefully, it seemed. Perhaps we might trade goods with them."

Snorri Thorbrandsson nods, even though peace-keeping has never been his strength.

Hallstein's eyes blaze, eliminating any hopes for unity in this decision. He wants nothing more than to prove that his god will help him defeat the Skraelings.

"We'll fight them if they come, of course," he says. Several of his men bang their mugs in agreement. "And kill every last one!"

Finn looks thoughtful. "You're both right. We must be prepared to trade. And if they won't trade, we must be prepared to kill."

The men look to Finn, slowly nodding as they feel the power in his words. I'm proud to have married such a wise man.

All the men hit their mugs on the table. Finn has won a peace, for now. Conversations begin about how to trade and how to hide the weapons.

The women and I collect the dirty bowls and mugs, loading them into our wagon to wash at the stream. My Snorri is safe in our hut, where another slave girl watches him. Women beg to watch over him, since he's the only child here, until Freydis has her baby.

I can't believe Finn noticed nothing, from the upheaval among the women to Hallstein's lusty advances. The men's unrest fills his mind now, I tell myself. It's not that he doesn't care.

I dread nightfall. I pray Finn returns to our hut by then. Otherwise, I'll be alone with my child, my seax, and my faith in a God who would make Thor quiver, if Thor were real in the first place.

Chapter Four

In the fading blue evening light, the men lean against the longhouse, sharpening weapons and sharing stories. I usually love this time of year, when I can watch the blue melt into the purples and corals of the sunset. But tonight, I ignore the beauty and use the light to watch for my enemies.

Near the woods, a low shadow moves near the trees. It could be the wolf.

Deirdre gives her dove's call nearby, the signal that Magnus is in their hut, watching over her.

I can't see Freydis' hut, which is past the men's houses. Hopefully Ref is back from the longhouse, ready to protect Freydis and the babe inside her. These Viking men are starved for female company. And when Vikings need something, they feel they can take it. Odin, the god of wisdom, rewards bravery, even when it's driven only by the cowardice of lust.

As he often does, Finn lingers in the longhouse after the evening meal. How he missed Freydis' threatening behavior tonight, I cannot understand. During the meal, she slammed half a stale loaf of bread on the table in front of Hallstein. Then she pulled out her own curved knife and slowly sawed off a piece. She stuffed it in her face, a hateful grin twisting her lips. Hallstein and his men sat as if tied to their seats. She ate every bite, leaving nothing for the men.

She gets her boldness from her father. I smile every time I remember my father-in-law. Eirik never feared for his own life, especially where his family was concerned. If he could only be in this hostile camp tonight, I could sleep soundly. But Eirik is dead.

I go back inside our hut to check on the fire. Snorri sleeps soundly, tucked into his cradle. His round stomach is full from the long feeding I gave him, in hopes he wouldn't wake if there's an attack.

Seax in hand, I go to the door and secure the deer hide. Then I drag a bench to the side of the door and climb up on it. This way, I'll be taller than any man who comes inside. My seax will cleave his skull before he can look around.

Hours pass before I hear the men leaving the longhouse for the night. Hallstein boasts loudly about what he'll do to the Skraelings, should they return. There's no talk of women, so I begin to hope they've forgotten any plans.

But a voice sounds nearby, lower than the others. It's the tall, yellow-haired man, who always talks as if he has straw in his mouth. The small stones in front of my door crunch as he walks by. He has wide shoulders and a large chest, with long legs. He reminds me of one of Eirik's biggest bulls. Maybe he's dumb as a bull, too—led by his desires, and not his mind.

The yellow-haired man has stopped outside my door, talking quietly to someone—perhaps Hallstein. One man gives a low laugh.

Then...nothing.

Snorri turns in his cradle. There's no movement outside.

I bring the seax above my head and hold it, frozen. I was foolish not to tell Finn. What if he comes through the door first, and I don't recognize his steps? What if I kill the one protector I have in this lonely, strange land?

A small, scraping noise starts at the back of the hut, near the midden pile. Someone could get in that way, but surely no one would do that, no matter how needy. It's full of dung and rotting food. There's only a small door connecting it to the house, where we throw our waste out. It's barely big enough for a person to get through, unless he bashes the frame apart.

Should I go to the back or continue guarding the most obvious entrance? The scraping turns into a chopping sound, as if someone's hacking at the wood.

I'll stay at the front. By the time someone hacks up the small frame and squeezes through the back opening, I'll be right there to lower my seax.

My nose tingles, a sneeze building. Halldis always told me, "The trolls will drive you mad with the little things." But I hold the sneeze in. I don't believe in trolls anymore.

Logs topple in the fire, sending sparks through the hole in the roof. I focus on the small patch of sky, the same color as a baby seal.

A woman's cry drifts through the air, from the direction of Freydis' hut.

My arms begin to cramp. I twist the seax down, resting it between my feet. I can still bring it straight up into the face of anyone who comes in.

Stiffness seeps into my legs. The chopping stops, but I can't stop clenching the seax. My legs are numb when a man's boots crunch on the door stones.

"Gudrid," Finn whispers. Thank God he speaks first, before entering.

"Here," I answer. His beautiful curly head comes into view. I collapse onto the bench, dropping my seax. He catches me before I slide onto the floor. His jaw is clenched, and his blue eyes are dark as night. The sinews in his arms tighten, strong as ship's ropes.

I wait for news, unable to speak.

"One of the slave women was attacked," he says.

I nod.

"But now the women are safe." He pulls my head into his chest, stroking my hair. "It won't happen again. I talked to Hallstein."

He had time to talk to Hallstein?

"They're leaving in the morning. They must pack tonight."

From the hard glint in Finn's eyes, I know Hallstein won't dare fight him on this.

"Should I have Deirdre come to stay with you tonight?" He pushes my hair out of my face and carries me to our straw-stuffed bed.

"No—only you." Surely he will stay with me.

Finn's eyes soften to light blue. He pulls down the wool blankets and curls up behind me. Later, when he drapes the cold mesh chainmail over me, I barely stir. Leif's chainmail. Finn must have borrowed it. And Leif loans nothing, unless he's sure he'll get it back someday.

Chapter Five

Before the morning sun creeps through the crack under the door, Snorri whines, as if he doesn't have enough strength to push his voice out any farther. I can't stretch my arms, numb from the heavy chainmail. Its links are pinned tightly to my body by Finn's arm.

"Finn." I straighten my left foot into his leg.

"Mmmm?" He's not fully awake yet.

"I can't get up." Snorri's whining spirals higher and higher.

"Yes." He rolls over, freeing me from his arm.

I push the chainmail off, but he wraps his arm around me again.

"Fi—" He rolls over on me and stops my words with a long, meaningful kiss. It's as if he is trying to speak all his feelings with his lips. Sadness wraps the kiss—a sadness loaded with the possibility of death.

Snorri's cries are so high, we can hardly hear them. His arms flail above the sides of his cradle.

"I must go to him." I pry Finn's arms off my sides, sorry to abandon those plush, salty lips.

Finn smiles lazily, then walks to the cradle, wearing only his long, walnut-colored tunic. He brings Snorri to me, placing him gently in my arms.

"Thank you." I move my shift to nurse my hungry, red-faced child. He immediately latches on and drinks as if he's never been fed before.

"You've done well with him." Finn's eyes shine as he strokes Snorri's soft curls.

I wait for him to continue.

"We must leave here soon." He made this announcement to the entire camp yesterday, so why is he telling me again?

"And if we don't find Vinland?" I ask. He must worry about Leif's response if our ships return empty.

Finn won't say what I long to hear—that we'll go home to Greenland, to Brattahlid, and the only family I have. I can never feel safe again, until I stand on Greenland's shores.

His eyes deepen. Finn is a planner, a man who likes to know the next step. But he wasn't planning on the Skraelings. He wasn't planning on Hallstein. He doesn't know the next step.

Snorri sighs, and I open his tightened fingers, shifting him to the other side. Finn stands and begins dressing, taking with him his warm scent of sea and pine. I wish he could wear the chainmail today, but it fits outside his clothing, and would be an obvious sign of fear. Instead, he straps his sword on one side and his knife sheath on the other.

A triple knock sounds on the door frame. It must be Magnus. He comes every third day, to accompany the women for the washing at the creek. Magnus is the most trusted man for the job, because of his blindness. No one can sneak up on him. And he can't watch us as we bathe, so we have privacy.

Snorri's head pulls back, drunk with my milk. I kiss his forehead and pass him back to Finn. Soon Nerienda, the oldest woman in the camp, will arrive so I can go to the creek. Leif practically forced Nerienda on us when we left, because he knew of her skills with woodland plants. A slave woman from Wessex, she knows which plants lend soups flavor and which plants kill. But Leif also knew of her fame as a midwife, and he wanted her with me when I gave birth in this friendless land.

Deirdre says Nerienda is lazy. True, she doesn't like mundane chores, like carding wool or milking cows. But she has jumped from her bench, even faster than I could, to keep Snorri from touching one coal on the fire. I don't question her care.

I gather our dirty clothes into a basket Deirdre wove from vines in our woods. Finn stands in front of the door, as if hesitant to let me go out. Perhaps last night made him fear for my life. He has said nothing of who was attacked, but I know the women will tell me the details soon enough. I put the basket down and wrap my arms around him, kissing him full on the lips, before Magnus raps again on the frame.

"Coming, Magnus." I take the large basket in both hands, feeling Finn's gaze on my back as I shut the flap.

Outside our door, three women trail along behind Magnus like little ducklings. Deirdre and the two slave girls. So all the younger women are safe and accounted for, except Freydis.

We walk silently to the creek. As we begin scrubbing our clothes with our horse chestnut soap, I finally ask about Freydis.

Deirdre's only too happy to share. "Ref said she never came home last night. But I told him she can certainly take care of herself." She gives a short laugh.

"It's not like her to run from danger." I rub at Finn's dark blue trousers, a little too harshly.

Deirdre falls silent, thinking. The sun reflects off the water, lighting up her white hairs.

I continue prying. "I heard a cry last night. Was it Freydis?"

"No, a slave was attacked, in Nerienda's hut. She fought him off, though. Hallstein did it, the fiend."

I don't mention the scratching outside my hut last night. Perhaps Hallstein tried to get in through the midden door, then gave up.

"Your Karlsefni came." Deirdre's tone is hushed. "He pulled the old man off the girl and held a knife to his throat, saying he'd be dead if he didn't leave today. Hallstein was too drunk and tired to argue. Stupid old oaf." She curses in Scottish.

So Finn reached the slave girl in time, but not me. Whoever scratched at my midden heap could have gotten in. And, if Finn knew Hallstein was too drunk to fight, why did he spread that chainmail over me? Was he worried about the yellow-haired man?

"Still, it's not safe for Freydis to be out in her condition." I wring the clean clothes and place them in the empty basket.

Deirdre gives me a look, which seems to say, "Better her than you, my friend." She, too, puts her washing aside and unclasps her shift to wash herself. Her milky white skin speaks of lush green hills and druid's chants.

"She's like a sister to me, because of Thorstein." I struggle to unclasp my own shift. Deirdre helps me with the gold brooch, and her fingers enclose mine.

"I know this," Deirdre says. "But she needs no protection."

"Nor do I." My voice raises, and Magnus turns toward us. As I pull my hand away, my brooch slips into the cold water.

Immediately, Deirdre hands me her soap and kneels, fingers searching the murky creek bed. I can't escape her loyalty, even when I am upset with her.

In a couple of moments, she straightens up, triumphant, with the dirty brooch between her fingers. She rinses and rubs it several times before handing it to me.

"I know how you feel about Freydis." I begin to shiver in the cold water. "But she's still with child. And that makes her vulnerable, even if she doesn't understand that."

Deirdre nods, looking out to sea.

I continue washing my shoulders and arms. Deirdre offers to wash my back, because the other women are already dressing on the bank.

I lower my voice. "I will go to the woods now, but you can't tell Finn. He'll be distracted by Hallstein and his men today."

The soap moves over my spine as Deirdre answers, simply, "Yes."

I look at my hands, a golden tan now, since the sun shines brighter in this land. We brought no mirrors here. I wonder if I look the same as I did in Greenland. My hair has grown, surely, but has my face altered greatly? Leif loved my eyes, saying they were soft and green as the mosses in the forests. He had smiled as he said it, one side of his mouth crooking down slightly, like his sister's.

Deirdre squeezes water over my back, bringing me into the present. I have to find Freydis. I finish washing, then dry off on the bank with the others. Magnus motions for us to be still, then points toward the woods. The wolf stands at the edge of the trees, observing us. Magnus drops his hand to his sword.

"No." I cover his hand with mine. He obeys immediately, crossing his arms instead.

As the wolf watches us, I wonder if her presence portends something else, as it did with the Skraeling boats. Finally, she turns and runs into the woods—as good a place as any to begin my search for Freydis.

"I have to gather berries." I turn to Deirdre, handing her my clothes basket. She nods briefly before trailing Magnus and the women back toward camp. Even though she heard Finn's command for the men to gather berries, and even though she knows I have no basket to put them in, Deirdre won't go against my wishes.

It's not hard to follow the wolf. She moves slowly into the forest, as if she knows I'm behind her. Still, I keep a healthy distance between us. She leads me into an area I've never seen, pale green with thick ferns. It's a sort of clearing, with trees arching overhead. I half expect to find runic stones standing around, it seems so hallowed.

The wolf stops near a tree. In its branches, I catch a familiar flash of red.

"Freydis!"

She's obviously tired, from the way she drags herself down, clinging sideways to the slim trunk. Thankfully, she wasn't up very high. But no woman with child should have climbed that tree in the first place.

"They found him?" Her voice is hoarse.

"Who?"

She leans against me, looking confused.

"Hallstein? Yes, Finn found him and told him he has to leave today." I try to comfort her. "Did you see him last night? Where were you?" I pat her head, like she's a small child.

"No, Hallstein? No." She sighs loudly, sinking into a sitting position. "I need food."

"Of course." I search the underbrush for berries, finding none. I hesitate to leave Freydis on the forest floor with my wolf around, even though she's nowhere to be seen.

Freydis senses my distress. She picks up several fern fronds. "I can eat these leaves for now." I'm surprised she knows they're edible.

I wait until she's eaten several, then help her to her feet. We walk back in silence. Since she's so exhausted, I hesitate to ask more questions. "Maybe Hallstein has shipped out," I say. As much as I doubt this, I hope for it.

Sunlight blinds us as we emerge from the forest's shadows. A group of men stand near the longhouse, Hallstein speaking loudly in the middle. They fall silent as we approach, then raise fingers and point.

"There she is! We call for an *Althing* meeting!" Hallstein's voice grates on the air.

I pull Freydis to a stop, almost tripping her. She grips my arm and whispers. "No matter what they say, it's not true."

"What's the meaning of this?" Boldness fills me and I become chieftain's daughter once again.

Finn takes my other arm, giving me a clouded look. "She has been accused."

"Accused? Of what?" I focus on Hallstein. "She's been hiding in the forest from *your* men!"

A sneer twists his face. "Oh, she wasn't afraid of my men, *Gudrid*." The way he says my name, so intimately, makes me want to strike him down.

I stare into his dark, hateful eyes. "Then what do you accuse her of? She did nothing wrong!"

His lips curl as he returns my stare. "That woman slit my man's throat last night."

Chapter Six

Freydis' knees give way, and Finn reaches around to hold her up. Ref pushes his way through the crowd and grabs his wife by the waist. As the men press closer, I recognize the one advantage we have—their ignorance.

"As long as she is with child, she can't be accused. This is the old Icelandic law." I move in front of Freydis, hoping my words alone will shield her.

The men fall back, and Finn's eyebrows raise. No one questions my understanding of the old laws, since my father was a chieftain, and so was Eirik. None of these men had the status to attend the Althing meetings, except Finn and Snorri Thorbrandsson.

Hallstein stumbles toward us. His bony finger points again. "Blood for blood, that's the only law I know."

"Old man, you should be packing your ship." I wrap my fingers around my seax, and his eyes widen. I'm not such a soft woman after all. "Although it won't be your ship for long, once Leif hears you've accused his sister of murder."

The men fall silent, considering my words. Finn moves closer. "Gudrid speaks truth, Hallstein. It's time for your men to go. Your man was outside *my* hut, with his own knife in his hand. Doubtless, he planned to attack my wife."

I tremble as he says the words, trying to contain my surprise. So the dead man was found near our hut.

Snorri Thorbrandsson steps up beside Finn, showing support. "We'll bury him properly. But you go now, or we'll force you out." He holds up his fist, a symbol of the hammer of Thor and of judgment. All Finn's loyal men hold up fists, joining him. Hallstein knows better than to cross Snorri Thorbrandsson, a man well-known for his fearlessness in Iceland and Greenland. Once, when he was shot through the neck with an arrow, Snorri simply broke off the end, pulled out the arrow, and sat down to eat his evening meal. He bears the scar to prove it.

Hallstein turns, muttering something to his men. Some go to the huts, others to the ship to continue loading. I stare at his hunched back, wishing I could kick it to the ground.

Ref walks Freydis back to their hut. Finn tells two of his larger men to follow them for protection. Then he grabs my arm, walking me deliberately toward the forest. He drives me off the path, into some brush, before he speaks.

"Where were you and Freydis?"

"She was in the woods, and I went to find her." I yank my arm away.

He clenches his jaw. "Hallstein's largest man was found behind our hut, on the midden pile. His throat was slit, and Hallstein says it had to be a curved knife like the one Freydis uses. Maybe she saw him out back and killed him. You know how quietly she can walk."

Yes, I do know this. The facts make sense. But the way Finn is talking to me does not. It's as if he's trying to convince us both that Freydis killed the man. True, it's nothing for her to kill—she enjoys it. And I know she would kill for me. But she told me Hallstein was lying before she even heard what he had to say.

In the forest, the first words out of her pale mouth were, "They've found him." I'd thought she was talking about Hallstein, but she was talking about the dead man—and how could she know he was dead, unless she was there when it happened?

Finn strokes my hair, but his gaze rests on the camp behind me. "I knew you were in danger last night. There was talk of unrest among the men."

Fury rises in me. Why didn't he come into the hut with us? Where was he when we needed his protection? His hands move over my arms, but I pull away.

"We must go back." I'm suddenly chilled, thinking of the many violent things Hallstein could have done to me—could still do before leaving. Even the Althing laws may not be enough to stop such a spiteful, gnarled man. What if he tries to hurt our son?

"Of course." Finn looks at me, waiting for something. He is tired from leading these brawling men. But he doesn't realize how much power he wields over them. He has kings in his bloodline, and the men instinctively feel his royalty. Finn is a stronger leader than my father was, or even Eirik the Red. The steel in his disposition could shatter the iron most of these men are made of. When his mind is made up, no one would dare go against him. No one except me.

As he strokes my hair, his rough shirt slides down, revealing the end of the tattoo on his upper arm. He got the tattoo when he traded in the Arabic countries. I love seeing the Midgard serpent, Thor's greatest enemy, wrapped around his arm. The serpent bites its tail, like the oceans surrounding the earth—a fitting tattoo for a sailor.

I touch the tattoo, lightly. Finn catches my hand. "What's this law you spoke of? About a woman with child?"

"There is no such law." I continue caressing his arm and raise my eyes to meet his gaze.

A curl drops over his eye, and he brushes it away. He pulls me roughly into his chest. "My little skorungur." His lips press against my forehead.

Reluctantly, we leave for camp, where we find Hallstein's ship loaded and ready to sail. It's one of Leif's larger cargo knarr. If Hallstein doesn't fill it with goods before he returns it to Leif, he will never sail again.

I pray that Finn finds Vinland in the south, so our return to Greenland will be honorable. Brattahlid is the one place on earth I feel completely unafraid, largely because of Leif. He is fiercely protective of me, and has been since I've been in his charge. When he talks with me, he always knows the right questions to ask, bringing out stories I've never shared. My disloyalty to Finn makes me sick. He stands right beside me, unaware of these poisonous thoughts.

I give Finn a final touch, then we return to the longhouse. Outside, Freydis rocks back and forth, rubbing her stomach. I walk toward my sister-in-law, drawn to her sadness. When I hug her, her eyes are empty, as if she's never seen me before. I lead her into the longhouse, hoping to find soup to warm her.

Instead, the dead man is laid out on a bench near the table. The women wash his large body. His eyes are closed, but his fist is still clenched. They've removed his knife.

Nerienda prepares the herbal infusions to rub on the body. I, too, know these ingredients, from my days spent as a volva, but the oldest woman in camp prepares bodies for burial.

She shuffles over to me as my eyes sweep the body. A long, darkened gash mars his neck. Without a word, Nerienda touches my hand, and I know what she's asking. I nod, and Inger puts a dampened white cloth on the wound, pulling it up over his face. Freydis doesn't need to look at this man again. I want the ground to swallow the evil in his body. I want him out of the camp.

"We'll take him beyond the forest," I say.

The slave women gasp. Several men will have to neglect chores to move this large body to the outer edge of the woods. And it won't be a proper burial, as Snorri Thorbrandsson promised. But I won't have Freydis going mad from looking at his grave every day.

"No." Finn stands in the door frame. The sunlight lights up the little hairs on his arms, making his hair look as light as mine. Freydis puts her hand on his arm, like a child waiting for judgment.

"The body can't be in the camp. And so we will burn it."

Chapter Seven

After the preparations, Deirdre brings Snorri to me for feeding. I'm thankful to escape the smell of death and step into the sunlight. Finn stays in the longhouse, speaking with the women. Hallstein's ship still lurks in the inlet, like a beached whale.

I overhear Finn saying the dead man had been sick. I never saw any signs of this, but Finn knows no one will argue with him. He's lying, probably because he knows I want to protect Freydis.

Finn also says he won't prepare the corpse for the otherworld in the pagan ways, burying goods and animals with him. And yet, the funeral pyre is an honorable tradition, reserved for noble men. This wicked man's pyre will use up much of our precious winter wood.

Snorri Thorbrandsson looks me full in the face as he walks into the longhouse, his bald head reflecting the sun's rays. Although burying the man with no goods will make him a liar to Hallstein, Snorri Thorbrandsson won't disagree with Finn. His lot was cast with my husband when this journey was only a dream, discussed over bonfires at Brattahlid. Finn even named our son after him. Snorri has taken so many voyages, he fears nothing—not a watery grave, not Skraelings, and certainly not Hallstein.

Snorri's orange-red beard reflects his fire-starting ways. Even though he's older than Finn, he has the strength and determination of a young man. Snorri and his brother feuded with the wrong people in Iceland, so they were banished. They became merchants, traveling to Greenland to collect walrus ivory. When Snorri's brother died of illness, Finn stepped in as his new trading partner. Sometimes I think Finn became Snorri's replacement brother, as well.

Back in our hut, I sit to nurse my baby, lost in the past. Finn doesn't know Snorri asked me to marry him shortly after Thorstein died. That long winter, Snorri watched my every move at Brattahlid, hoping for a favorable answer.

But Eirik realized that Finn, who came from a wealthy family, was a better prospective husband for me. Finn impressed Eirik when he shared his beer and supplies that lean winter. So Eirik encouraged me to accept Finn's offer, knowing I would be well provided for. He also hoped we would stay on and live at Brattahlid, sharing our bounty with him.

"I promised your father I'd watch out for you if anything happened to your husband," Eirik had said. His eyes shared the smile on his lips. "But who knew I'd care for you so much? I married you off to one of my sons to keep you in our family, then he went and died. And men keep asking for you, Gudrid. So I have to pick the best of the lot. Thorfinn Karlsefni's the best. And I'm trying to talk him into staying here to gather more ivory."

Eirik wanted me to live in Greenland forever, because I softened his relationship with his wife, Thjodhild. She and I could talk together of Christianity. And Eirik and I could talk about everything else. Thorvald Eiriksson once told me, "I don't honestly know how those two ever married, Gudrid. But you bring a space between them. We can all breathe when you're around."

Leif didn't stand in the way of my marriage to Finn, because he was married himself. He'd been tricked into marrying Gunna of the Hebrides when she discovered she carried his child. All his gifts couldn't buy her silence. She wanted to be married to a chieftain's son, and she knew Leif wouldn't leave his child fatherless.

Snorri's coos bring me back to the present. He plays with his hands instead of nursing, grinning up at me. My stomach grumbles of its emptiness. I hope Freydis has eaten by now, but in her nervous state, I doubt it. Maybe Ref has brought food into their hut. He cares for her in such a tender way, even if she doesn't deserve it.

I kiss Snorri all over his face, then walk to the door. When I pull back the deerskin flap, one glance shows the inlet is empty—Hallstein's ship has gone. I thank God, because the threat of mutiny has sailed with that ship.

In the longhouse, the body has been moved and the men eat their mid-morning meal. Freydis and Deirdre stir the porridge, which reeks of cumin—Freydis' favorite.

The men who stayed share a bond of respect for Finn. Laughter spills over easily, and they drink more beer than they should.

Snorri Thorbrandsson watches me from his bench. He thinks I don't feel his stares. I'm used to ignoring them, since he means no harm. Nerienda takes the baby, hoping to feed him some oat porridge. I let her try, since he didn't nurse as long as usual.

Finn bends over a crude map. He prepares for our southern exploration to Vinland. He won't let us stay here, where we are vulnerable to Skraelings.

"Eat," Deirdre says. She gives me a bowl of porridge, with a man-sized helping inside, and walks me to a bench along the wall.

The over-spiced porridge nearly gags me. Deirdre must have let Freydis dump the cumin in. She probably had a moment of compassion for the accused forest child.

Freydis, sitting close beside me, hands me her own piece of cheese and bread. Deirdre busies herself serving the men, so we can talk. Yet I can think of no words to comfort Freydis.

Her hair is wild, as if she hasn't bathed for days. I need to take her to the creek and scrub her off.

She brushes the strands out of her face. I touch her stomach—small and hard. Perhaps too hard?

"How much have you eaten today?" I ask.

She looks at the ceiling. "Ref fed me."

"What? What did he feed you?" Ref shakes his head at me from the table, as if he can hear what I've asked. His unusual eyes, one green and one blue, reflect concern for his wife.

"Something...I can't think what."

"Has Nerienda checked you lately?"

"No." Her red overdress is too bright for her hair, and shows the lack of color in her cheeks.

"You eat some of this porridge right now, then go with Nerienda. I will put the baby to sleep and come to you." I hand her my bowl. She takes the wooden spoon, fingers shaking, and eats a small mouthful.

"Not enough—eat it all." I take the spoon and guide it to her mouth, again and again.

She watches me, her freckles standing out against her pale skin. I've never seen her so unable to fight. She continues to eat what she is given, without another word.

I instruct Nerienda to heat milk and to warm a stone for Freydis. Nerienda can feel where the baby is in a woman's body, making sure it's in the right position. It's a painful process, though, and Freydis will be more comfortable with the warm stone under her back and the milk to warm her inside.

Nerienda happily hands the baby to me, since he decided to spit the porridge all over her overdress. He snuggles into my arms, his baby smell drawing me in like a bright flower draws bees. I love having such a quiet, easy child. As I stand to leave, Finn touches my back. I stop next to him.

Finn pulls me into the crook of his arm, under his tattoo. His hand fits around my waist, under Snorri's curled-up body. His warm grip is strong. The men understand this language even better than words. It says that I belong to him.

Snorri Thorbrandsson looks down at the map, reddening to the top of his head. I feel sorry for him, with no wife to make his clothes, and no brother to watch his back.

The men bring their bowls over for cleaning. Still, Finn holds me. His extended grip sends me a message too—he's saying that he sees me. Yet I fear what he would think if he could see deep inside me, with these thoughts that constantly pull me from him.

Leif's deep, slow voice intrudes into my head...the way he says "Gudrid," nearly worshipful. My face begins to heat.

I pull myself away from Finn's grasp, kissing his head so he doesn't notice my face. Snorri already sleeps in my arms. Deirdre notices my blush, and comes to me as if I had called her.

"Please take him to the hut." I hand Snorri over, then rush outside. Milking my cows, my only inheritance from my father, will clear my head.

The air is sweet and fresh, the afternoon sky a deep blue. The soft ground almost hums with fertility, as I walk behind the longhouse to get my bucket. My cows have deep summer grass now, so their milk is perfect for butter, cream, and cheeses. And it's so much richer than goats' milk. Despite the bull's fierceness, I'm thankful we brought my animals along.

The dead body lies nearby on a bench, covered with a deerskin hide. Thoughts spin through my head, as I wonder what happened to him.

Whoever killed this man didn't care that the murder would be discovered, since his body was left lying on the midden heap, for all to see. A coward would try to hide him. The person who cut his throat was aware of the consequences. Perhaps ready to face judgment? Or certain there would be none?

Because Freydis doesn't usually lie to me, I want to believe in her innocence, even though she's been strangely timid since she's been accused. This fear isn't good for her babe.

Since no one in the longhouse can see me, I creep toward the body, lifting the deerskin. After peeling back the white face cloth, I search the large face, with his scarred yellow beard and closed eyes. His paleness, coupled with his long, hulking body, brings to mind the frost giant stories Halldis used to tell me.

I feel no anger toward him for trying to attack me, just pity that he had to die. The dark wound travels from one side of his neck to the other. But it wasn't slit—the cut is too deep. Freydis' skinning knife, properly used, would only make a surface cut. A man's knife made this mark, with its jagged, ripped edges.

I pull the cloth over his face once more, then cover it with the deerhide. They'll have to burn him tonight or the body will begin to smell, now that the warmth of summer is on us.

Freydis knows something about this man. But even as I think of questions I need to ask, her cries ring throughout the camp.

Chapter Eight

Many possibilities race through my mind as I run toward Freydis' hut. Perhaps Hallstein left a man behind to attack her, as retribution for killing his man. Perhaps she miscarried when Nerienda checked her. I should have stayed with her, instead of fleeing outside to cover my shameful thoughts of Leif.

I duck under her doorframe, far too low for someone her height. The men didn't take as much care building her hut as ours.

Inger holds Freydis' legs, while Nerienda rubs her stomach. The old woman doesn't look around, recognizing my step. "I had to turn the child."

Freydis' face is even whiter than it was earlier. As I get closer, her colorless face blurs into my mother's as she died. The smell of fresh vomit in a nearby bucket brings me back to my senses.

"You turned the child already?" I ask. "But she has a few more months."

"No." Nerienda's hands rub in a circular motion. "She has only a month and a half, at most."

This is distressing news, but I won't speak my thoughts in front of Freydis, shivering on her bed. I find a soft rabbit-hair blanket and drape it over her.

If she's that far along, her baby is too small. Its position might not even make a difference.

I lay my hands on Nerienda's, stopping her motions on Freydis' stomach. "I will help her." Nerienda nods, instructing Inger to fetch a brew of herbs that will ease her pain. Even though the heated rock has been placed below her back, she's draped both arms around her stomach, crying with each cramp.

Freydis' fingers wrap loosely around mine as I take her hand. I point to the light-haired slave girl called Linnea. "Broth."

She jumps from her chair to obey.

"Freydis, I want you to look at me." She opens her eyes—heavy with such pain, I want to absorb it for her. Her pains must be relentless.

I touch her stomach and imagine it softening, like an over-ripe plum, instead of the apple it is now. I used to chant as I did this, when I worked with Halldis. Now, I pray over her out loud, to comfort her.

Freydis' mouth opens a bit, which is good, because she's been clamping her jaw. Inger comes up behind me, placing the warm herbal tea in my hand. I pull Freydis' head up, pouring a sip into her mouth. She manages to hold it down. It will take Linnea some time to make the broth, so I put both hands on Freydis' stomach and press lightly, just enough to bring warmth to her.

"This baby will be a strong son to his father." I speak like a volva, soothing and assured. "He'll have your beautiful hair, the red hair of his grandfather, Eirik."

Freydis groans, her hands fluttering to encircle her stomach. I focus on every word I say, willing it to become true.

"Perhaps he'll wield a sword like his mother," I say. Her lips turn up into a half-smile.

I know this isn't the time to ask Freydis questions. But I lean down toward her ear. "Thank you, for whatever you've done for me."

Her small nostrils flare and her eyes focus. "But...you don't believe me?"

"Of course I do." I can't meet her relentless cat-stare.

"My knife is missing." She's like a child who's lost a favorite toy.

No one has come forward with the knife, but I wonder if they would. Everyone assumes it's the weapon the killer used. Maybe someone is hiding it, to protect Freydis.

"I will find it." I stroke her curls from her head.

She nods and closes those shining blue eyes, breathing hard.

Finally, Linnea brings the broth. I force Freydis to drink some of it. I'm afraid the baby has no nourishment. Who knows how long she was in the forest, with nothing to eat, sitting in one position in that tree? And her recent vomiting spell will only make the cramping worse.

The slave girls chatter in the corner. Their disrespect brings heat to my face. I point to Inger. "Would you milk my cows for me? Do you know how?"

"Yes, m'lady." She drops the 'm'lady' so I can hardly hear it. When she leaves, Linnea goes silent, twisting her skirts in her hands.

"And you." I motion for Linnea to come closer. Her long, fair hair looks identical to my own. "You take this stone and reheat it." She stares at me with pale green eyes so widely set, I can't look away from them.

As she takes the stone and leaves, Nerienda joins me. "She's the one Hallstein attacked. That girl fought like a wild animal. I couldn't get my club quickly enough to protect her. If Karlsefni hadn't come, she would be carrying a child of her own now."

I ignore the jealousy that springs up—Finn was there for Linnea, but not for me. Surely he hasn't been watching her?

"There's a rumor…" Nerienda says.

I spoon more broth into Freydis' mouth, wondering what the old woman has heard. "Yes?"

"We hear you've charmed a wolf. It was seen around your hut at dusk, not looking for food—just circling." Like all Vikings, Nerienda is superstitious about wolves. In pagan stories, the wolf Fenrir kills the great Odin himself.

So, my wolf was ready to protect me, when my husband was not.

"Nerienda." I force a smile. "You know you can't listen to rumors."

"Well, I saw that wolf myself one day." She's determined to get information from me. "A beautiful animal, bigger than the ones in Iceland. Healthy coat. It looked at me, but ran back into the woods."

"I suppose the wolves in Straumsfjord are smart enough to leave Vikings alone," I say. "Let's hope the Skraelings are, as well."

At the mention of Skraelings, Nerienda falls into her own thoughts. I tend to Freydis, giving her broth here and a drink there, until Linnea brings the heated rock to me. She hands it over, and it's exactly the right warmth. This is hard to do, and it shows me she's careful with her tasks.

I settle Freydis on the bed, covering her with the blanket and the white reindeer hide Stena gave her. Looking around her hut, I realize she's brought all sorts of objects with her from Brattahlid. Eirik's iron helmet hangs on a nail. How she was able to get this, I don't know. Rightfully, it should have gone to one of his sons, since helmets are costly. This one was specially hammered around the eyepiece to fit Eirik's wide-set eyes. I know Freydis can't use it, since it would be huge on her. Does Leif know she has this?

A pillow, covered with red silk, sits on a chair. It's probably from one of Leif's voyages to Europe. I've only seen silk once before, when Finn traded it to a man in Greenland for numerous ivory tusks.

I sit next to the bed, thinking about Nerienda's words. Freydis will have the baby sooner. This will make it difficult to move camp, especially given her weakened condition. I wonder what Thorvald, her kind-hearted brother with the chestnut-colored hair, would have done if he were still alive.

The answer becomes clear. The women must not go. Nerienda was telling me this, without ordering me to stay. But Finn has to search for Vinland, to find the riches Leif expects on our return. Grapes alone would bring my husband unbelievable wealth.

Deirdre carries Snorri in, his face red and crinkled as he cries out. Freydis doesn't wake, finally in a deep sleep. I don't know how much time I've spent in this hut.

"Many thanks," I whisper. I settle back into the chair. Ref made it for Freydis, and it's perfectly curved to fit my back. He's a wood-worker, with skills well-known throughout Greenland. Today, he's probably building the funeral pyre.

Adjusting my yellow overdress, I talk with Deirdre, since everyone else has gone to do chores.

"The milking?" I ask.

"Inger finished it. She makes the butter now. She's honored that you asked her to handle your cows."

I laugh, and so does Deirdre, even though sometimes she seems as awe-struck by me as the slave girl.

Deirdre needs to know the truth, since she will need to stay behind, too. I speak quietly. "Freydis won't be able to ship out."

As I say this, Deirdre's blue eyes get very large, and she looks to the bed where Freydis' fiery curls fall over the side.

"But the men plan—"

"I know their plans. They can still go. But the women should stay at Straumsfjord for Freydis. She helped me with Snorri's birth, and besides, Leif would want us to stay." I want Deirdre to come to this decision on her own, although I will command her to stay if I have to.

"Yes, we must stay." She twists her silver necklace, with its complex, woven strands. How did a slave come to own such a rich piece of jewelry? "But Karlsefni would want Magnus with him, would he not?"

True, Finn relies on Magnus to know the right direction. Magnus is the reason our ships have made it this far. When the seeing stone won't change color, when there's no sunlight or starlight to steer our ships, Magnus can feel where the land is. No one questions him.

"Yes, he'll need him."

Deirdre twists the necklace tighter. "But who else could he trust with us? All the men are…they are empty without women."

Maybe the women should stay here alone. But we would never survive, even with the wolf, because Freydis can't fight now. There is one man who could be trusted, though.

"Snorri." Deirdre voices my thoughts. Truly, Snorri Thorbrandsson is the only man who could defend us like ten men.

I nod slowly, knowing what this could mean.

"You'll be talking to Karlsefni soon?" She speaks with her Scottish tongue, so easy for her when she's worried.

"Tonight." As Snorri finishes nursing, I feel he's drained the last of my strength.

Freydis groans in her sleep, so I go to her, holding Snorri close to me. I brush the sweat-coated hair off her forehead. Looking at her small stomach, I can picture what's inside it, although I don't want to. I can do this because when I worked with Halldis, we offered a dead servant woman to Thor. Halldis performed the holy songs and chants, explaining that they would sanctify the woman before we looked in her body. Then she used her sharpest knife to cut the stomach open. This was necessary because she died of a strange illness during pregnancy, one that none of the midwives had seen before. We were trying to avoid more problems for other Icelandic women.

This is how medicine went in Iceland. We looked at the dead to find how to help the living. The volva believed the gods had created cures for every disease; it was up to us to find the plants they'd placed on earth for healing. We found that grinding and mixing the Angelica plant with water and wine would help children vomit up what was clogging their breathing. We also learned that certain bell-shaped flowers, when the seeds were ground, would quicken the heartbeat.

Now I can picture Freydis' child, not stretching its arms and legs as it ought to, but lying very still, curled in a tight ball. She has probably never felt the babe kick.

My baby dropped into the right place just before I gave birth. I wouldn't let anyone turn him. Nerienda went along with my wishes, giving me honor as a chieftain's daughter, and as Thorfinn Karlsefni's wife. I hated giving birth in our sparse, makeshift hut, with nothing familiar around me.

Finn attended baby Snorri's birth in the only way acceptable. He stood right outside the hut, listening to my every cry, and shouting words of comfort to me. He didn't care if any of his men heard him. He told me later that it nearly broke him, hearing my cries. Nerienda swore he had more pain than I did during the birth.

Deirdre takes Snorri from me so I can think. As she walks out, loneliness overwhelms me. I walk to the wall, taking down Leif's sword. I can easily picture his long fingers, with their blonde hairs, as he handled it. Leif likes doing tricks with swords, to show how quickly he can kill someone, should he need to.

Finn walks into the room, almost as quietly as Freydis. He takes the sword and turns it in his hands, thoughtfully studying the worn, rune-carved blade. "Do you remember how to use this?"

I nod, feeling the warning in his words.

He places the sword in my hands. "Show me."

I thrust the heavy iron sword, wishing it were lighter metal, like Snorri's steel blade. Finn guides my hands from behind, teaching me new movements. His gentle, firm touch nearly breaks me. Why can't I always feel his love this way, strong as an unseen shield?

Finn replaces the sword, finally satisfied with my ability. "The burning will be tonight after the meal. Freydis will stay in her hut. I'll have Deirdre watch over Snorri. But you will come with me."

Chapter Nine

I hardly notice as the evening meal comes and goes. I try to ignore how long it takes for Finn's strongest men to lift the heavy body onto the funeral pyre. But I can't turn my eyes away from the stars tonight, burning hot against the black sky.

As a young girl, I believed the stars sang to me through the hole in our longhouse roof. Halldis couldn't explain this, even with her trolls. Orm said, "This child is connected to the world in deeper ways than the volva, Halldis." They began asking my opinion before making decisions, thinking I had a supernatural source of power.

Tonight, I recognize a large star I've seen in Greenland many times. Its buttery yellow glow makes it seem almost friendly. I talk to it in my head, as if I'm talking to God. Finn wants me to chant the burial songs, since I'm the only one who knows the proper runes. I explain this to the star. I'm not being disloyal to God, because I have to support Finn.

The men gather around the pyre, some looking at it, but most looking at the ground—a sure sign they have no respect for Hallstein's man. They should be watching the fire and sending well-wishes with him as his spirit leaves for Valhalla.

Halldis' deep purple cape drapes over my shoulders, soft as a dove's wing. It was the one thing I kept when she died. I chant the funeral rune, murmuring at first. My words gather strength as they flood back into my mind. I'm once again a teenager, preparing for testing by the volva. Halldis made me memorize every healing or hurtful chant they used. I know she loved me, because she trained me to replace her.

I can almost feel her wand in my hand again as I sweep my arms upward, to move the man's spirit to Valhalla. But it saddens me to know he's only going down, into the fires of the earth, and to his eternal doom. I look at the yellow star, shining steadily on us. Finn stands by my side, his eyes on me during this entire ritual. He's anxious to be done, so his men can start preparations for their voyage.

Afterward, we walk back to our hut in silence. A lone howl rings through the woods.

"I'm glad that's over." I take Finn's arm outside our hut's entrance. I want to know his thoughts on the strange funeral.

"You didn't want to say the runes." Finn's hand slides into my own.

"No." My first husband, Thorir, known to all as The Eastman, had once forced me to use my abilities to make him look better, and I have always hated him for it.

The Eastman and I had only been married for six months when we had to accompany my father and a shipload of friends to Greenland. Father wanted to leave Iceland and all his debts behind, to settle near his friend

Eirik the Red at Brattahlid. Eirik had convinced Father that Greenland was a land of opportunity for Icelandic outcasts.

When The Eastman, a Norwegian seaman, agreed to captain my father's ship, I was part of the bargain. He married me right before we sailed for Greenland.

We had to overwinter at Herjolfsnes, a small village in southern Greenland, because Brattahlid was still a sea voyage northwest of us. Our voyage that far had been horrible, with the shivering disease taking many, including Orm and Halldis, who had only come along to protect me. Our number had dwindled to sixteen. So we stayed with Ulf, the only farmer in Herjolfsnes with room for all of us.

That winter was very lean, and Ulf wanted some kind of guarantee his crops would prosper the next year, to replenish his stores. Even though my father said we'd leave in spring, Ulf didn't trust him, knowing of his debts in Iceland. If he had no promise of good harvest, he planned to put us out.

One day, over the noon meal, Ulf said the Little Prophetess was coming into town. He wanted to invite her to his farm, hoping she would predict good fortune for the next year's crops.

My father voiced his disapproval. He had cast aside all pagan practices when my mother's sacrifice failed to save the farm. The volva couldn't explain why the farm didn't prosper, after he'd offered his most valuable sacrifice. But I could explain it—Thor was dead. There never was a Thor, or any other Norse gods, for that matter. My mother died for nothing. Even though Orm and Halldis had filled my head with Icelandic myths, trying to explain why her sacrifice hadn't worked, they had never convinced me.

On the ship, my father made attempts to kill himself, the weight of what he'd done to Mother almost crushing him. Every day, I tried to forgive him. I had believed in the Christian God, after spending hours listening to a monk tell stories from his Holy Book. He explained how Jesus Christ was the only perfect sacrifice, a human who was perfectly God and man. While my father never understood Jesus, he hated anything to do with Thor and the volva.

The Eastman believed in the Norwegian gods he had always known, but he never feared them. Horrifying my father, he encouraged Ulf to have the Little Prophetess over. "I've never seen a live witch." He laughed in my face. "I would love to see her mighty powers."

Fear gripped everyone in the household the day the Little Prophetess arrived. Her requirements were well-known in the town. Before telling the future, she had to talk with everyone on the farm. She needed a high seat, with a cushion of chicken feathers. She wanted the hearts of every animal killed for the meal.

Her dark hood had a strap with so many red gemstones, it looked like blood when the light hit it. Her white gloves were made from cat's skin, as was the lining of her hood. She had tall boots, and a belt that tinkled from the charms hanging on it. The belt itself was a large strip of aging touchstone felt, so it glowed in the darkness.

Her wand was tall as she was, and it glittered with rubies, with a bronze ball on the end. She often pointed it at the fearful servants, laughing as the gems' bloody red hit their faces.

I remained unimpressed. Halldis had looked more otherworldly in her simple purple robe, her copper hair her best adornment.

The Prophetess came close to me, her old-woman breath hot on my face. I could see all her missing teeth as she spoke. "So, how are things between you and that big, strong husband of yours?" Her familiar tone revealed she wouldn't mind having The Eastman as her own lover. The volva were known to be driven by lust.

"Things are very *pure* between us." I refused to give her the details she wanted. The Eastman scolded me later for my impudence. I didn't care. I would not be drawn into her wickedness.

To everyone's surprise, she decided to stay overnight. Father had stormed out of Ulf's house to stay with a neighbor while the Prophetess was there. I was glad of this, because I feared he would do something rash that would end Ulf's hospitality. In the cold of winter, we would be hard-pressed to find another place to stay. Ulf was the wealthiest farmer in Herjolfsnes, with much influence on the town.

"Your papa's not a very good guest." The Eastman loved to goad me about our poor condition, since my father was no longer a chieftain.

I never answered The Eastman on these things. It only made him worse. Instead, I found some task that moved me away from him. He couldn't stand the way I avoided all his spoken arrows. I treated him the same as I would a wild dog in Iceland—I didn't look in his eyes, and I walked right past him as if he didn't exist.

The next day, the Little Prophetess demanded to cast a magic circle. She asked all the women in the household if they knew the ward songs, which, of course, no one did. I refused to tell her I'd known them since I was twelve years old.

But The Eastman pushed me forward. "My wife is skilled in magic rites, having grown up with a volva foster-mother." His teeth shone in his wide smile.

"I won't take part in these actions, since I'm now a Christian," I said.

The Little Prophetess smiled as well. Then she talked to Ulf. She told him she wouldn't tell his future unless I agreed to participate. Ulf strode over to me, laying his heavy hand on my shoulder. "Gudrid, we need to know this. If you can't do it, you and your father can leave. And take all your father's friends with you." He dropped his threats carelessly.

That was the first time I used my skills to guarantee safety for those I loved.

I sang the ward songs. The servants thought my voice unnaturally pure and high, and they called me a *valkyrie*. The Little Prophetess herself was speechless. She declared I'd summoned spirits out of nowhere, making her prophesying easy.

She proceeded to give Ulf a good prediction for the farm. I left the circle, and prayed in my room for the spirits to leave the house, picturing a giant broom sweeping them out. As I did this, the Little Prophetess sighed loudly in the center room, saying the séance was over.

The Eastman forgave my impudence that night, because he wanted to share my bed. He was humbled and slightly awed by my power. He had his way with me, but in our marriage he never broke the icy surface of my deepest thoughts.

Finn compliments me, dragging me away from those memories I've tried to forget. "You remembered all the chants." He's proud of me.

"Of course, I hear them in my dreams sometimes." I pull my hair back, wrapping it in a knot.

"And that's all you dream about, my wife?" He takes my hand and kisses it. "Old women's chants and runes?"

"I suppose you dream of grape vines and plenty of wheat!" I laugh, hoping he'll change the conversation. But Finn has known me long enough to understand what I'm doing.

His voice lowers. "Gudrid, are you happy to be my wife?"

"Yes." My answer comes too quickly.

"You think of him."

"Who?" I tuck a strand of hair back, trying *not* to think of him.

Finn doesn't answer. His hand stays wrapped around mine, its strength and warmth flowing into me. I'm thankful for the deep darkness, which covers my blush.

I touch his chin and beard in the darkness like one blind. Then I run my hand into the curls at the back of his neck, picturing his dark blue eyes and his forehead wrinkling.

"*You* are the reason I like to be alive," I say. "You and our son."

I reach down into his shirt, touching his tattooed arm muscles. He pulls me into him, and we kiss silently before going inside to the baby and Deirdre. She'll be anxious to get back to Magnus, to hear about the funeral.

Later that night, we talk. I tell Finn the women will have to stay here to help Freydis. It's what her brothers would want. When he finally agrees, we discuss who needs to stay behind. Finn would leave everyone but Magnus, if I'd let him. He's nervous about the huge number of skinboats that came ashore.

He stops rubbing my back. "Snorri Thorbrandsson."

"Yes." I act as if I hadn't already figured that out.

"And I'll choose the others…only those I trust."

While he talks aloud, wondering what men are respectable enough to keep their hands off the women, I wonder if I can tame my wolf. Would she stay close to camp, if I put out food? Perhaps she would protect me, since she's been around my hut.

When I finally go to sleep, much later than Finn, I dream of Leif. These nightly dreams aren't troubling—in fact, they comfort me. Tonight, Leif seems so close I can almost smell him. His beard is short, starting to grow in as it did when he'd returned from Norway clean-shaven. His hands reach for me….

Snorri wakes me during the night to feed, but I fall back into my dream easily. Now I'm on the hills of Greenland, skies sweeping around me. I go into the longhouse, where Eirik sits at the head of the table, pounding his glass and yelling at Thjodhild to fill it, like she's a common slave. In these dreams, I have conversations with Leif that make no sense. We talk of Straumsfjord and the things we've found here. My wolf stays by my side. Our children play together—babies I haven't given birth to yet.

I know I'm sleeping later and later each morning, wishing to live in my happy dream-world. I cling to these dreams, hungry as any nursing child, because I am sure Leif is having them, too.

Chapter Ten

When I wake, much later than Finn, I determine to go check on my cows. Magnus feeds and cares for the few sheep we have in a pen near his hut. It's been nothing short of a miracle the sheep haven't been attacked yet. It's quite mad to think that my wolf, a predator, might be protecting them. But I wonder anyway, because nothing else explains it.

In the pasture, Linnea carries two splashing buckets of milk toward me. Her rough-spun clothes somehow draw attention to her face, like a frame on a painting. She doesn't speak, waiting for me to say something.

"Many thanks." I take one pail.

She smiles, revealing the whitest teeth I've ever seen, with a small gap between the front two. She's undoubtedly the most attractive woman here, and yet her beauty is a curse, not a blessing.

Linnea is a Swedish slave. I'm surrounded by slaves from all over the mainland. I'm also beginning to wonder if these women were taken in raids, or if Leif hand-picked them for some reason.

She continues walking down the hill, toward the longhouse. I follow her, noticing the empty bench out back. I've promised Freydis I'll find her knife, and I plan to do it.

As Linnea goes in the back door, I put down the bucket and search the ground beneath the bench. Nothing. If any of the women removed the knife, they would've told me. And Hallstein said his man's throat was slit, but he had no knife to prove Freydis did it.

Behind our hut, the midden pile is covered with a bucketful of fresh waste I emptied this morning. Normally, I would gag at the smell, but I hold my breath and creep closer.

Freydis loves that knife. If her weapon is behind our hut, it would prove she was there the night of the murder. And if I find that knife first, I'll make sure no one else knows where it was.

Smoke rolls out the hole in the longhouse roof. Linnea and the women are preparing the mid-morning meal. Even if they see me, they know better than to question Thorfinn Karlsefni's wife. Deirdre's still in my hut, watching Snorri for me. Hopefully she won't hear me.

I turn sharply at a noise near our midden heap. The wolf stands just behind it…perhaps rummaging through the scraps?

She sniffs the air, then trots right up to my side. Finn would be furious if he saw how close I stand to her. She surprises me further by rubbing her head into my hand, like a small pup. Something seals between us, something I can't explain, but I know it won't be broken. I slowly rub between her ears, pulling out pieces of shedding fur.

We stand there, mutually happy, for some time. Finally, she lopes up the fenceline, back into the woods. I go over to the spot where she'd been nosing around.

I find nothing more than the pile of excrement, molding food scraps, and ashes from our fire. I turn in a circle. One low-lying evergreen bush grows near the fenceline, so I go to examine it. It's the only place, except the midden heap, where anything could be hidden. I pull up the edge of the bush, and a curved metal blade glints in the sunlight. Picking up the dirty wooden handle, I look for blood stains. The blade seems clean, although it could have been wiped off after the kill.

If I cared about following Althing law, I would take it to Finn, so he could report it to the men. Instead, I carefully tuck it into my tall boot. I walk stiffly toward Freydis' hut, so the knife doesn't poke my foot. She's probably still inside today.

A few men stand around guarding the camp. The hunters and fishers left before dawn, to stock up on food before shipping out. As I pass the men's huts, Snorri Thorbrandsson comes out, head down. But his gaze shifts to my boot, which is probably bulging, even under my skirts. His light brown eyes travel curiously up to my face. His thick, unruly beard shines bright orange in the sun. Again, I feel a strange sadness that he has no woman to trim his beard.

"Gudrid." He nods, then covers a smile with his free hand. I get the feeling he's laughing at me. He walks on toward the longhouse, swinging his sword. He practices with it every day. He's probably heading over to meet with Finn, as his right-hand man. Although Finn's right-hand man is left-handed. I smile, amused at my own pun. Snorri

Thorbrandsson holds his weapons in his left hand, and when he eats, he spreads himself all over the table, taking the space of two men. Some say it makes him a fiercer warrior.

Freydis wanders around her hut in small circles. She's rubbing her stomach again. I call out to her, so as not to alarm her, and hold out my arms as I approach.

Freydis walks into my embrace. Her soft hair glints in the sunlight, and she smells clean. Someone helped her bathe, thank goodness.

I cup my hand to her ear. "I found it." She doesn't expect me to waste time explaining how. I put the knife into her hand and her long, bony fingers close around it.

"Many thanks, sister." She pulls herself up to her full height, as if new strength has flowed into her. She's as tall as her brothers, and at least a head taller than I am.

"And how is the mother-to-be?"

She gives me a half-smile. "A little better. I'm so thankful for you and Nerienda—the wisest of birthers from Greenland."

I beam at her compliment. A blush begins at my cheeks and slowly spreads down to my throat.

"Ah, only a true princess can blush like this!" Freydis says.

When Finn traded with the Arabic men, they had a saying that only those of royal blood could blush so deeply. Finn must have shared that idea with Eirik's family at some point—quite possibly when boasting of me.

"I saw the wolf again." This will distract her.

"It seems to follow you, Gudrid! I'm not surprised— who doesn't love you?" She deliberately compliments me again, then winks as my blushing continues.

"I think she'll protect us when the men are gone." I pretend I don't notice her enjoyment of my embarrassment.

Freydis' eyes narrow, for she begins to understand what I'm saying.

I speak softly. "Your baby will be early, so we're staying here."

She raises her chin, a determined look coming into those harsh eyes. "I have my knife back, at least."

Of course, instead of thinking of her baby's safety first, she thinks of her ability to protect the camp.

I feign confidence. "Snorri Thorbrandsson will stay, I'm sure. And Finn will pick some men."

"Ref might stay?"

I look past her eyes, fringed with long red lashes, and try to understand her thoughts. Does she want her husband here? It seems she does, for some reason. How he comforts her when she hardly acknowledges his existence, I don't understand.

"I'll ask Finn." This means Ref will stay.

"Thanks for everything." I know she speaks of her knife—possibly more important to her than Ref. I hope someday she'll tell me if she cut that man's throat to protect me. But for now I'll tell myself she's innocent, just because she said so.

She begins circling her hut again as I leave, and I hope she doesn't try to hunt today. It's one of her favorite pastimes, for good reason. She's faster and quieter than the men, often felling three deer to their one. And sometimes she doesn't even use her bow, but her knife. No one knows how she gets close enough to slit even the bucks' throats. I think she falls out of a tree on them, or somehow coaxes them to her.

Before I check on my baby, I stop at Nerienda's hut. I'm actually staying away from him longer, in hopes he'll start drinking from the deerskin bottle we've made, or eat more solid food. It's never good for babies to rely too much on their mothers, especially when their mothers are Vikings.

Nerienda stands in the small room, strands of wool carelessly wrapped around her spindle. I laugh to myself, because her housekeeping skills are as poor as my own. We both value time with people more than chores. So far, I've been able to avoid spinning, since no one ever trained me how to do it. Besides, the women here would laugh me out of the hut.

"Gudrid!" Nerienda's smile crinkles her yellowed face. "How's Freydis today? I haven't…."

She tries to unwind some wool, leaving strands hanging all over the place. I would help her, but I'd only make it worse. I pretend not to notice her disgust with her task.

"I haven't been able to see her this morning." She throws the entire pile of wool back into her basket, spindle and all. She sits down on her bench and sighs, rubbing her hands together.

"She's better." I smile. "She walks around and is impertinent with me, as usual."

"Does she know?"

"I told her. She wants Ref to stay behind."

Nerienda rubs each of her fingers, working the stiffness out of them. "Of course she does. That man would bring every meal to her bed, if she'd stay in it long enough. He went and bathed her himself, I heard."

We both chuckle as we envision this. Freydis hates bathing. Deirdre says it's the forest child in her.

Nerienda stops laughing, the wrinkles in her forehead deepening as she frowns. "If the babe lives to breathe once, I'll be surprised."

I nod, but try to be hopeful, picturing the healthy births of Stena, Thorvald's wife. She was short and tiny, but she had endless reserves of strength. Though it took an entire day for each of her deliveries, her babies were perfect and chubby, all crying loudly as soon as they were born. We didn't have to teach them to suckle, either, as they all latched on quickly.

Thorvald bragged to Eirik, Leif, and anyone else who would listen that reindeer herders were stronger than Nordic women. Leif eventually told him to stop talking about it, because he was insulting his own Norwegian mother.

But Thorvald couldn't stop marveling at his children. Everyone else did, too, as they were exceptionally beautiful, with their dark eyes that turned slightly downward and their perfect honey-colored skin.

Stena left Brattahlid after Thorvald was killed, taking with her my chance to watch her babies grow up. She couldn't bear to stay near Thjodhild. Her mother-in-law insulted her daily, calling her a Lapp and a Skraeling to her face.

Nerienda stretches and stands, noticing my attention has wandered. "I'll go and help with the mid-morning meal."

As I start to follow her, Linnea rushes in, gasping for breath. "They're here—many this time. Karlsefni needs you." She points to me.

"Find Snorri and hide him!" I shout at Linnea. Then I run into our hut, grabbing a sword from the wall. By the time I reach him, Finn stands in the middle of the beach. He is completely surrounded by Skraelings.

Chapter Eleven

Skraelings wander around the rocky beach and up toward our huts. Some look through the fence at my sheep, some at the men's weapons, and many stare at my hair.

Snorri Thorbrandsson is poised to cut the hand off anyone who gets too close to Finn. All our men are uneasy, gripping their weapons. The sword, cold and solid, rests in my hand, giving me a small measure of comfort.

A woman with unnaturally huge eyes and reddish hair sits on a pile of furs in one of their narrow boats. She's probably their magic-worker, for she wears an elaborate necklace of shiny, dolphin-colored stones, and is surrounded by young men. She points to me, motioning in a circular movement to the furs.

Trade. They want to trade.

I push through the natives and whisper in Finn's ear. The Skraelings tighten their circle around him, closing us in.

When a native leans over the fence to touch a sheep, the small flock startles, wildly tearing back and forth. Magnus edges toward them, protective of his favorite animals. Other Skraelings eye our men's axes. It's as if a group of curious, uncontrolled children has been unleashed on the camp.

Freydis runs out of her hut, carrying a pile of red silk from Leif, which she hands to Finn. As soon as the old woman sees it, she clambers out of the boat, holding onto her men's shoulders. They bring the pile of furs up and present it to Finn, waiting for their valuable reward.

I can almost hear Snorri Thorbrandsson's aggressive thoughts as I watch the spectacle. We could kill them all now, while they're weaponless, in such a tight group. A few Skraelings sit in boats waving long sticks in circles, but they would be no match for our swords, axes, and knives.

A tall man with a long black tail of hair reaches out to take the silk. He has to be their leader, given all the furs he's wearing.

Finn places the silk in the man's hands. Their thin leader pulls out a knife, and Finn's hand flicks to his thigh. Snorri holds his sword in a double handgrip, stepping in front of Finn. But the Skraeling man begins to cut off a long strip of silk. He wraps it around his head, then turns and speaks to his people. He passes the fabric to the old woman, who takes out her own bone-handled knife and cuts strips for all of them.

The Skraelings all begin swinging their sticks, which swish loudly as they complete a circle in the air. They like their colorful head-wraps.

We stand frozen until the woman cuts up all the silk. A few Skraelings continue watching the sheep, but most edge closer to observe our weapons.

My wolf chooses this moment to begin her patrol of the fenceline. She runs out of the forest, ears high, back hair bristling. I back up toward her, aware that if she wants to attack the men, I can't stop her. But at least Finn's men will see I'm with the wolf, and hopefully think before trying to kill her.

The old woman shouts in their nasal language. The sticks clatter into the boats and their people jump in. How did the woman know the wolf is with me? I turn to see where my wolf is.

She has come to a dead stop at my side, panting slightly.

None of our men come closer, afraid the wolf will attack. But as soon as the boats have sailed out of sight, I lean down and tell the wolf to get home. I don't know why I do this, but somehow she understands, following the fenceline back into the woods.

Finn walks up, a strange look on his face. His mouth is set, but his eyes are smiling.

"Your beast saved us all." I'm shaking as he puts his arm around me. "Perhaps you're safer in the woods than I thought," he whispers. He brushes my ear with his lips.

Finn turns to his men. "We need to talk—now."

They slowly sheath their weapons, following Finn to the longhouse. Inger and Deirdre run ahead of them, in order to get the mid-morning meal started.

As the men pass me, they give me looks—some respectful, some bordering on hatred. My wolf stole their chance to wreak some havoc on the Skraelings. As Snorri Thorbrandsson passes, he dips his head toward me so slightly, I'm the only one to notice. But it's a movement that shows his approval, something I'll need when Finn leaves us.

Linnea stumbles out of the woods, holding Snorri. She hands him to me, her skirt ripped and her face flushed. Many of the men stare at her in this disheveled state. She's certainly in the bloom of life. She'll be safer if she gets married as soon as possible. I'll ask Deirdre if she's interested in anyone. Linnea is probably the age I was when I first married.

My baby nuzzles into me. I touch the cleft in his chin that matches Finn's. I've only seen Finn once without a beard, when he first arrived in Greenland. It had been the fashion to be clean-shaven in Norway, where he traded. His strong chin seemed to contradict his genuine compassion, and I'd been enchanted.

I turn into our hut to feed Snorri.

"I just fed him!" Linnea immediately looks ashamed at her outburst.

"You did?" I ask. "How?"

"I put cow's milk in the deerskin bottle—to keep him quieter for the Skraelings." Again, I'm pleased to see she's careful with her duties.

"Thank you." I marvel that my son finally eats from someone other than me. This gives me freedom, along with a strange sadness.

Snorri squirms in my arms, reaching for the grass. I put him down, holding his hand. As he tries to walk, I can tell he's getting stronger, his thin legs straightening up.

Linnea stands too, watching him with a motherly smile. Deirdre comes out of the longhouse.

"We are needing the two of you." She holds Snorri's other hand, and we try walking him to the house.

Deirdre whispers, "When Linnea smiles, you have a twin."

Perhaps this is why I worry about the girl. She looks much as I did, when I was younger. No wonder my baby loves her. Did Leif love her too? Does Finn notice her youth, wishing I looked more like her? Such thoughts are poison to me. But perhaps our similarities caused Hallstein's attack. He was drunk, and could have easily mistaken Linnea for me in the dark.

This radiant girl, full of the youth I've lost, must be protected from future attacks. We'll have to watch over her closely when the men sail for Vinland.

My Snorri stumbles in the doorway, then looks up at me and grins. His eyes are bright green today, like the northern lights in Greenland. He's so determined to succeed, just like his father. Or perhaps like me.

Finn stops talking when his son comes into the longhouse. He quickly starts again, but his pause makes me happy. Though I know he loves us, loving words don't come easily for him. I'm learning to watch for these small gestures that show his affection.

Deirdre sits next to Magnus, and not with the other women. She's determined to be with him as much as possible before the trip. Those two are joined at the hip.

They have the strangest relationship. Magnus barely talks at all, while Deirdre chatters all the time. Somehow, they balance each other. Halldis would have said it's like Thor and the Midgard serpent—Thor destroys the serpent, but before it's over, the serpent's poison also destroys Thor. Thus, they're equal in strength, with differing abilities.

I pick up Snorri, carrying him over to the women standing around the kettle. I scoop out a bowl of soup, made with deer jerky. It's a colorless dish, with no vegetables, save cabbage. Perhaps, if we could talk with the Skraelings, they'd show us other plants to grow, and how to thrive here. We can't survive another lean winter.

The old Skraeling woman may be the key. We communicated when she was motioning about trading. If I could spend time with her, I could learn to speak their language. Languages are easy for me, perhaps because I had to memorize so many chants and runes as a girl. And my grandmother was Scottish, so I learned that language early.

As the men discuss the trip, I know Finn's thoughts. He won't want to go, with the Skraelings returning more often. And what could we trade next?

Bjarni, an old man with a shock of white hair, speaks. "It's time to head south. Leif expects a haul of goods. Besides, I know Vinland's south of here. Hallstein was a fool to go north." Bjarni was the first sailor to spot this new land, so many years ago. He didn't explore it then; he just told Leif about it and sailed with him on the first voyage to Vinland.

"But how long will it take to find this legendary place?" A light-haired man talks around a mouthful of cheese.

"Tell me why we should we risk our lives just to repay a chieftain's son?" A slave shouts from the corner. His dark eyes, hair, and skin set him apart from the rest of us. He's probably some kind of native Sami or northern Greenlander. Of course he feels no allegiance to Leif, a rich chieftain.

Freydis listens from the back bench. She gives a loud huff and pulls the hair off her eyes, glaring at the bold slave.

"We promised to bring back a shipload for Leif," Finn says. "And I keep my word."

"Hear, hear." Several of the men bang their cups.

"But our wives?" Magnus puts his arm around Deirdre. She hasn't even gotten up once to refill the soup bowls.

Snorri Thorbrandsson speaks up. "I'll stay behind. I'll keep ten of you with me. The Skraelings probably won't come back, after Gudrid's wolf—"

The dark-eyed slave interrupts. "That beast is unpredictable. Who's to say it won't kill us all in our sleep?"

Finn says, "That *beast* has been patrolling our camp. It's protected our cows; maybe even our sheep. And now, our people. It's harmless for us."

I could jump up and hug him, but I stay on my stool near the fire, watching Snorri play with a large wooden spoon. He's easy to please—a blessing in this sparse place. If he were at Brattahlid, he'd have his choice of wooden horses, ivory figurines, or golden rattles to play with.

"Which ten men?" The red-haired man who speaks is someone I've barely noticed. I should know all the men's names, but I don't. I deliberately avoid their side of camp and don't make conversation with them. On our voyage from Greenland we were so packed on the ships, I learned not to smile at any man. These Vikings take a woman's smile as an open advance.

Finn points out the ten, naming them, including the dark-eyed slave, Suka. Why my husband would choose him to protect us, I can't imagine. Perhaps he's skilled in some way.

Suka's eyes narrow and a sour look crosses his face, until Snorri Thorbrandsson returns the glare, his eyes bright with all the violence he's capable of.

Most of the men who have been chosen to stay behind are eager to protect us. Some even say "Good-night" to women for the first time, after the meal. I don't like their familiarity, and I don't know what's going to happen when Finn is not here to control them.

Finn pours most of his soup out on the midden pile, a sure sign he's anxious.

I touch his shoulder. "Could we talk?"

He nods, picking up Snorri on our way out. The boy squeals, and even says something like *far*, calling for his father.

It's my chance to voice all my fears. The tall pines along the forest form a dense barrier, making me feel trapped without a full view of the ocean. Iceland had no trees on its rough cliffs. I'd sit on those desolate ledges as a child, watching the waves for hours. Even inland, on Eiriksfjord at Brattahlid, we could see the ocean and sky meet in a perfect blue line.

Finn notices the faraway look in my eyes. "We won't be gone for long, Gudrid. I'll make sure of it."

"I know, my sweet husband. But I was wondering about your choice of men. Suka has no respect for position. He's even worse than Hallstein."

"Snorri chose Suka. He's our fastest runner."

Runner? Why would we want to run? I thought we needed men who could stand and destroy huge groups of Skraelings.

"You saw those larger men, Sindri and Tyr?" His voice is calm and soothing. "They were King Olafsson's guards. There are no better men with swords. They're also close to Leif and want to prove their loyalty to him by protecting his family here."

Not wanting to scorn Finn's comfort, I take his hand. "Thanks for choosing them."

"I promise to come back in at least four months." He's determined to make me feel better.

So much can happen in four months. But he's right, he needs time to explore the coastlines further south, to go ashore and look for grapes and wheat when they're ripe.

He kisses me on the forehead. "You'll be safe." Snorri kicks at his father's side with his tiny boots. "You know I wouldn't leave if I didn't feel sure of that."

His rough beard brushes against my face as he kisses my forehead again, longer this time. I take his face in my hands, moving his mouth to mine, willing myself to believe I'll survive these four months without him.

Snorri grabs at Finn's beard, jabbering away at us. I'd do anything for this child. I certainly would have killed that yellow-haired man. Chill bumps spread up my arms to my neck, because even if our ten men *can* handle the Skraelings, what if Hallstein and his crew decide to come back?

Chapter Twelve

Lately, I've been exhausted just trying to survive at Straumsfjord. I don't even care to wake some mornings. In Greenland, family surrounded me, like a protective circle. On the farmstead, we all lived so close, knowing when to amuse or when to console.

Here, I wonder if the women are kind to me only because of my position. Deirdre will always be loyal to me, and to my baby—it's her nature. But the slave women were chosen by Leif, and might harbor hatred for me, as Suka does for those in power.

Freydis is impossible to understand. I'm in her good graces now, and she still looks up to me. But what if I can't deliver her child into the world, healthy and strong, as promised? Freydis' hatred is like an unchecked flame, ready to spark into a blaze and destroy without reason.

I've lost my purpose in life. When I was a girl in Iceland, following in Halldis' footsteps, I knew my destiny. I would be the next high volva, loved and feared by the villagers. But when I believed what the monk told me about Christ, I no longer wanted that position or the powers I had to embrace to make it possible. My hatred of my father was misplaced. It was Thor I hated, and all the gods and goddesses that ruined mortals' lives just for fun.

Thor *is* real—he's an evil spirit that whispers into the volva's ears when they're in trances. He encourages the powerful to take pride in slaughtering the innocent.

I tried to tell Halldis that only one God was willing to kill himself for humans—the Christian God. But since I didn't have a book of Holy Writings, I couldn't explain everything as the monk did. Halldis finally agreed to let me worship on my own and not join her in chants. As she died, I knelt next to her bed, praying over her. I hope she believed in the end, for I can't imagine heaven without her beautiful red head there.

Snorri Thorbrandsson could be a friend to me here. I believe he would be loyal, because of Finn, but what if he lets his passions take over? He and his brother were outcasts for a reason, offending as many neighbors as Eirik the Red did.

Finn has been out fishing for at least two hours now. I should get up, but instead I stay in bed and try to sleep again. Nerienda wakes me when she comes in, carrying a bowl of porridge for Snorri.

Her warm hazel eyes flicker with surprise, but only for a moment. She stokes the fire for me. It's a small but much-appreciated gesture on this chilly morning. It seems the fogginess outside hangs in the damp air of our hut. I should hunt for berries, help with the mid-morning meal, and check on Freydis and her baby. Today, though, I really don't care what I'm supposed to do.

I have my own baby to care for, and I'm doing a poor job of it. As Nerienda takes him out of his cradle, I can't even remember putting him there after nursing last night. It's not good for him to sleep so late these mornings, instead of walking to gain strength. What kind of mother plunges into her own homesick thoughts and dreams, neglecting to care for her own son?

Nerienda senses my mood. "You have encouraged Freydis. I felt her baby today—it's dropped some. She thinks she's ready to go into the woods and hunt." She places Snorri on a chair, tying his waist to the back with a linen belt so he won't topple out.

I smile, but my mouth is stiff, and won't even curve up. All the bones in my body ache. But I don't think I'm becoming ill, at least not in my body. My mind struggles with a sadness I can't pull under my control.

Nerienda loads up the spoon with porridge. Snorri opens his mouth wide, ready to eat. I try to speak, but a cough chokes me.

She turns sharply. "Are you ill? You're far too pale."

I nod, not really saying yes or no. "Maybe I'll just sleep today."

If she understands why I request this, she doesn't show it. "I'll take the boy to my hut. Linnea knows what he likes."

It seems the very act of feeding my own child would be too much today. Nerienda unbelts Snorri. She wets a cloth and washes his little body with it, then dresses him in his long red woolen tunic. That way, he can relieve himself whenever he needs to. He's getting old enough to use a pot for this, but I've been too busy with my own fears to show him how.

Finn comes in as Nerienda pulls leather boots on Snorri's feet. He sets down his basket of fish and goes to his son, kissing him on the head. I want to get closer to the fire, but it's probably warmer staying wrapped in my wool blanket.

Finn hesitates as he sees me, doubtless wondering why I'm not out gathering berries. I'm too tired to make up an excuse, so I roll over and close my eyes.

Nerienda clatters around some more, picking up the bowl and dropping the spoon. Finally, she shuffles out the door.

"Gudrid?" Finn approaches our bed. I roll over and stare at his white woolen trousers, noticing there's a hole in the knee. A Viking wife maintains her husband's clothing, and I haven't even done this much. But Halldis never trained me to do mundane chores, knowing that as a chieftain's daughter, I would have slaves to do them for me.

Finn's rough hand traces the slant of my cheek. "Is something wrong?"

Yes, everything. Everything is wrong. I'm living in the wrong place, raising my son in a land I don't want him to become familiar with. I don't have family anymore. And I haven't laughed in a year.

Finn lies down next to me, trying to understand. He touches my forehead. "You're sick?"

"No." I smooth my hair around me like a protective hood. I will tell him my fears. "What if Hallstein comes back, Finn? He wanted to attack me. You must have noticed that Linnea looks almost exactly like me—he made a mistake that night, a drunken mistake."

He pushes the hair off my face. "Yes, I have thought of this."

He has?

"It's why I'm also leaving Bjarni with you." His eyes are dark and serious.

"The old man?" I try not to laugh. "What use is he to a group of helpless women? And wasn't he close friends with Hallstein?"

"They were friends once, when they used to sail together. But they've fought since Hallstein decided to go north. And Bjarni knows Hallstein's tactics better than anyone, so he's useful to your group."

Bjarni used to sit at Eirik's table, boasting about how *he* was the one who'd given Leif the idea of looking for Vinland, because he'd seen it first. I'd always thought he was cowardly for not going ashore when he found it. He's a proud, useless old man, and the idea of relying on him for protection makes me want to sink deep under my blankets.

Finn's eyes rest on me, waiting for my response. But I can't give him one. I can't even look into his eyes long, for fear he'll see how desperately I want to keep him near me.

Suddenly, he says the words I've been longing to hear. "I won't go south, if you ask me to stay. I'll break my promises to Leif, so we can go back earlier."

I can't agree to this. The entire trip will be a waste if he goes back empty-handed. We've found very little we could give Leif in return for the use of his ships. Still, I know Leif, and he would let us stay on at Brattahlid, because he looks on me as family. But Finn is not family. I don't know how Leif would deal with Finn's failure.

Yet it's so tempting. New strength rushes into me, just thinking of the comforts of Greenland. I prop myself up on my arm, meeting Finn's eyes. He's ready to do what I want. I could change our future by manipulating his sympathy for me.

But I can't. He might despise me later, when we're safe in Greenland. He would wonder if he missed finding self-sown wheat fields in the south, or grapes for rich wine. He would despise me when the men mock him for shortening his trip for his wife. He would become like Freydis' husband—people would start calling him "Gudrid's husband."

"No." I look away from those steady blue eyes. Then I force myself to repeat it and look directly at him. "No. We stay here."

He straightens his back, gazing into the fire. When his eyes fix on mine again, they are filled with resolve. I didn't stand in his way, and he loves me for this freedom.

He leans down and pulls me into a hug. "We'll leave in a few days. The sooner we travel, the sooner we come back. Summer is almost over and we must return before winter. But there's enough firewood stored, if we don't get back in time." He lowers me to the bed again. "There's still one more thing the men need to do before our journey. I'll have them start working on it today."

Perhaps I should ask what it is. Perhaps I should get out of bed. But when I close my eyes, all I can see is a tangled black tree with feet dangling from it. And a girl, knife in hand, scared to death of being alone.

Chapter Thirteen

It's dark when I open my eyes again. Finn snores lightly, his arm thrown over my body. Snorri's regular breaths sound from his cradle.

I carefully push Finn's arm to the bed. Groping around on the floor, I latch my fingers around the oil lamp. I slide out of the blankets, holding steady so I don't spill the oil. I take a twig from the kindling and hold it to a smoldering coal, planning to light the lamp outside.

I'm dirty. I don't remember how long it's been since I've bathed. At the very least, I'll be clean for my husband before he leaves me.

Outside, I blow on the twig until it lights the felt touchwood wick. I'm using our precious whale oil for this late-night bath. I hope Finn leaves at least one fisherman with us, so we can collect more oil for winter. Although Deirdre could probably fish, if she had to. And I'm a quick learner, as Eirik loved to tell everyone. He taught me how to ride horses, how to string a bow, even how to cook his favorite carrot soup, because Thjodhild refused to make it for him. She claimed it would turn his red hair an ungodly shade of orange.

The air is chilly and crisp as I walk to the creek—too crisp for summer. Fall will come early this year. I look up at the stars. I'm comforted to recognize *Friggjarrokkr*—the distaff of Freya—with her three stars, evenly spaced. Since I don't have to walk by the men's huts, I take my time stargazing.

Out of nowhere, I feel a low presence next to my side. Without lowering my lamp, I know it's my wolf. Her rough fur brushes against my hand. The wolf, like Snorri Thorbrandsson, knows exactly where I am at all times. It's as if she has my scent buried in her nostrils. She must not have young, because she would spend all her time hunting to feed them. Maybe now she looks on me as her pup—or does she know I have a pup of my own?

We walk together until we reach the creek. The water is probably freezing. I take a rag out of my pocket, planning to wash myself without dousing my entire body.

I find a safe place for the lamp, in an open spot between two small trees that loop over one another. This way the wolf can't easily knock it over, should she start sniffing at the whale oil.

My brooches loosen without incident, and I drop my shift to the ground. I can barely see where the waterline begins, but I step on the moss until I feel the shallow water start to flow over my feet. It's bracing, but the coldness revives my spirits.

I leave my seax in my leg sheath and wash under it, since I'm never comfortable enough to remove it. The wolf sits on the ground nearby, so I begin to talk to her. Or maybe I'm talking to God.

"Only four months. I'm strong enough for that." I squeeze the rag over my hair, then rub my face. "Suka or

Suki or whoever that Viking-hater is will have to submit to
my authority, as Finn's wife. Snorri Thorbrandsson will back
me." I move the rag in circles over my arms. The wolf hasn't
moved. "And Snorri will be under my authority, too."
Though truly, because Snorri is Finn's trading partner, he's
as much a leader as I am. I can't let him take charge, though,
because where would that lead?

The wolf jumps up, alert. I slip down into the water as
my lamp flickers. A man steps into its light. His long hair is
the color of golden flax seeds, pulled back from his face, and
he has a ruddy complexion. In fact, he looks like a younger
Leif. Why's he wandering around the camp?

"Someone here?" He even has a deep voice like Leif's.
He's not very observant, because my wolf sniffs at his boot
even as he peers into the darkness of the creek.

If I don't say something, he'll doubtless take my lamp.
"I am here—Gudrid, wife of Thorfinn Karlsefni. I'm bathing,
so don't come any closer."

His eyes continue to search the darkness for me, but he
has recognized my voice. "Many apologies," he says. "I'll
leave you. I'm guarding tonight."

My wolf now crouches in front of him, barring his way.
I don't know how to tell him this without scaring him to
death, but if he steps forward, she might bite him.

"You must go back the way you came," I say. "Don't
take another step toward me or I'll report you to my
husband."

"Of course." He turns awkwardly from the creek. He
tramps back through the brush, as my lamplight flares. Soon
it will be gone.

My skin is covered with gooseflesh and my lips feel
locked in place with the cold. I climb out of the water, taking

my brooches and dropping them in the pocket of my shift. My stiff fingers couldn't fasten them now. I pull the thin shift up around me, wishing I had my cape to cover it. My light finally goes out, so I wait until my eyes get used to the faint starlight.

The wolf patiently watches me, then walks over to the creek and drinks from the water, as if she's been waiting for me to finish using it.

I walk back to camp, watching my footing around the stray rocks and limbs. I'll go behind the longhouse to get to our hut, so the guard won't see me. He should be patrolling the shoreline now.

Passing the bench in back of the longhouse, the presence of the huge dead man deepens my chill. I pray out loud.

"Please protect our camp, God in heaven…from Hallstein or the Skraelings or anything seeking to harm us. You are all we have in this hostile land. And thank you for your Son. Amen."

My prayer seems too simple. I'm not eloquent, like the monk was. If only I could write poetry in runic form to God. Or would that be offensive, since runes are used for pagan magic spells? I'll never know, unless I have a Holy Book and learn to read it.

Once I'm back in the hut, I pull on a pair of Finn's woolen trousers and two of his heavier tunics. The fire is dying, so I add pine cones and stir it up. Finn still snores, and Snorri breathes softly under his reindeer skin covering. I curl my body into Finn's, planning to sleep, but I can't. Memories of Leif spill into my mind, uninvited.

Eyes closed, I can smell the curious scents of Brattahlid—its damp stone walls, incessant smoke, and the cinnamon sticks Thjodhild always kept on the table. I remember Leif breezing into the longhouse where I'd worked with Thjodhild. He grabbed my hand, saying, "If Gudrid doesn't come outside on this glorious day, I won't plant your flowers, *Modi*." He loved using his baby name for his mother when he wanted something.

Thjodhild looked up from the coat she was stitching for Thorstein, for our upcoming trip to Vinland that winter. Her eyes were the palest blue I'd ever seen—the color of faded violets.

"But of course, Leif." She gave in to her charming son, as usual.

As we walked out, Leif's hair tumbled free, full of the scent of outdoors. I'd been married to his red-headed brother for only a few weeks. Leif was married, too, and their son had been born in the winter, right before my father died.

Though Thorstein the Red was many things to me, he was never thoughtful, like Leif. Leif knew the things that pleased me, like running in the fields, or standing under the barley-barn roof during storms. I loved questioning him about the medicinal practices in Norway that were years ahead of our herbal cures. He paid attention to those things each time he traveled, so he could share what he'd learned with me.

All these things he knew, and still knows about me— things I haven't shared with any of my three husbands.

I can't even remember what we talked about that day. I only remember the way the sunlight hit Leif's beard, his hair light as Thorstein's was red, or Thorvald's brown. How two people produced such different-looking sons, I never understood. The only things the brothers had in common were their light eyes and ruddy skin.

From his lingering glances and smiles, I realized Leif found me attractive. But that day, he planned to act on his feelings. When we reached the middle of the field, he planted his feet, towering over me. I looked up into his soft gray-blue eyes. Pain filled them, yet desire shone brighter.

His fingers laced under my hair, and he leaned down to my lips. The enticing smell of him nearly overwhelmed me, until I pictured Thorstein's wrathful face...and Gunna's new baby. I turned my head. We couldn't hurt our family like this.

He raised his eyebrows, but released his hold on me, reaching for my hand instead. We both turned toward the deep blue line of the horizon.

"Don't let Thorstein stay away too long, Gudrid. You know he'll do anything for you, just like every other man in this camp."

I disagreed, because Thorstein was determined to travel to Vinland, even though I'd repeatedly told him that revenge was no reason to risk our lives.

Leif knew my thoughts. "Well, he'll do what you want sure enough, after this pointless trip. He'll be begging for your advice." He chuckled, tightening his long fingers around mine.

I smiled, letting Leif's inner sunlight fill me up one last time. I knew I couldn't be alone with him again. If anything did happen between us, Thorstein was just hot-headed enough to kill his own brother.

"Thorstein has no idea how to sail properly," he said. "Father taught us all, but he never learned. My brother wasted all his time preening his hair and bathing, in hopes of garnering attention. I told him women were more attracted to the sweat of hard work."

He was right, but I knew I shouldn't let myself laugh at my husband. "Well, he *is* the baby."

"And well does my mother know *that*." Jealousy charged his voice. It amused me how all three brothers fought for their mother's approval. Anyone could see she loved each one the same.

We walked on in silence, my hand swallowed up in his grip, his rough fingers caressing my own.

"Come back to me, Gudrid."

"For what? We're married. You have a son."

"Things change."

It sounded careless, but it was the Viking truth. We had both watched family die that winter, people who should have lived long lives. The illness had spared no one, young or old. Perhaps we clung to each other because we still grieved over our fathers.

"I'll always come back to my home." Even as I said this, I turned away from his light, into myself.

I roll from one side to the other, trying to forget Leif and think only of Finn. I wish for sleep to come. But I never sleep alone—Leif is always right beside me.

Chapter Fourteen

I feed Snorri before dawn, then snuggle him back into the cradle before going out. I need to clear my head from all this dreaming, so I will milk my cows and do something helpful for the camp.

Two of my cows are giving milk now—I call them Amber and Crystal, names of my favorite stones. Amber lost her calf, and her milk is starting to dry up, so we'll need to breed her again soon. Crystal's both fatter and more difficult. She has to be bribed away from her calf with hay.

Amber comes right over when I walk inside the fence, eager to be milked. I put my stool down and rub my hands together to warm them. I've only gotten two good pulls when she starts kicking her back leg, moving uneasily. Turning, I see Freydis running up the hill, her hair flowing around her like an erupting volcano.

"Is all well?" She had better slow down before barging into my pasture. I pat Amber's side, murmuring words to calm her.

"Have you seen what your husband has been doing?" Freydis gasps for breath and holds her stomach. She takes so long fumbling with the latch, Crystal lows from her shady spot beneath a maple tree. "The men worked on it all day yesterday! Wait until you see it!"

"I've seen nothing, because I came straight over here." I turn back to Amber.

"You must come with me!" Freydis yanks my arm so hard, my bucket spills. Amber's sad, dark eyes fix on me, anxious for the sweet relief of milking.

Once Freydis gets like this, I can't deny her, or she becomes a thorn in my foot. I pat Amber's side again, planning to come back later. Holding my bucket and stool, I latch the fence, then follow Freydis back down the hill. She is too thin, because her shift hasn't tightened at all over the child. From behind, her overdress hangs in loose folds that drag the ground.

I leave my bucket and stool in the longhouse, then we walk all the way past Freydis' hut. Near the shoreline, her arms fly open, as if she's embracing the air. And there, perfectly built, is a stockade. Log after log, sharpened, tied together, ends dug into the ground. A perfect protection, reaching from one end of the beach to the other, with only a small portion at the edge of camp unfinished.

Finn. Finn has done this for me.

Freydis' large eyes take it all in. "Imagine the work! Last night, Ref said he was exhausted, but I had no idea why. I'd been out hunt—well, I didn't even see the logs when I went in for the meal."

She knows I want to scold her for hunting. But I'm too awed by Finn's determination to keep me safe. She sighs next to me, as moved as I am.

"I dare any Skraeling to come ashore now!" She wraps her bony fingers around my arm and squeezes it like a small girl.

"Thank you for showing me this, Freydis."

"'Thank you for showing me this?!' What's wrong, Gudrid? Why all the formal talk?"

I remain silent.

"Not that I'm mocking you, of course." That's exactly what she's doing. "But you don't seem yourself these days. Nerienda noticed it, too—not just me. Are you worried about something?"

I'd like to know who in this camp is *not* worried.

She raises her eyebrows. "Don't give me that look! There's nothing to worry about, now that we have the stockade, and Thorfinn chose the best men to guard us. Have you seen Sindri and Tyr? They look like brutes. And of course, we all know Snorri Thorbrandsson and his ways. Not to mention that brown-eyed man, Suka. He looks like he wants to kill something."

Probably us.

"And Geisli? Now *there* is a man." She sighs, again like a silly girl.

I haven't met Geisli yet, but Freydis would do well to remember her own husband. "I thought Ref was staying behind?"

Freydis rises to the bait, as always. "Of course Ref's staying! He's a man among men!" Then she rubs her stomach, probably remembering he's given her a child, too.

"How is the baby?"

"How should I know? I've never had one before. All I know is what you midwives keep telling me." She glares at me, as if it's my fault I haven't taught her more about childbearing.

I look up into her eyes. "Does he move inside you?"

"Not so much. But Nerienda says he's dropped."

I put my hand over hers. Then I put my other hand on her stomach—it's still hard, with no kicking. I bend down and speak to her stomach.

"Your mother is a real handful." There's no movement in response.

Freydis smiles, her freckles crinkling all the way up her nose. "Gudrid, you'll be the death of me yet!"

Freydis very well could have died for me, if she's the one who killed Hallstein's man. I pray I can redeem myself to her by keeping her and the baby alive during the delivery.

We walk closer to the shoreline, examining the heavy log wall. The men have done a week's work in a day. Although many of the logs were already felled in the woods, hauling them to the shore and burying the ends should have taken days. No wonder Finn slept so deeply last night—he was exhausted.

Freydis speaks my own thoughts. "I pity the man who would stand in Thorfinn's way. He appears so gentle and peaceful, but when it comes to you, there's no telling what he'd be willing to do. You do have that effect on people, you know." She shoots me her crooked grin.

I start walking toward the longhouse again. Freydis always makes me uncomfortable with her obsession with my personal life. "We must get our chores done."

"Yes, do go finish milking your cow—goodness knows she needs you." She laughs, then half-runs toward the forest.

Once I have a full bucket, I carry it to the longhouse, where Inger waits to make butter. Her hair is so dark, it looks out of place among us. But her light eyes and skin tell she's Norwegian. She is pretty, but not beautiful, like Linnea. Her hands are red and cracked from all her time spent cooking over the fire, and from the spinning she's probably done most of her life. I'll find a salve for her to rub on them.

She doesn't say anything until I walk toward the door, then speaks so quietly I can hardly hear her. "It's a perfect stockade."

And I see that Finn has made us all feel safer, with his one huge gesture. I want to sit on the bench and cry without stopping. I want to find him and throw my arms around him. But, mostly, I just want the next four months to be over.

"I'm sorry, m'lady, to upset you." Inger's clear blue eyes show her surprise.

"No, don't think of it." I hope she soon forgets this weakness she has seen in me.

"Yes'm." She turns back to the churn.

I have a sudden yearning for my baby—to hold his solid little body, to sprinkle kisses on his lips and eyes, to feel his soft fair skin.

The fire has died in our empty hut. Deirdre should be here. Perhaps Snorri is with Nerienda. Urgency presses me to run toward the old woman's hut. Something is wrong; I can feel it.

Nerienda meets me at her door, holding Snorri. "Gudrid." Instead of saying more, she passes my baby to me.

He's burning up, and his eyes are glazed over. Dear God, don't let this be the shivering disease that took so many in Greenland.

"How long?"

"Not long," she says. "He was just tired this morning. He wanted to be held."

For a healing woman, she should have known to send for me when she realized he was feverish. She knows as well as I do what can happen if we leave the fever unattended. I try not to let my anger spill over.

"I'll get the garlic." She bustles toward the longhouse, probably sensing my black thoughts. She'll make a paste from the garlic and mix it with oil, then spread it over Snorri's feet to draw the fever out. It's the traditional way. If that doesn't work, I've hidden another cure—a powerful, expensive one.

But first of all, I'll pray. In the middle of the camp, holding Snorri high, I raise my eyes to the heavens. I ask the God who lives there, the God who sees even me, to heal my only son. I beg Him. I've watched all my parents die, even my godparents. I've been with two husbands as they took their last, rasping breaths from the shivering disease. I can't let my son die.

Finn comes up behind me and puts his arm over my shoulder. He doesn't interrupt my prayer, as it's obvious I pray for our boy, lying limp in my arms. Snorri feels like a hot coal. We have to sponge him off with cool water.

"Finn, please run and get Linnea. Or Inger—she's in the longhouse. We need water from the creek." The deep concern in his eyes mirrors my own.

He doesn't answer me before racing off. He is a quick runner, light on his feet, like a deer. I've never noticed this before.

I cradle Snorri. His eyes fix on the clouds instead of me. As I reach the door of our hut, Linnea runs up, holding a small ceramic jar. "Inger's gone for water. I have the paste. Nerienda's coming soon."

I carry my baby to our bed. He looks fiery, wearing the bright red cloak Thjodhild made for him before he was even born. I strip him down, then lay a light piece of linen over him. Linnea hands me the paste, and I rub it into his feet, praying all the while.

Suddenly, he has a bout of diarrhea, which spurts everywhere. We'll have to put a covering on his backside, like the Europeans do, just to contain it. Without my asking, Linnea leaves, saying she will fetch water and cloths. I stand motionless, splattered by the blast. The smell of my son's sickness fills the small hut.

Snorri Thorbrandsson barges through the door, not even calling out first. "I saw you and the boy." He draws closer and rubs the paste on baby Snorri's feet. He motions to the corner. "You change clothes."

Unfortunately, we have no large furniture to stand behind in our hut. But the mess on my shift makes me take the chance, because I'm afraid the stench will make me sick, too.

I secure the deerskin flap to the wall with a piece of bone through a leather loop. Turning my back to Snorri Thorbrandsson, I pretend he can't see me. Trusting he won't look, I undress and drop my soiled clothing into our basket. I'll have someone wash it with hot water soon. With these illnesses, I've noticed those who handle the dirty clothes are next to get sick.

I wipe down with a wet rag before pulling on a clean shift and my overdress, holding it up until I can secure the brooches. My leather shoes have also gotten dirty, so I take them off, looking around for my fleece-lined slippers.

Someone knocks on the door frame. I unhook the deerskin, still bare-footed. Finn stands there, probably wondering why I've secured the door. He looks over at Snorri, then back at me. Whether he notices I'm wearing a rust colored overdress, instead of the green one I was just wearing, I don't know.

"Nerienda will come, and Deirdre." He doesn't look me in the eyes. There is something he's not telling me. Linnea mentioned Nerienda was coming, too. She should have been here by now, if she's only a few steps away in the longhouse.

Suddenly, I divine the source of his worried tone. "It's Freydis."

"Sometimes you understand too much, my wife." Finn sighs, his eyes meeting mine. "Yes, Freydis is having early birth pains."

But she and I laughed together just this morning, enjoying the security of the new stockade. Something must have happened when she went hunting.

"Tell Nerienda to stay with her. I'm a healer, too, and I can care for my own son." I still can't believe the old woman delayed when she knew my son was ill.

"And Deirdre?" he asks. Deirdre would probably rather be with me, but Linnea is more instinctive in knowing what I need next.

"She also must stay with Freydis. Linnea and Inger can help me."

Finn looks again to Snorri Thorbrandsson, who holds our baby on the filthy bed. I don't want to think of what he's sitting on. I'll remind him to change when he leaves. But Finn must leave our hut now, because he can't get sick before the trip. There will be no healers on his ship, since we're both staying behind with Freydis.

"Could you go find Inger? She's supposed to be at the creek." Commands come easier when my child is sick.

Before Finn even turns, Inger and Linnea come in, each bearing the kind of water we need. Cool for Snorri's overheated body, and warm to clean everything.

I tell Finn to go ahead and work with his men, since he doesn't know how else to help. He must finish the stockade, so they can ship out as soon as possible. He can't delay searching for Leif's camp in Vinland because of our baby or Freydis, or he won't get back before winter.

The girls and Snorri work together to clean the baby, securing rags on him to stop the diarrhea. They also take blankets from the bed and burn the ruined straw. When I try to help, Snorri Thorbrandsson says, "No—you're clean." He makes me sit down in the chair to wait.

Already, Snorri Thorbrandsson steps into the space my husband will leave. And this isn't a bad thing.

Chapter Fifteen

After many bouts of diarrhea, my boy finally tosses into a fevered sleep. I slump in my chair, exhausted.

Linnea speaks in her quiet way. "We must stop the diarrhea. I've seen this before in children."

She's right. I search out my wooden herb chest, filled with spices, healing powders, and dried leaves. Pulling back a hidden sliding panel, I find the root I seek. I tell Linnea to cut off a small piece and grind it into powder, before mixing it with water.

She fingers it tenderly. "I've heard about ginger root, but I've never seen it. This must have been costly."

It was. Finn could sell this for a large sum, having traded for it in Persia. Even Icelanders, so close to the mainland, don't have this root yet. I took this from Finn before we left. He wasn't able to inventory his goods before leaving Greenland, and I'm hoping he'll think he lost it somehow.

When Linnea leaves to grind the root, I touch Snorri's forehead. Still hot, but not as hot as before. I send Inger to mash more garlic and replace the paste. She will also stir eggs in a bowl and put the mix on cloths we can wrap around Snorri's feet. This is an old Scottish cure that Deirdre taught me.

Deirdre. I should be helping her with Freydis now. Hopefully, Freydis won't go into labor yet. There are herbs that can stop the pains, but Nerienda would know of those, too.

I wonder about this sickness of Snorri's. It's too early for the coughing illness that usually comes in fall. It can't be something he ate, because he eats so little. I pray it's not an illness that spreads quickly.

Snorri Thorbrandsson comes back in, rubbing his hand over his bald head in a gesture that always makes me think he misses his hair. "Freydis' pains are slowing."

I nod, glad of his report.

He pulls up a chair near baby Snorri, looking at him, then at me. Snorri Thorbrandsson's eyes are difficult to describe. They're usually light brown, but today they resemble dark wildflower honey. He looks distressed, and it's clear what he's thinking about.

I'll relieve him of the burden of telling me. "I understand what has to be done."

Snorri Thorbrandsson nods without speaking. We both know that Finn cannot return to this hut, which means we'll be apart until his return.

"He took a chance coming in before." Snorri's eyes rest on mine.

I stand, offended. "He didn't touch the baby."

"No." He readily agrees with me. For being such a valiant warrior, Snorri Thorbrandsson is almost as thoughtful of me as Deirdre is.

I sit down again. "You must tell him."

"I plan to." His eyes reflect the fire.

As he rises to carry out his mission, he knocks his chair over. The baby starts awake, but then falls back into his dazed sleep.

"Sorry." Snorri keeps his eyes down as he leaves.

I move to the wall bench, my eyes heavy. Inger and Linnea come in, bringing the smell of fresh garlic with them. Inger rubs paste on baby Snorri's feet and wraps them with cloths, while Linnea holds him close to the breast, much as I would.

"Is he cooler?" I ask.

Inger just barely shakes her head.

"We'll give him the ginger water, then." I stand, strangely weak.

Linnea holds Snorri out to me. His skin has gooseflesh and his color looks mottled. I can't understand why the fever hasn't broken.

She hands me the deerskin bottle. "I mixed it like you said."

I hold the bottle to his mouth. Rather than gulping, he takes tiny sips, which is best for him anyway. Maybe his stomach will be calmed by the ginger.

Both girls look to me for instructions, but I have none. "It's good that he drinks," I say.

They both nod, eyelids drooping from exhaustion.

I speak of something other than the sickness. "The stockade? Is it finished?"

"Geisli said it will be complete sometime today." As Inger speaks, a blush colors her cheeks.

Geisli...the same man Freydis was impressed with. Inger's blush says much about her feelings for this man.

Although these girls are old enough to be married, I want to protect them from it. I had no mother to prevent my marriage to The Eastman. Orm and Halldis had found a good match for me, but my father disapproved. And everyone knows the chieftain has the final word.

My godparents thought I should marry Einar, a boy whose father had become rich in Iceland. Einar had brought a shipload of wares from Norway for Orm to examine. While loading them into Orm's barn, he saw me walking past and started asking questions. Who was I? Was I a good cook? Would my father let us marry? Orm was surprised but impressed at his boldness.

When Orm brought word of Einar's proposal to Father, he rejected it, because Einar was the son of a slave—even if he was a prosperous slave. Orm made the unwelcome suggestion that Einar's wealth and status could raise my father's standing. With his endless feasts and parties, Father was running the farm into the ground. But, in return for Orm's good advice, Father took me from my godparents and brought me back to live with him again.

Once I moved in, Father set about choosing a husband for me. He had to find someone willing to travel, because he planned on sailing to Greenland. He found what he wanted in Thorir the Eastman, a Norseman with a good family name. The Eastman knew how to joke with my father, when no one else dared. Father never saw the darkness in him, because he hid it well.

We married the winter I was fifteen. Halldis took me aside before the ceremony, to explain the ways of men with women. But her Orm was gentle and kind, nothing like The Eastman. Once we married, he raged like a bull, not only in his desire, but also with his hateful words to me.

I learned how to control him, in my own way. Still, I didn't grieve when he died of the same illness that took

Father, Orm, and Halldis, because I didn't want to have his children.

The Eastman was a flirt. Even though he was only with me, he flirted endlessly with the slave women at Eirik's. Women loved him, because he would entice them with flattery, making them feel beautiful.

Leif once remarked on it. "That Eastman would have children all over Brattahlid, if he made good on all his advances." It's funny that Leif was so concerned about my husband's unfaithfulness, yet he too would have become guilty of the same thing, had I let him.

I feed Snorri as much ginger-water as he'll take. He sips at the bottle, his lips strangely red. If there is a rash in his throat, I would know better what to do, but the hut is too shadowed to tell. I can't take him outside in the sunlight or he might get more chilled. Inger and Linnea continue cleaning his things with hot water, making sure all the blankets have been changed. They are some of the most efficient slaves we've ever had. The slaves at Brattahlid tended to be lazy. I suppose it's different here, where we must rely on everyone just to survive.

I hum quietly to Snorri, old Icelandic songs my mother sang to me. He enjoys it, stretching his arms and legs, ready to snuggle up.

But he grows still warmer. I put him down in his cradle, taking off everything but his cloths for the diarrhea. He still has gooseflesh, so I place another linen cloth over his chest. He looks up at me with dull eyes.

"Girls." I speak quietly.

They immediately stand by my side.

"I want you to look in on Freydis for me. I need to know how things are going for her. You've done enough here for now." They'll need sleep before their morning chores.

Both girls nod. Inger takes the basket of dirty clothes as they go. Darkness falls outside the hut. The night meal has probably come and gone.

Tiredness washes over me. I would be content to curl up on the fresh straw on my bed and go to sleep. But I need to stay awake to watch for changes in Snorri, and to feed him more ginger water.

A knock on the door frame startles me. As I pull up the flap, I wonder how the girls can be back already.

But it is Snorri Thorbrandsson, ready to continue his vigil over his young namesake. I notice he's changed his clothes. I'm strangely glad he thought to do that on his own, since I forgot to remind him.

"How's Freydis?" I lean against the doorframe.

"Better." He still doesn't come in, shuffling his feet. "Are you hungry? There was salmon tonight. I brought some."

He passes me a plate heaped with salmon, turnips, cabbage, and bread. The food looks tasty, but as I think of my baby's illness, I can barely chew more than a few bites.

When the girls finally return to tell me Freydis is doing better, Snorri remains planted outside my door. This irritates me.

"Shouldn't you be rallying your ten men?" I raise my voice toward the closed deerhide. "Preparing them to protect the women when Finn leaves tomorrow? Telling them who's going to be in charge?"

"I'm doing that right now." He maintains his post. It takes me a moment to understand his meaning, and when I do, fresh boldness fills me. Snorri is loyal to me.

As the night wears on, I give Snorri Thorbrandsson a task. The girls have long since gone to their own beds, and my eyes feel like they have sand in them.

"Snorri, will you come in and feed him ginger water if he wakes?"

"I will." He has been waiting for my invitation. As he sits on the bench, I collapse on the bed, fully clothed.

"You told Finn?" I close my eyes, remembering my husband's sad kiss the other morning.

"I did."

And? What did he say? Finn won't see me again for months. He won't know if his son gets better or worse. Baby Snorri could be running instead of walking when he returns. Or he could be dead. Such is the way of illness, with our limited understanding of things. I hate sickness as much as I hate Thor.

"Many thanks." I don't need to ask Snorri the questions that plague me.

Snorri looks at me, eyes so filled with concern, it threatens to undo me. I sometimes feel that he sees behind all my cold requests.

"He knows you love him; now go to sleep." His suggestions are more like commands—commands I don't chafe to obey. Black silence sweeps me under, and I sleep.

Chapter Sixteen

The constant patter of rain on the sod roof wakes me. Snorri has covered the fire hole so rain won't pour in.

I stumble over to my baby's cradle and put my hand on his head. It is slightly cooler. I'll let him sleep, instead of waking him to change his cloths or feed him. He isn't horribly smelly, so the diarrhea has slowed.

Snorri Thorbrandsson sleeps near the coals, on a pile of blankets. The bowl of garlic paste sits near his hand. He sleeps like a horse, with his arms and legs straight out to the side. I look away before laughter gets the best of me.

I wonder if it's wise to eat anything, but my stomach leaves me no choice. Just an egg or piece of bread should quiet this rumbling emptiness inside. I wonder where Finn had to sleep last night. Probably in one of the men's huts.

My purple cape hangs on its post on the wall. I drape it over my head to protect it from rain, then put on my leather boots that come up to my knees. I love these boots. Made from the softest reindeer skins, they wrap my ankles tightly. Not only do they keep my legs warm, but they're the exact color of perfect honey mead. They were a gift from Stena when I married Thorstein the Red.

As I go out into the light rain, I breathe deeply the smell of fresh, wet earth. By the edge of the forest, the stockade looks finished. Finn will be able to leave soon—maybe even today.

Inger and Linnea have already been busy, judging from the fresh milk filling the bucket on the longhouse table. I search Ref's carved wooden cabinet on the wall and find some jerky and cheese from yesterday.

Footsteps splash in the mud outside the door, and Finn strides in. He stops abruptly, watching me.

"Finn." I grip the cheese and jerky.

"Is he well?"

"He's getting better." I fight the urge to run to him. "Snorri Thorbrandsson helped with him last night."

He nods, and the rain runs down his long eyelashes, onto his chest. If I could only touch that chest, feel the strength of his arms around me….

"We leave today." His eyes don't meet my own. He looks at my muddy boots instead.

"You must." I need to encourage him. "The stockade is finished. Have you packed enough food? And weapons? And what about some garlic? And herbs from Nerienda?"

"Linnea checked the supplies, and made sure we had the right herbs."

"Hmmm." That should have been my job. Finn must have noticed her youth and beauty if she helped pack. She draws the eye. But why am I so jealous of a slave girl who likely dreams of being in my position?

Finn looks up, eyes the color of storm clouds before snow. He clamps his lips, as if he's holding back words.

"I'll go out the back." I feel I've offended him somehow. But I didn't speak of my jealousy aloud.

His hand circles my arm before I can take a step.

"Don't do this." I know the pain of leaving drives him.

"Do you think it matters if I become sick?" His scent, woodsy like juniper, yet salty like the sea, surrounds me. "Nothing matters, until I get back to you."

I fight the frantic desire to turn and be pulled into those strong arms, to feel his urgent lips on mine. I don't want to be left behind, without my anchor. And yet he must stay healthy.

"I can't." I pull my arm away, slipping out the door into the rain. It quickly drenches me, the heavy drops pounding my head. Surely Finn knows what I'm feeling; that I couldn't be the one to make him sick.

Since I grew up surrounded by rocks and cliffs and sea, I know how to pull the strength of the rocks into myself. I become hard and untouchable, locking all my emotions inside. I won't come out until I see Finn's face again.

Water puddles beneath me as I stand in our hut. I'm still gripping the jerky and cheese. In my clenched hands, the rain didn't touch it. Snorri Thorbrandsson sits awkwardly on a bench, holding my baby. He stands as I come in, giving me a bright smile. Hope floods me.

"Fever's breaking, for the babe sweats." He's almost tender as he rocks Snorri back and forth in his sturdy arms.

Dropping the food on the table, I go to him, holding out my arms. Snorri Thorbrandsson awkwardly tugs at my cape, which drips water everywhere. I pull it off my shoulder, then take my boy. Sure enough, baby Snorri has small beads of sweat on his face, and his skin has returned to a healthy color.

The worst is over now. Snorri has changed the cloths on my son. He's also stoked the fire, straightened his blankets, and fastened back a corner of the deerskin, letting fresh air into the hut. I don't need Inger and Linnea anymore, since Snorri Thorbrandsson knows just what to do.

He stretches and yawns, leaving his mouth wide open like a fish biting for bait. Realizing how crude this looks, he covers his mouth a bit too late. "Shall I check on Freydis?"

"Of course. Eat something, too. I brought the jerky and cheese." I smooth my baby's curls, enjoying the life in his eyes.

"Only a little." He cuts off large pieces of each. Once again, I stifle my laugh.

"They leave today." I'm sure he already knows this, since he talked with Finn last night.

"Yes." His jaws work, chewing the jerky.

I wait, knowing he has more to tell me.

"I'll be talking with the men today." This answers my unspoken question.

"Good. What of our bathing and washing? How can we do these things, without Magnus as our guard?"

"I have thought about this. I could come, or your wolf. Do you have a way to call her?" he asks.

My wolf always comes when she's needed, but I haven't tried calling her yet. "I could go into the woods and see. But someone would have to stay with Snorri."

"I'll tell Linnea." He pulls a blanket off the floor and positions it over his bald head. So the hardened Viking warrior worries about getting wet. Snorri Thorbrandsson is a riddle...a man-slayer blessed with compassion.

"Many thanks." He is out the door before my words reach him. I don't want to go into the woods, leaving my baby behind, but everything must be in place when camp leadership transfers. It's an important, risky day—the ten men left behind must respect Snorri Thorbrandsson and me as they respected Finn.

Most of the men will accept this readily, but I wonder about the old man, Bjarni, and that Skraeling from Greenland, Suma. Or Suki? I can't remember. Today Snorri has to show his dominance, much like the head wolf in a pack. I find it difficult to picture him this way, after watching his gentleness with my sick boy.

I cradle my baby, thanking God his fever has broken. I ask him to watch over Finn as he sails, and to protect Snorri Thorbrandsson and the women as we stay. I try to make a rune song for these things, one I can remember during the long months without Finn.

After rubbing more garlic on Snorri's feet and nuzzling him a bit, I place my drowsy baby back in his cradle. Linnea bursts in the door, sopping wet.

"So sorry, m'lady." She hangs up her cape. I find a thick cloth and hand it to her, then search for a dry shift and overdress. Hers are soaked through, clinging to her like bark on a tree. I finally settle on my light yellow overdress, thinking the color will flatter her as it does me.

"Freydis recovers. He asked me to tell you." She dresses in the middle of the room, with no fear of someone walking in.

"Thank you." I'm unsure if it was Snorri Thorbrandsson or Finn who told her this. "Is there anything else?"

"Yes, m'lady. The men have shipped out."

Those simple words tear at me. *Alone, alone, alone,* pounds in my head.

"I must go out. Watch the baby." I put on my wet cape as she starts combing her hair. She uses my favorite ivory comb without asking. "He's getting better, so let him sleep."

I remind myself that Linnea is very attentive to details, and she's doubtless the best person to leave with my recovering child. Nerienda's delays bothered me, and now Linnea's boldness annoys—am I being unreasonable with my lack of sleep? How many days has Snorri been sick? One? Two? At this point, the days and nights blur together.

Outside, the rain hasn't slowed. As my feet sink into the mud, I can't bring myself to look at what it's done to my favorite boots. I pull my skirts up, jumping onto a tiny patch of grass between houses.

As I pass the longhouse door, I'm surprised to see how few men are gathered at the table, listening to Snorri Thorbrandsson. So many have sailed. Inger and Nerienda are probably serving them the mid-morning meal to refresh their spirits.

I stop at the edge of the woods, waiting. Will my wolf find me even if I don't call? Will she sense my sadness?

The ocean is dark as charcoal, and the wind whips rain around me. I won't move until she comes. Even though my head is covered with the hood on the cape, wetness seeps through the wool.

I missed watching Finn ship out. I didn't come to the point to wave goodbye. He wanted a kiss, a reassurance of my love, and I could not give it. If he never returns, will he die wondering if I loved him?

I finally turn, defeated. But as I wipe rain and tears from my eyes, I see her. She sits close to the new stockade, watching me with her yellow eyes.

I walk toward her, not caring that she's wild. She doesn't move. I stop short of her and wait, hand at my side.

She comes up and puts her nose into it. Her muzzle feels like the blue velvet curtains Thjodhild gave me when I married her son.

The wolf jerks her head toward the forest and I yank my hand back. Suki runs out of the trees, his long black hair flipping water on me as he passes. He runs at top speed, and I'm truly impressed. My wolf isn't. Her wet hackles form spikes.

Suki has a bag on his back, probably carrying game of some sort. He looks back at me scornfully.

Who does he think he is? The way he flew by me shows disrespect. His eyes are dangerous, and my wolf doesn't trust him.

"Told you he wants to kill someone." Freydis has crept up behind me. The wolf ignores her, like she's some kind of forest animal.

Freydis' eyes look sunken, as though she hasn't been drinking enough. If her body gets too dry, the pains will be much worse.

"You're looking at me that way again." She sighs. "I had to get out of that hut. If Deirdre tells me one more thing about how healthy Scottish women are, I'll…I'll pull her hairs out, one by one."

"Calm down." I use the same tone I use with my cows. I won't scold her for not drinking enough, but I'll make sure Nerienda does. Right now, Freydis wants to talk.

"I'm so thankful Ref was able to stay." She catches herself. "Of course, I'm sorry Thorfinn had to go. But you know Leif."

Yes, that I do.

"And I know your husband. He'll find Vinland in no time and bring back plenty of treasure." She pats my back.

"I have to get back to camp." The rain trickles to a stop, and I push my wet hood back, holding her gaze. "And don't think about looking in on my sick child, either."

"I won't." Her lip droops. She wanted to escape Deirdre and stay with me.

Our trails between the huts are thick with mud now. It's surprising Suki could run so quickly without falling on his face.

Back at my hut, I wave Freydis on to her own, knowing full well she'll head back into the woods instead. But she stands with her mouth open, pointing.

At the top of our stockade, the tall Skraeling leader climbs over, red silk tied around his head.

Chapter Seventeen

Freydis flies into the men's hut, knowing there are weapons hanging on its walls. Snorri Thorbrandsson gives a shrill whistle from the longhouse to rally our men.

I run straight to Snorri's cradle. He babbles to himself, playing with his toes. Linnea sits on the bench, staring right past me. I turn. Behind me, the Skraeling magic woman shifts on her feet. She truly must be magic to make it into the camp without raising alarm.

The woman is short, with a tight-fitting wrap and a shawl protecting her head from the rain. Her hair reminds me of a red squirrel, and her large cow-eyes watch me. The unnaturally white shade of her face makes me think she's painted it somehow.

She struggles as she balances a large pile of material over one arm. She motions to me, pointing to a leather dress on top of the pile. It has tiny red and white beads sewn along the sleeves and bodice. I've never seen any beads like these, in Greenland or Iceland.

It would have taken a whole season for one woman to bead this, so they must have many women, unlike us.

I point to the chair behind her. She sits, holding her clothes in her lap. Her large eyes are disturbing, anxious with her need to communicate. I wonder how she knew which hut was mine. Perhaps she divined this by magic, or realized I had the only baby in camp.

"What is your name?" I ask.

Her eyes are empty as she stares at me. Perhaps I need to talk to a younger Skraeling, one more accustomed to change.

"My name is Gudrid." I motion to myself.

Linnea must have picked up Snorri, because now he chatters on the bench behind me. She'd better keep hold of him. We have to stay calm with this stranger. One false move, and I'll have to kill her before she kills any of us.

"Gud-rid." I point to myself. Then I point to her.

"My…name….Gud-rid." Her cracked lips form the words. She doesn't understand.

I turn, looking around the room for something to trade. Our hut is sparsely furnished, because I keep telling myself we won't be here long.

Snorri laughs loudly at Linnea as she makes a troll face at him. As I wonder about trading milk for the dress, a shout echoes in the camp. It's a Viking war whoop.

The chair crashes down, the clothes fall to the floor, and the old woman is outside before I can even turn around. Linnea cradles Snorri and rushes to my side. Do we stay in the hut or go to the woods? The woods are too far, so we move into a huddle under the bed, pulling the blankets down low. What kind of life is this for my son, always having to hide under things and keep quiet?

I carefully slide my seax from its sheath, ready to thrust it up through the bedding if I have to. Steps sound in the doorway. But then Freydis whispers my name.

I peep from under the blankets. She holds her precious knife in one hand and a spear in the other. She's also somehow strapped a shield on her back. Freydis embodies the rune about the *disir*—ruthless female spirits. "Malicious disir stand on both sides of you, and wish to see you wounded." Even the bravest warriors flee when the disir are roused.

"Gudrid." Her long legs get in the way as she tries to kneel to my level. "I saw where that Skraeling hag went— should I go kill her?"

"No, Freydis—*no*. Who gave that shout?"

"I think it was Bjarni. Some Skraeling tried to take his sword. He pulled his spear and ran that fool through. I watched from the back of the men's hut."

"Are they fighting now?" Given Freydis' lust for violence, she'll probably join them if I don't stop her.

"No, the Skraelings ran for their boats. Only a few had crossed the stockade anyway. What a quick kill! I like that old man."

I breathe out a long sigh. Snorri nuzzles into me, ready to nurse. I pull down my shift, happy my son's healthy enough to feel hungry again.

Freydis goes out like a warrior, spear held high, once again forgetting she's with child. Once Snorri finishes eating, Linnea asks with her eyes, and we finally crawl out from under the bed.

Deirdre comes into the hut soon after, running toward me with her arms out. "Gudrid!"

We embrace. I think she's gotten more white hairs this week. I forgot she had to say goodbye to Magnus, as I did to my Finn.

I cling to her, breathing deeply of her comforting, rosewater smell. She has become like a mother to me since we've been here—helping with my birth, showing me how to feed Snorri, and staying by my side. Though Halldis loved me, she was more my teacher than my comforter. And I have so few memories of my own mother.

There is one I cherish, though. When I was only four, my mother combed my hair in front of a mirror Father had brought her from a raid. Her face, reflected behind my own, looked so similar. Only her eyes were different. They were bright blue, while mine were green as the grapes Father brought back from Europe. Our hair was exactly the same color—the clear yellow of Icelandic poppies.

"You'll grow up to make your mother proud." Her voice was musical as she smiled down on me. I've wondered many times why she was so sure of this. It's easy to say things like this to your child, hoping for the best. But she said it as if she knew the future.

Deirdre pulls back and looks at my face. "Are you well? How is the boy?"

"He can nurse again." I twist at a wayward strand of hair.

She looks at me in that way she has, head cocked slightly to the side, and I know she sees far deeper than my face.

"But how are *you*?"

I sigh, pulling my hair back.

"It has been much for you, with the baby's illness and Karlsefni's departing." She speaks my thoughts. "And Freydis with her pains...and the Skraelings."

Snorri squirms in Linnea's arms, and she steps out of the shadows. "Soon it will be mealtime, m'lady."

I welcome the change of thought. "Linnea, please feed Snorri something, but no cheese or butter yet. Maybe just broth with softened bread."

Linnea nods and gathers my son into her arms. Deirdre chatters on about the men shipping out, Freydis and her birth pangs, and several men in camp who seem to be getting sick. I listen, but can't really understand the words. Darkness seems to close around me. My body collapses to the floor.

When I wake up, I'm on my bed. Deirdre stands over me, holding a cloth to my forehead. I believe Snorri Thorbrandsson sits on the bench, but everything looks fuzzy.

"You are ill." Deirdre explains how my head hit the floor.

I can't concentrate on anything. The room moves in slow circles.

Deirdre pulls the cloth from my head. Blood colors the light fabric. I wonder where it came from.

Snorri Thorbrandsson walks to the bedside, bringing another cloth. Linnea sits, rocking my baby's cradle. Or is that me sitting there? Snorri's hand on my forehead reminds me of another man's hands, a man who stood with me, even when Thorstein the Red did not.

"Leif." Surely I didn't say that aloud? Snorri Thorbrandsson leans in close, his eyes sparking yellow as my wolf's in the firelight. Hurt fills his gaze. I have altogether too many men in my life.

Chapter Eighteen

Dreams torment my feverish sleep. Men go walking through my mind. Husbands, as well as men who only *wanted* to be my husbands.

I see Thorstein, with his red hair, only a shade darker than his father's. The shivering disease took him, just like the wife of the farmer we were staying with. Unfortunately, the farmer thought he needed a new wife. I knew the only way to be safe was to be under Eirik's wing again. Somehow I convinced that lonely farmer to return me to Brattahlid, with the bodies of Thorstein and his men. Thjodhild loved me for bringing her youngest home. Perhaps she felt guilty for urging Thorstein on the very hunt that carried him to his death.

I see Einar, and the way he looked at me that summer. He was determined to marry me. But my father was far more determined, and blinded by his pride.

The Eastman appears to me, just as he often did, with one hand on his sword and the other on his hip. This always seemed an aggressive stance to have with one's wife. His almost white hair hung down to his shoulders and matched his long beard perfectly. He was extremely fond of both, saying it showed his pure Norwegian heritage. He thought I wasn't as well-bred as he was.

Now I'm back at our first winter at Brattahlid, joking about Leif's unexpected marriage and eating Finn's delicacies around the roaring fire. Eirik the Red was never stingy with two things: fire and food. His slaves worked hard all summer, chopping plenty of wood for the long winter months. Eirik's rich laugh filled up the room. I've never felt more loved, or more at home. I miss not only Leif, but the family I left behind.

And now I see Snorri Thorbrandsson, his hand hoisting me from our ship onto Leif's. The Eastman wrecked our ship on the rocks outside Eiriksfjord because he was drunk. But that shipwreck wasn't the first time I'd seen Snorri.

My mind takes me back, further than I want to go. Back to the bottom of the tree, Yngvild's hand touching mine, Mother's flowing hair blowing on the breeze. But Snorri Thorbrandsson stands outside the circle of people with his older brother. He never takes his eyes off me, not even to look at the sacrifices. When I jump up with my knife, his hand flies to his own. I suddenly recognize what Snorri was to me in Iceland, and what he is now, in this strange land. He's like my brother. He has seen my past, he knows the horrors of it, and he'll protect me. I sink into a deep, comforted sleep.

When I finally wake, I lightly touch my throbbing head. The tightly-wrapped cloth on my forehead makes my whole face too warm. I strip it off, examining it. It appears the bleeding has almost stopped. I roll over to check on Snorri, and my bedclothes stick to me. I'm covered in the fever-sweat.

Snorri isn't in his cradle. What time of day is it? I look up, toward the hole in the roof. Quick-scudding clouds fill the bright blue sky. How many days have I lost over these past few weeks?

Perhaps I should bathe. But the very idea of plunging into the cold creek water makes me shiver. I'll find someone to bring in water and heat it for me.

I put my cape on, even though my shift is thin underneath. I'm too hot and weak to dress myself. Maybe Deirdre or Inger or one of the slaves could help me.

As I lift the door cover, fresh air rushes into my chest and fills it, taking my breath away. My head swims, and I brace my arms on the doorframe until the feeling passes. Silence blankets the camp. It must be about time for the mid-morning meal.

I peer into the darkness of the longhouse, barely making out a woman's form at the table near the back. My steps seem to drag as I hold onto the walls.

Inger rushes out to hold my arm. "M'lady! You're awake! Nerienda said you mustn't be up for a few days yet!"

My voice sounds foreign to me, raspy and low. "My head is well, and my fever's broken, Inger." I don't care what Nerienda says—I'm as much a healer as she is.

Inger takes my scolding, recognizing my authority. She helps me sit at the table and pours a bowl of soup for me.

"Is Snorri eating well?" I sip at the warm green broth.

"Oh, yes'm, he is. Nerienda made up this special broth for him and the others who suffer with this illness. It has spinach juice in it. Helps if you can't keep water down. Do you like it?"

Not really, but I'm glad Nerienda actually thought to make it up. Spinach juice can work wonders. But what did Inger mean by *others*?

"Who else is sick?"

"Quite a few. Some of the strappiest men are down now. Strange illness. Your Snorri got over it quicker than the rest."

Thank God for that, as children are usually the worst hit, between the fever and the fluid loss.

"And where's my boy?"

"Oh, Deirdre bathes him at the creek. Geisli watches over them." Her eyes brighten.

"I don't think I've met Geisli." The lukewarm soup seems to curdle in my stomach.

"Well, he said to me he saw you once, at the creek it was, in the night." Her words jumble together.

Ah. The boy-man with the long fair hair and the deep voice like Leif's. The one my wolf decided not to attack.

"I really should meet all these men who were willing to stay behind," I say.

Inger continues stirring the soup with sure, strong movements. "Freydis is quite taken with Bjarni since he ran that Skraeling through." I'm sure this bit of gossip was dropped straight from Deirdre's mouth.

"And how is Freydis?" I hand my half-full bowl to Inger, and she takes it out back to dump it.

She turns back to me. "Nerienda wants her to stay inside, away from the sickness. But Freydis hates it."

Of course she does. The red-haired forest child would live in a tree if she could. But she must care for this child — this grandchild of Eirik's — more than she cares for herself.

I glance at the stack of clean bowls, and Inger answers before I ask. "Oh, I've already taken her soup, m'lady. She ate it fairly well."

"And where is Linnea?"

"She's with Nerienda, spinning. Shall I fetch her?"

"Yes; I need warm water in my hut to bathe. But don't be gone long or your soup will burn." I don't have strength to stir it myself.

"Yes, m'lady." Inger rushes out. Though she is short, her movements are quick and efficient.

Snorri Thorbrandsson comes in and sits next to me, like a bee that always flies back to its hive.

He speaks first. "You're too pale."

"But I am eating. And I'm warm." Now he can answer to me. "What of the men? What was Bjarni thinking, killing a Skraeling? They could retaliate when our men lie sick."

"I know, I know." Snorri rubs his beard. "We're planning for this. And Bjarni did what any of us would have done."

"Not all of us. I was almost trading with their wise woman." It seems Snorri doesn't see the whole picture. "Now we can't drop our guard—we must watch for their skinboats day and night. That old fool!"

Snorri holds my angry gaze. "I wasn't sure about keeping him here, but your husband is a smart man. Bjarni has his own talents."

"So I've been told. All I've seen are talents for killing, and not for peace."

"Perhaps so…but sometimes killing's necessary, Gudrid."

He says my name so earnestly, I can't think of a response.

"Some men have to be killed, or they'll kill you." His eyes flick to the back door of the longhouse—where the dead man was laid out on the bench.

"Do you know something about the murder?" Perhaps my boldness is a result of those feverish dreams I had earlier.

"If I did, to be sure, I wouldn't tell you." He laughs as if he's made a great joke.

Well.

He recognizes my offended look. "Wouldn't be safe for you, you know."

My eyes drift down and shockingly fixate on his tight leather pants. Everywhere Snorri Thorbrandsson goes, women laugh about his pants. Truly, they must have been fitted to him by someone.

I look up sharply, and his eyes crinkle, a friendly light amber color now. "Wondering about my pants, I suppose?"

"The women have wondered, yes." I should be embarrassed, but I'll treat him like the brother he was in my dream.

"They're leather—made from a bull I had to kill in Iceland, years ago. My mother sewed them for me. A reminder. So you and I have both seen our fair share of bulls."

He rubs his beard and looks into my eyes. "What do you recommend, besides killing?" He's quite serious now.

I'm not used to a man asking me for advice. Of course we have to protect the camp. And my baby. I won't hesitate to kill a Skraeling, if one comes near my child.

"I just want to be in a place where we don't have to think of these things. Where we don't have to hide like cowards, or fight with our backs against the wall."

"Well said, Gudrid." He doesn't correct me, or explain why we have to stay and find more goods. He just agrees. I'm flattered.

"I do know what you want." He searches my face, his cheeks reddening. "I guess I won't forget that anytime soon."

It takes me a moment, then I understand. "I said it out loud?"

He nods, his lips in a tight smile. "I'm sure the women think you were crazed with fever. But I think I heard the truth in the way you said his name?"

"Snorri, you can't tell anyone, especially Finn. It was...it was just a mistake."

He looks offended. "I've no reason to tell him."

"But your loyalty to Thorfinn—"

"Has a lot to do with you." He holds my gaze.

I can think of nothing to say to that. His face is much the same as that young teen, watching me at the sacrifice. He had wanted to protect me then. I suppose this is his chance, while Finn is away, to look out for me. But even if Finn trusts him, he doesn't know the whole story.

Linnea comes into the longhouse, breaking the silence between us.

"Sorry, m'lady, but your bathing water's ready in your hut." She stirs the soup, then cuts slices of meat and cheese for the mid-morning meal, which will be late today. From the hot water pot, Snorri fills two small bowls. He knocks things around in the wooden cabinet until he finds chamomile. As he drops the dried flowers in the water, his hand brushes mine.

"Take this and get some sleep in your hut, but first clean yourself up, for the love of everything." He grins.

"I have to check on Snorri first." I know he jokes, but I can think for myself.

"Deirdre has him. A bouncier boy couldn't be found in all of Greenland. He has truly recovered. Please, sleep. The time will come when we'll all have to stay awake." He speaks like an oracle predicting the future.

I sip some of the weak tea, ignoring Snorri's eyes on me. I nod to him and Linnea before leaving. But instead of going back to my warm bathing water, as I should, I feel I need to maintain my power around here. Ignoring Snorri's order, I walk to the creek, searching for Deirdre and my baby. I don't like taking direct orders from men, or anyone else, for that matter.

At the creek, no one is in sight. I wander farther into the woods, not really caring where I'm going. I keep a sharp eye out for more rabbit traps. Deep in the forest, the men chop logs, adding to the stockpile of wood. The thought of another winter scrounging for food weighs on me. When I reach an overturned tree trunk, I sit on it to think.

Ferns and moss blanket the moist forest floor. A few trees already change color. At least we've had adequate rain this summer, and will probably get more in the fall.

A yellow head emerges from the trees. Geisli walks down the path—young, carefree, and completely unaware I'm sitting here. When the path winds around, putting him right next to me, he startles and pulls his sword.

"Stop!" At my shout, he quickly sheathes his weapon. He should have been paying more attention.

"Sorry…thought you could be a Skraeling hiding out here."

"Didn't you already comb the woods? Are you on guard?"

"Yes, m'lady. I did. But Skraelings are good at hiding, or so I hear."

I stand, looking up at him since he's taller than me by two heads. "From who? Who has even had dealings with Skraelings?"

Leaning on a tree, he thinks better of it and stands straight again.

"Bjarni, m'lady."

The old man who probably stood around when Skraelings killed Thorvald Eiriksson? The old fool who nearly got us all killed today, starting a war with the Skraelings?

"Any other advice from the esteemed Bjarni?" I put my hands on my hips and step closer to Geisli.

"No, m'lady." He steps back, looking confused.

"Do you know where my son is?" I thought Geisli was supposed to be guarding Deirdre as she bathed the baby.

"At camp, I suppose. I took them back there for mid-morning meal, before I had to chop. If you don't mind, m'lady, I have to switch off for guarding now." His eyes are a piercing blue, matching the sky that peeps through openings in the trees.

"Shall I walk you back, as well?" he asks.

I fight the urge to slip my arm under his. He has a very captivating presence, so much like Leif. I crave a man's touch—it's my greatest weakness. The Eastman used to taunt me, saying, "You're a woman who'd go mad without a man, Gudrid!"

After the events of the past few weeks, I wonder if I already am.

Chapter Nineteen

I spend the next two weeks with my boy. I can't be near him enough. I had never noticed how much his nose looks like Finn's. Every time I pick him up, I pray for Finn, knowing only too well he could be sick, lost, or even dead. We wouldn't know it for months. Unease fills the spaces created by Finn's absence. It seems we are prey, just waiting for the Skraelings to return.

When I feed baby Snorri at meals, I watch the men. It has almost become a game for me. Bjarni's quite interesting. That skinny old man eats enough for three men. He also never sits still. He probably has worms. I plot sneaky ways to have him drink a fennel and wormwood brew, to rid him of them.

Geisli's like a light. The men position themselves around him, like rays from the sun. He's a leader, like Finn or Leif. And the women can't take their eyes off him—I've even caught Nerienda gazing at him like a young girl.

Suka, the Greenlandic Skraeling, spends most of his time glaring at everyone. To my astonishment, Freydis is the only person he seems to find tolerable. Something about her flame of hair seems to draw his attention endlessly. I wonder if Ref notices Suka's devotion to his wife. But he's rarely at meals, determined to keep a very personal and constant watch at the stockade. He's always aware of the babe Freydis carries.

Tyr and Sindri intimidate everyone around them, so they usually have the bottom half of the long table to themselves. Snorri Thorbrandsson's the only one who dares talk with them. He loves hearing their stories about how weak the king of Norway really is, and how he's totally dependent on his Viking guards.

The men have bad habits, like eating with mouths wide open and telling stories unfit for a woman's ears, although Freydis sits there soaking up every gruesome detail. I do fault Eirik for this one thing—he treated Freydis as a son. Brattahlid was filled with women who could have helped her appreciate the strengths of womanhood, but he only nurtured her violence.

At least Halldis taught me to glory in those strengths— the ability to bear children, to tap into our deepest feelings, and to communicate in ways most men can't. I've tried to share these thoughts with Freydis, but she'll have none of it. She was born with the bloodlust and aggression of a man. She doesn't see how she angers most men with her superior skills at hunting and killing.

I have to be careful watching Snorri Thorbrandsson, because I can't help laughing at him sometimes. He has excellent manners, fit for the king's table. But his left-handedness makes him awkward. He tends to drop things— particularly around me, but I pretend not to notice. He keeps his beard combed out and free from crumbs, unlike the other men, who don't seem to mind their unkempt looks. His bald head looks soft and sleek, like my son's cheek.

And yet, despite all his clean habits, he's the most
dangerous man I've ever seen with a sword. Even Leif
wouldn't stand a chance against him. Sometimes he
practices with two swords. One day, I saw him thrust with
one sword and defend with the other in a move that would
have sliced a man's head off. He is very precise. I'm proud
that Finn named our son after such a warrior.

I spend as much time as I can with Deirdre. She
comforts me, with her idle gossip and her true tenderness
toward me and my child. As summer ends and the days
start to get colder, we take breaks to sit in the longhouse
with mugs of warmed milk. Often, Inger and Linnea join us,
asking my opinion on things ranging from herbal cures to
marriage. I find myself thinking of them as my own
daughters as they share about the families they left behind.

One night, the men decide to make a bonfire, to burn
the smaller, scraggly limbs they've chopped. After Snorri
eats a good meal, I put him down in his cradle, praying over
him as I always do. It's so good to have my son healthy
again. Everyone remarks on how sure his steps are and how
plump he looks.

Nerienda offers to stay in the hut with my boy. For the
first time in two weeks, I agree to let someone else watch
him. But I firmly tell her that she must find me right away if
anything goes wrong. The old woman has fallen out of my
good graces, but I must give her the chance to make it right
again.

The sharp evening air pulls me into it, invigorating me
with promises of fall. I could look at the stars and sing rune
songs the whole night through. I miss the northern lights of
Greenland, with their bright heather purples and apple
greens. So far, we haven't seen any here.

The men carry out benches and circle them around the fire. Geisli and Inger share a bench. Freydis sits on the ground, with her long legs crossed. Ref is nowhere in sight. Suka sits across from Freydis, but as the evening wears on, he moves to the bench behind her. This isn't a good thing, but I take comfort in the fact that Freydis seems oblivious to him.

Deirdre sits by me in the deepening dusk, confiding how much she misses Magnus. As she describes his loving gestures over the years, I recite rune songs in my head to distract myself. I can't think of Finn right now, or I might fall back into the sadness that threatened to overtake me before he left. I have to be strong for whatever comes next. And Snorri Thorbrandsson was right, the Skraelings will be coming. It doesn't take the gift of foresight to see that.

As I become quieter, so does Deirdre. Finally, she yawns, muttering about how she's too old to stay up so late. I hug her and wish her good sleep.

My bench isn't empty long. Snorri Thorbrandsson straddles it like a horse, so close I can smell the spice oil he uses. The masculine scent makes it hard for me to think. He's like my brother, I tell myself. He's only here to protect me.

I look up at the constellations and name the familiar Icelandic ones for him. I feel his eyes on me, instead of the stars. I pause in my lesson.

"Are you well?" he asks.

"Why do you ask?"

The peeping frogs call loudly tonight, and smoke laces the air. My boots press into the rain-softened dirt. The fire is nearly white-hot, like the fire in a blacksmith's forge.

Snorri's hand covers mine. He doesn't answer me, but asks another question.

"Can I help you, Gudrid?"

I need touch so badly. But not from Snorri Thorbrandsson.

My eyes fill with tears and I can't give him an answer. Shame and anger rush through me. I hate this loneliness that makes me weak.

I almost run back to my hut. But I want to be outside this breathtaking night. I use my long sleeve to brush my eyes, trying to laugh.

"No one can help me, Snorri Thorbrandsson, except Thorfinn. You know this."

He falls silent, but he doesn't remove his hand. He is not so bold with me as Leif has been. He knows Finn too well, and respects him too much.

I keep my mind busy, thinking of the things I love about Finn. His tattoo, his eyes, his chin, his smell....

But right now all I can smell and feel is Snorri.

So I pull my hand out from under his, placing it on my lap. I look around, half-expecting my wolf to sense my unease and show up on the edge of the woods.

Snorri gives me a long, measuring look, then walks over and talks with Bjarni, who pokes around at the already roaring fire. The old man can't sit still for two moments.

I look around for Freydis. She sits on the bench, wrapped in a man's cloak. And Suka sits right next to her. If Ref came back from guarding right now, I don't want to think of what could happen. I walk over to her, extending my hand to pull her up. "Freydis, you shouldn't sit on that hard bench too long. It's not good for your babe."

She seems to wake from a deep sleep. "You know, you're right, my fairest Gudrid." She pulls herself up. "I'm stiff all over. I think the baby's gone to sleep before I have tonight!"

She sheds her borrowed cloak like water, dropping it carelessly on the bench. I can't avoid Suka's angry glare as he gathers it up.

"Should I walk you back?" I rub her lower back.

"No." She drops her voice. "Perhaps you want to stay here?"

"I don't. I've had my fill of sky and smoke."

"Good." She looks at me proudly, like I've passed some kind of test. "You're a better wife than I, and a true chieftain's daughter."

"Nay, you are too." I wrap my arm around her, walking her toward the huts. Ref strides toward us, holding up a lamp. It's a good thing I pulled Freydis away from the fire, no matter how much Suka hates me for it. Freydis links her arm in Ref's. At least one of us sleeps with her husband tonight.

Chapter Twenty

The ocean is black as my lava-bead necklace when I wake the next morning. I can only see part of the flame-red sky from my hut.

I take Snorri to Nerienda's hut after I feed him, so I can again feel useful and do chores. Last night's fire still smolders a bit, and the smoke hangs in the air.

There's a rocky outcropping deep in the woods where I often go to pray. I feel driven to visit it before milking. The small overhang drops off to the ocean, almost like Iceland, except the trees crowd it here. I settle myself there, thanking God again for Snorri's health and asking for Finn's protection as I watch the dark waves. Out of the corner of my eye, I catch a movement in the forest.

Bjarni picks mushrooms near a fallen log, not far from me. He hasn't seen me yet, because his eyes are fixed on the ground. I don't remember good mushrooms growing there, and I know most of the forest plants. He smells one, then brings it to his lips.

"No!" I shout. I run to save him from poisoning himself.

"Gudrid?" He looks at me strangely. Wild, unwashed hair strings down his back.

"Wrong mushrooms." I step closer.

"What? No, these are right." He opens his hand, picking one to eat.

I knock his mushroom to the ground, only to pick it up again so I can examine it. It's a bright red puffed mushroom, covered in white spots. Suddenly, everything becomes clear—the cause of Bjarni's jumpiness, his perpetual disheveled state, and the reason he was left behind. Bjarni is valuable to us for only one reason. He's a *berserker*. Only berserkers dare to eat these mushrooms all the time.

"Sorry." I return his mushroom, because it won't poison him. He eats a couple bites, and his teeth start chattering.

I'm torn between thanking him for doing this and telling him to stop for the sake of his health. But from the looks of him, he doesn't have much longer on earth, even if he is a mighty berserker. They're supposed to be impenetrable by sword or spear, killing everything in sight. They also wear skin hides, usually of bear or wolf.

Wolf. I hope he remembered to bring his own hide, or I just might have to kill him myself. I know he wouldn't hesitate to slay my wolf. Which do we need more, the wolf or the berserker?

The old man's entire body shakes, and I do feel sorry for him. After so many years, he's probably unable to stop eating the mushrooms. He is lucky they grow in this land, as well as Iceland and Greenland.

"Bjarni, come with me and have some gruel. Linnea makes the best."

He looks at me with watery eyes, not understanding.

I hesitate before taking his arm. I've heard stories of what these men can do in battle. Some have been so crazed, they've torn off their own friends' arms.

But Bjarni seems worn out, not full of energy. He's just an old man, who happens to be shivering on this sun-warmed morning.

"We're going back." I use my volva voice and put my hand firmly on his arm. My command should work on him, since he grew up in the days when priestesses ruled the Viking lands.

He says nothing, but trails along with me as I start walking. My wolf has found me again, because she's standing where I sat on the overhang. I try not to look at her, so she won't think I need her.

In the longhouse, Inger, Deirdre, and Nerienda sit at the table, drinking warmed milk. The bright fire crackles, and the comforting smell of warm gruel fills the air. Deirdre's mug hits the table when she sees what I'm bringing into this calm house.

"Bjarni needs something warm." I stop any possible comments by giving her a meaningful look.

"Yes, m'lady." Inger jumps up for a mug of fresh milk.

I try not to look at Bjarni, but I'm sure he's quite a sight. He's skinny and shaking, his white hair so filthy it sticks out everywhere. And his unwashed body gives off a sweet, rotten smell that must be the mushrooms. It's so strong, I might have to vomit if I don't get away from it. I sit down and take Deirdre's mug, burying my nose in the rich smell of the milk. Her eyes widen, but she doesn't utter a word. I pull Bjarni's arm until he sits in a chair.

Freydis comes in, holding her stomach. She takes a long look at Bjarni, then sits next to me.

"You know?" she asks. So she's been hiding this from me.

"I do now. I found him with the mushrooms."

"He's one of the fiercest old Vikings I've ever seen." She's awestruck with the old man. "He's a weapon for us, you know." She wants to convince me that berserking is acceptable.

"I'm sure he is. And how are you feeling today, Freydis? Have some milk to warm you." Even as I say this, Inger brings over another mug.

Out in the camp, a bell starts ringing. It must be that huge, rusty bell Magnus was trying to hoist onto a pole before the men shipped out.

Everything happens at once. Bjarni knocks over his milk, grabbing the rest of his mushrooms from somewhere and cramming them in his mouth. Freydis jumps up and runs out the back of the longhouse. The other women circle around me, waiting for instructions.

"Linnea has Snorri?" I look at Nerienda, who's been strangely quiet since I came in.

She nods. "They're in my hut."

"I'm going to get them," I say. "You go to the woods— deep into them. We'll meet you." At least I hope we will.

Bjarni's entire body is having tremors. He bites a piece off his mug, then roars. I run out the back door as he charges out the front.

The dreaded bull stands at the top of the hill, bellowing and slamming against the fence. Finn and Snorri Thorbrandsson discussed this bull in Greenland. As they'd talked about the possibility of a Skraeling attack, Snorri had said, "We could just let that hard-headed bull of Gudrid's go in front of us, and it would kill every Skraeling in sight. Of course, when it turned back on us, we'd have to kill it ourselves!"

Maybe I could do that—hide nearby in the woods until the Skraelings are in the camp, then let my bull out. It would truly run over any people in the way. But first I have to know my son is safe.

I run behind the huts until I get to Nerienda's. No Skraelings climb over the stockade yet, and I don't see our men, so the fighting must be near the shoreline. I value every second I have to retrieve Snorri and Linnea.

Inside the door, I see nothing but darkness. "Linnea?" I shout. "*Linnea!*" Oh, please, God, let her be here.

She crawls out from under a bed in the back, pulling Snorri out by the arms. I grab him, motioning toward the door. Linnea grabs an axe from under the bed first. I move Snorri to my left arm, then pull out my seax and wield it in front of us.

We run to the woods, not looking left or right. Freydis has positioned herself in a tree on the outer edge of the forest, with her sword and spear and that shield strapped on her back again. I doubt this would protect the baby, but I don't have anything better to offer.

I take us through the trees, slowing as we near the outcropping. I'll have Linnea climb down and hide under it with my baby. Even if the Skraelings do get that far, it's protected from their arrows and completely hidden from view. Reaching the edge, I hold Snorri while Linnea shins down the rock face, knocking small rocks loose. Once she reaches the ground, I kiss Snorri and drop my boy the short distance into Linnea's outstretched arms.

I place all my trust in this slave, knowing this isn't the first time she's had to hide for her life. She knows how to stay quiet and calm, like a true Viking woman. But now, also like a Viking, I must do my part to protect our camp.

I pull up my skirts and tuck them in my belt, not caring that my legs are exposed. Now is the time for speed. I race toward the camp and up the hill. The fighting has moved behind the stockade. Bjarni, his white hair streaming wild, jumps on Skraelings like a mad animal. I can see the blood from here.

The bull stops its ruthless banging at the fence as I approach. I don't dare look in its eyes, giving it a challenge to kill me. Once I open the gate, there will be no turning back. I wish I had a way to warn Snorri Thorbrandsson. I must do this at just the right moment.

Suddenly, a heavy flaming object flies into the camp, then another, and another. The natives shoot them with some kind of catapult, right over our stockade. If those land on the sod roofs, the whole camp could burn to the ground.

Slain Skraelings litter the ground near the stockade, but our men fall back, toward the woods. The only way to stop the fireball attack is to move the battle far from the shoreline.

Now is my moment, while our men retreat into the woods. If the bull does what I expect, charging toward the Skraelings at the bottom of the hill, I should be able to escape up a tree. If it doesn't do what I expect...I will die.

I hold my breath, silently unlatching the fence.

As the gate falls open, the bull snorts and runs. Its intimidating bulk moves past me, straight down the hill. I jump the fence and run as if my feet had wings. I scramble up a tree, panting and watching the attack.

The Skraelings yell at each other in their guttural tongue, but not fast enough to save the ones in the crazed bull's path. It gouges at the crowd. Many men fall to the ground, like grain cut with a sickle. Finally, one of the Skraelings stabs the bull with a spear, and others join him.

While they are distracted, I climb down and run toward the woods. If I die, I'll die protecting my son. I scramble over the edge of the rocks, just in time to see a small group of Skraelings approaching the forest edge. The tall leader walks behind his men.

Sindri charges from the dark trees, wielding his axe. One of the nearby Skraelings grips a long rock slab, and he quickly turns, ramming it against Sindri's head. Our huge warrior thuds to the ground, blood pouring from his wound.

The Skraeling looks at Sindri's axe, curiously touches the sharp blade, then aims it at one of his friends. It strikes him in the forehead. He gives a muffled cry before dropping to the ground. The Skraeling who threw it starts wailing.

Their leader, shocked as I am, runs and pulls the bloody axe from his man's head, letting it dangle from his hand as if it's poisonous. He turns and walks straight toward our overhang. I duck below the rocks, clinging to a lower ledge. I pray he didn't see me in his distraction.

The tall, scarcely-clad man murmurs some kind of chant, then the axe goes flying into the ocean. He stands on the rocks directly above us. Linnea, watching me from below, holds Snorri tight to her bosom. He might not be able to breathe properly, but she has to keep him silent to save us all.

Greenlandic words fly through the air, shouted by a woman. Freydis. She calls to our men, deeper in the woods. "You cowards! These fools are easy to kill as sheep! Watch how it's done!"

The leader turns, running toward her. I hope Freydis has strength to do whatever she's planning. Killing two men would be easy for her, but I hope it's only two.

I don't hear any shouting from the Skraelings, just scuffling sounds in the leaves. When it becomes silent, I climb up again. I must check on her. As I begin to see over the outcropping, my breath leaves me and I lose my footing for a moment.

Our men stand in a circle, gathered around Sindri's body. And on the ground near him, I see a familiar shock of red, curly hair.

Chapter Twenty-One

Freydis isn't dead, but her baby is coming. It's still too early. She groans regularly, lying on the forest floor near Sindri's body. Ref stands above her, not knowing what to do next.

I start to shake when I realize Snorri Thorbrandsson isn't standing among the men.

"Snorri?" I ask.

Tyr, kneeling next to Sindri, turns to me. Unfettered tears course down his cheeks. He shakes his head, making me even more fearful that Snorri is among the dead today.

I turn to Bjarni. "Where are the Skraelings?" Surprisingly, he seems to be the only one calm right now. His berserker powers must have burned out.

"Ran—every last one of them. But not from us. They ran from Eirik's daughter. She stripped her breast and slapped it with her sword, right in front of us. She didn't have to fight. She was terrifying and powerful as the goddess Freyja herself." He gives her a tender look, as if she were his own daughter.

It's hard to believe the sight of a half-bare pregnant woman would frighten the Skraelings so much. Still,

Freydis' fearlessness was plain to see—and her intent to kill. And perhaps they thought her a magic woman.

From the regularity of her moans, Freydis is close to giving birth. "Bjarni, find the women and bring them to me." I stand. "Men, take Sindri's body and protect the camp. This woman has saved your lives today. Leave me alone so I can save hers."

The men obey, thankful to have something to occupy them. I have no time to wonder about Snorri Thorbrandsson. I cut off Freydis' shift with her own knife, only to see that she has fluid leaking out.

Suka stays behind, watching from behind a tree as if entranced. "Did you run from the Skraelings, too?" I shout at him. "Run, then, and get me some warm water!" There's a flash of brown as he flies to the camp. At least he followed this one command.

"Gudrid!"

Snorri Thorbrandsson's voice reaches me before he does.

"Here." My voice cracks. Relief floods me as I turn to see his familiar bald head and red beard.

As Snorri walks up behind me, fresh strength fills me. It's enough to know he's alive and nearby. I couldn't lead these men alone, if something happened to him.

"The women?" I ask.

"Coming. Bjarni found us. What should I do?"

"I need your cloak."

He hands it to me, and I barely have time to shove it under Freydis before she begins pushing. It'll be almost impossible to clean the golden wool after this, but she must have something cleaner than the forest floor under her.

The cord comes out first, twisted and dark. The babe isn't upside down, as he should be after Nerienda turned him. Suka places a bucket of warm water and clean cloths at my side. I'm glad for Suka's speed—he found hot water faster than I thought possible.

Nerienda and Deirdre approach, panting. Nerienda takes one look at the cord, then lowers to her knees in front of me. She's seen more births than I have, and I can only watch and pray she knows what to do. She takes my hand and puts the cord in it. "Push it up," she says, still out of breath.

I pour warm water over my hand and the cord, then try to push it in. Freydis screams. I can't imagine how this hurts, although it's almost as if I can feel the pain myself. My stomach cramps. Some part of the babe will come out soon.

Sure enough, the feet are first. I continue holding the cord, while Nerienda tries to grab the baby. I motion to her, and we switch positions, since I'm stronger.

After several pushes, the baby seems stuck. The head won't come out, because an arm blocks it. Nerienda says, "Move the arm." I hook my smallest finger and pull the arm down as much as I can. Finally, after more pushing, and much screaming by Freydis, the head emerges.

The eyes are closed, which is normal. But that's the only normal thing about this birth.

The boy is blue, and his skin is loose and wet. He's far too small, not fully developed yet. He's bruised all over. And he hasn't been alive for some time.

Freydis shouts like a wild animal. "Give me my child, woman!"

I overlook her disrespect, wondering how to tell her. But Nerienda does it for me.

The old woman crawls up to Freydis' face, putting her hand on her forehead. It's a calming gesture, but one strong enough to hold her down, should she have to.

She pulls Freydis' wet red hair aside and speaks into her ear, very low. I've cut the cord with Snorri's knife, and I continue holding the babe. We don't breathe, waiting for Freydis.

But she's quiet.

And then, she asks for the babe again. I hand him to her. When her long white fingers trace his slack jaw, I can't hold my tears back. Everyone is crying, except Freydis. She carefully places her baby on the cloak. Though she's just given birth, and shouldn't have the strength to stand, she staggers off into the forest. From the waist down, her clothing is cut off. She hasn't even lost the afterbirth. She could die if it isn't removed.

But Nerienda says, "Let her go."

And so we do.

Deirdre helps me up. She says my boy and Linnea are safely back at camp, guarded by our men. My wolf should be guarding the camp, too. I don't know where she was during the attack. She could have kept the Skraelings out of the forest, away from Freydis.

Freydis should have stayed in her tree. Why did she risk her life, and the babe's? To show the men's cowardice? To keep the Skraelings from going further into the woods?

I think of the Skraeling leader, throwing the axe so close to the outcropping, and I know the answer to my questions. Freydis revealed herself for me and my boy. When the leader went toward our rocks, she tried to distract him, knowing we were hidden there.

She was ready to give two lives for ours. It's too much. I stumble over a root, not watching where I'm walking. Deirdre grips my arm tighter and continues leading me toward camp. Snorri and Suka are gone. They must have left us soon after the birth. I hope Snorri Thorbrandsson will tell Ref, because I can't watch his face when he discovers his anticipated child is dead.

I have nowhere to go but to my own child, who still lives. My son, born without too much trouble, even after our difficult sea-voyage to Straumsfjord.

I long to feel strong arms around me. Not even human arms—God's arms. If only God could tell me this will somehow work out for good. But whatever foresight I'm blessed with tells me otherwise. Freydis will never recover. She had a wild look in her eyes, more crazed than any berserker, as she looked at her dead child.

If only Finn were here, he'd know what to do. He wouldn't have run from the Skraelings in the first place. Anger replaces my thankfulness for Snorri Thorbrandsson. Why did he let the men go into the forest? He knew the women were hiding there. He could have released the bull, instead of letting me do it. He could have stood and fought, despite the fireballs raining down. Maybe he *is* a coward, like Freydis shouted.

Deirdre has probably been talking to me the entire time we've been walking, and I haven't heard the first word. She must notice my anger, because she drops her arm. "Gudrid?" Her eyes are wide.

I'm torn. I need to be with my son, to touch him and know he's safe. But I need to find Freydis, before she hurts herself.

Snorri Thorbrandsson walks from the camp to meet us. He'll regret this day, the day I lost respect for him. I run at him, beating his broad chest with my fists.

"You did this!" I shout over and over, until exhaustion makes me drop my hands.

He pulls me into his coarse blue tunic, stained with sweat and blood. My fists haven't hurt him, and my words haven't either. This is the second time he's seen me after an unfair death. And he's ready to protect me again, even from myself.

Chapter Twenty-Two

During the next few days, I cling to the promise of protection I felt in Snorri Thorbrandsson's arms. But I'm very aware of Freydis' inability to escape madness after such a loss.

Suka stays with her in the forest, reporting on her when he comes in for meals at the longhouse. Ref admits he can't bear to be with her, since he can't calm her ceaseless ranting after the birth. She speaks of nothing but how good it'll be to have her firstborn in her arms, as if the stillbirth hasn't even happened. As if she hasn't touched her dead son's face.

I'm of two minds about Suka. He seems devoted to Freydis, accepting her in this maddened state. But at the same time, he does nothing but glare at me, and even at Snorri Thorbrandsson. He's said nothing to us directly, but I know he despises our authority. He's not the best person to influence Freydis right now.

But I can't complain—I can barely look after my own son as we try to handle the grief in our camp. Sindri and the red-haired man I barely knew were slain by the Skraelings. We burned our men that night, on two pyres near the shore. Tyr was crying the entire time I chanted. Those two were more like brothers than friends. I fear he may not overcome this grief, to guard as he once did. Later, Ref carved runes into their memorial stones.

The women whisper of future attacks, while the men plot at the longhouse table. But I think the Skraelings won't return. Freydis' boldness frightened them, but they also lost many in the battle.

We wonder what to do with the Skraeling bodies, mangled and bloodied from the Viking weapons and the bull's horns. I didn't realize how many had been killed until I walked along the beach that day, after the battle. Fifteen of their men lay dead. If we put the bodies out to sea, they might wash up ashore. Burning them would use too much valuable wood, since the fires have to be hot enough to incinerate a body. So our men finally decide to run carts far into the woods, digging a deep hole for them. They leave it unmarked.

Freydis' boy has a special grave in the clearing in the woods. His runestone is larger than the others, since he's a chieftain's grandson. I wish we could bring his body to the burial ground at Brattahlid so the family could weep over him.

Days go by, and Freydis keeps to the forest. I finally decide I must go to her. When Suka visits the longhouse for an evening meal, I ask him where she is. He doesn't want to answer me, but Snorri Thorbrandsson stares at him so pointedly, knife poised over his fish and beets, Suka finally speaks.

She is living in a cave toward the outer rim of the forest. Suka challenges Ref with a look and declares Freydis has no interest in seeing any of us. Ref pushes on his beet so hard with his spoon, the dark red juice leaks onto the table, but he has the good sense not to respond. Even in his silence, he simmers like a pot right before it boils over. Suka is a walking dead man. His life is worth next to nothing now, because he's a slave trying to steal a freeman's wife.

The next day, during the mid-morning meal, I go out while Suka talks with the men. Linnea is only too happy to watch over my Snorri. He takes endless delight in her, jabbering and grabbing at her hair. Sometimes I wonder if he likes her face better than my own. I scold myself for not spending more time with him, but how can I? Snorri Thorbrandsson and I are now the backbone of this camp.

I wear my soft gray shawl, one of my favorites, spun from long-haired rabbit fur. Its warmth shields me from the damp chill in the air. The ocean smells especially briny today. I close my eyes and imagine where Finn could be. Perhaps he's found Leif's settlement and has set up camp there. But perhaps he's drifting in the sea. I bring my attention back to my surroundings.

I can't enjoy the red leaves on the few maples in the forest. The seasons have changed, and Finn is still away. Once all the leaves are on the ground, the animals will have to go into their small barn. Or perhaps we will have to butcher them, since the bull is dead and there will be no more milk.

The trail gives out as I keep walking, but I can see where ferns have been crushed underfoot. They're not completely mashed down, which tells me Suka probably runs to and from camp this way.

I wonder how Suka will react if he finds me with Freydis. He's far too possessive of her. I walk faster, determined to get to her first.

Mushrooms abound in this part of the forest. I should have checked on Bjarni since the end of the battle. Every time I see him at meals, he looks off into space instead of eating. He's getting thinner all the time. The men talk reverently about the way Bjarni attacked the Skraelings, like a youth. They say he killed three men with his shield alone.

When I get to the creek, I realize it's too wide to jump. Groups of smaller fish swim in its clear water. Perhaps I should catch some for Freydis. A true Viking's daughter, she loves any kind of fish.

But I don't stop. I pull up my skirts and tuck them into my belt. I take off my shawl, which confines my arms, and tie it around my waist. Finn marvels at my small waist and always comments on it. "You've had a child, and yet my arms could wrap around you twice!" I know he lies, but I'm pleased he likes me so well. I blush to think of his praise.

I slide down the steep muddy bank, then step into the creek. The shallow water only comes up to my knees. I cross quickly, pulling myself up the other side with exposed roots. My wolf stands at the top, her head cocked to the side, as if waiting for me to speak to her.

"Good day, my friend." I try to be friendly, but still regret her absence the day of the battle.

She seems to sense my false good wishes, and lanks off toward the edge of the forest bordering the ocean. I pull out my skirts, which drape over my cold, muddy legs, and wrap my shawl about me as I walk. Ahead, the land drops off, large rocks replacing the leafy forest floor. I've reached the caves.

I hear Freydis before I see her. She makes a high, keening sound, like the wind through the trees when the weather changes. I walk along the top of the caves so I can talk to her. Leaf pieces litter her hair, as if she's been sleeping on them. The caves encircle the clearing where she stands, arms in the air.

It's no accident my wolf patrols this area now. She has positioned herself here. Does she sense my connection with Freydis? Or does she sense the madness that's overtaken her?

I steel myself against images of the blue baby that push into my thoughts. If Freydis doesn't come back to camp soon, we could lose her forever.

"Freydis!" I try to keep desperation out of my voice as I shout.

She stops her noise and looks up at me, recognition brightening her eyes—a good sign.

"Gudrid? My baby. I need my baby!" As she says this, she runs to me in an alarming way, staggering like she can't remember how to use her legs. She could be sick, especially if the afterbirth didn't come out. She's still under-dressed, but she wears men's trousers under her cut-off skirts. Just how familiar has Suka been with her? If he's taken advantage of her in this state, I'll make sure he's dead by morning.

I climb down, determined not to lie about her child. She must remember. She must accept the truth. Suka has probably been feeding her lies, given the way she still asks for the baby. He keeps her to himself by pacifying her, like a small child. I won't treat her that way.

"Freydis, the babe is gone. A boy. Think back. *Look* at yourself. The babe's gone, my sister."

The wild look blazes in her eyes. *"Neinn!"*

"Ja." I get closer and take her arms in mine. She's so thin, she almost slips from my grip.

Her body shakes with sorrow. She cries out—a horrifying sound because we're face to face—then goes limp in my arms. I hold her, praying against the lies and illness that have caged her mind.

Footsteps sound on the rocks above, and Suka's face appears at the top of the caves. He could easily be mistaken for one of the Skraelings here. He has the same slant to his eyes and wide cheekbones, though his skin is darker. His hand rests on his sword, and he's furious.

"You stop there!" I shout.

Freydis sobs into my shoulder, more like a grieving mother now than the wild animal she's been. Suka pulls out his sword. I'm not surprised he wants to challenge me here, where no one can protect me. He thinks I'm a weak woman. He thinks wrong.

Pushing Freydis back first, I tuck my skirts into my belt. I drop my shawl to the ground before pulling my seax from its sheath. Suka stands above me on the rocky ledge and laughs.

"You need time to adjust your skirts, wife of Karlsefni?" The sinews in his arms bulge as he flashes his sword around. "You know I can run you through before you can hoist that knife into the air, *blaudur!*"

He has to climb down to fight me. I'm counting on this.

Freydis crawls toward her cave. I try to provoke him. "Only a coward steals another man's wife. Maybe you couldn't find a wife of your own. Believe me, you can't run fast enough from your death, slave."

"In this land, I am free!" he shouts. "You don't rule me here, nor does your husband or even your chieftain lover, Leif!"

I don't correct him. He needs to know that Leif takes a personal interest in my safety. "You're a slave until death, *Skraeling!*" My voice echoes from the rocks.

It is enough. He jumps down off the lowest rock. As he straightens up, my wolf lunges from behind, where she was waiting in front of Freydis' cave. She attacks his sword arm, biting and shaking it. His sword drops. "Call off your wolf, woman!" he screams.

If I knew how, I might do that, to spare Freydis from seeing this attack. The wolf jumps at Suka's midsection, biting repeatedly. I don't dare lift my seax to her, or she might get confused and attack me. Instead, I run into the cave with Freydis. She rocks herself on the floor, peering out at Suka.

"He said he loved me, he loved me...."

I don't respond, holding my seax in front of us, so I'll be ready to face the winner of this struggle. Suka fumbles for his sword with his uninjured hand. I wrap my free hand around Freydis' eyes. It's too soon for her to see another death.

The sword clangs against the rocks as Suka drops it again. He's bleeding everywhere, it seems. His legs buckle. My wolf's fur is sticky as she jumps for him. I close my eyes.

Suddenly, Ref shouts from above and a spear hits the rocks. He's tracked us. My wolf runs through an opening on the far side of the rock bowl, uninjured. Ref and Snorri Thorbrandsson clamber down the rocks. When I call out, Ref runs toward us, the pained look growing in his eyes as he takes in Freydis' appearance. He's a broken man.

Snorri examines Suka, then picks up my favorite shawl and wraps it around the gaping wound on his arm. He looks at me and shakes his head. I wonder what he'll think of me if I've killed one of our men.

Chapter Twenty-Three

Freydis sits on the cold rock floor of the cave, unwilling to go back to camp. But Ref has determined to get her there, and he'll carry her the entire way if he has to. I've never seen this small man stand up to his hot-headed wife before. He's more Viking than I thought.

While Ref gathers Freydis' few things, Snorri and I rip up more clothing to wrap around Suka's stomach. He's lost so much blood, I don't know how his heart still beats. His eyes are closed, but his chest continues moving, if only slightly. It's selfish, but I hate that Suka's death would mean we'd lose another defender of the camp.

Snorri finally convinces Ref to help carry Suka back to camp on a blanket held between them. I'm to stay with Freydis until they come back. Ref's clenched jaw and tensed back show that he'd rather drop Suka to the ground and watch him bleed out. However, he wouldn't go against Snorri, undermining Thorfinn Karlsefni's commands.

I wrap my arms around myself to fight the chill, wishing for my soft shawl. In the back of the cave, I find another blanket, so I wrap it around Freydis' bony shoulders before I go about starting a fire. At least Suka has provided her with firewood. As I rummage about for kindling, it becomes evident Suka has been sleeping here. There are two mats, padded with leaves and blankets. They're so close together, they might as well be one. I don't think Ref has noticed this yet. I consider hauling out the leaves from one mat, but instead, decide to burn them.

I bring Freydis closer to the fire, growing hot with the leaves I threw on it. She strokes the blanket.

"What happened?"

I don't know if she asks about her baby or the fight with Suka. But when she starts cradling the blanket, she removes any question.

"You know, Freydis. You've given birth to a son."

I wait, hoping her mind will fill with the image of her child. She grips the blanket tighter.

"He was blue, wasn't he? Gudrid, was he dead?"

"Yes, sister. You were strong in the birth. But he wasn't healthy, even inside you. We buried him that day, in the forest. He has a runestone so you can see his place."

"Ref?" she asks. Maybe she realizes her husband grieves, as well.

"He needs you—he's been frantic for you."

"I must go to him." She awkwardly rakes her fingers through her tangled hair.

"You will. But we will clean you first." There's hot water in a pot over the fire, which I mix with cold water in the back of the cave. I search until I find a wool tunic that looks somewhat clean, and begin to wash her body. She hasn't cleaned herself since the birth, so the smell is worse than a dead body. However, it hasn't made her ill, as far as I can see. It's only on the outside. Perhaps God used this stench to protect her from Suka, as well.

"God watches over you, firebrand." I hum as I scrub, thankful she's coming back to camp.

"Whose god, Gudrid? Not mine." She pays attention now.

"I don't speak of Thor—but you know this already."

"Strange for you to say, volva." I'm glad she's getting some of the bite back into her words, even as she tries to hurt me with them.

"There is a God in heaven; that much we can see," I say. "Who else could have made the ocean, the sun, and the stars that we can't even reach? We both know it's not Thor, a god who can be killed by a serpent. Or Odin, who gets gobbled by a wolf at the end of the world."

"You're right about that, but no god cares much for humans, anyway. And where's the god who cared for my child? Don't tell me he protects me, only to take my babe. I couldn't respect a god who did that."

I won't argue with her on this, at least not now. Her anger shows she understands what's happened to her child.

"You need to eat, and soon." I stir the already-dying fire. "Do you have any food in here?"

"There's smoked herring in the bag over there." She gestures to the dark corner.

We eat the tough fish, then I put more leaves and wood on the fire, now sputtering in the damp of the cave. I pray the men return tonight. It seems to be taking too long.

The sun is mostly hidden behind thick gray clouds when it finally sets. This isn't a good sign for the weather tomorrow. The air holds a smell I've tried to forget since last winter, when our supplies were almost gone. Snow. And fall has only just started.

The leaves crunch on the rocks above, and Ref jumps down. He doesn't even look around the cave, keeping his eyes on Freydis. She gets up from the bed and runs into his arms. I burn another small pile of leaves, giving them time. While I'm moved by their unusual display of affection, I try to push down my own loneliness.

Ref speaks in his slow, quiet way. "We'll leave now. Is there anything we need to take?"

Freydis shakes her head, but I pick up her bag from the corner anyway. Ref pours water over the fire.

Outside, I climb up the rocks first, then Ref gives Freydis a boost so I can grab her hands. His lantern sits at the top of the rocks, throwing flickering light on our faces. The tight bones of Freydis' face seem sharper as the shadows fill her cheek hollows.

When they both get to the top, Freydis leans heavily on Ref's arm, still weak even after eating the fish. At the camp, she'll have to rest for days on end.

I want to ask Ref about Suka, but he and Freydis don't need any reminder of our attacker. I find my footing by watching how Ref's lantern dips and sways ahead of me. The forest is black and endless.

Hopefully my wolf has bedded down somewhere. Ref's spear didn't hit her—she ran too quickly for it. She gave me the advantage of surprise with Suka. If I'm honest, I know he would have defeated me if we'd fought. I may know how to use a knife, but Suka's larger than me, and a trained Viking warrior.

At the creek bed, Ref carries Freydis across. Once he sets her down, he places the lantern on the opposite bank. I slide down my side of the bank on the leaves and mud, then hitch my skirts up again, dreading the feeling of the icy water on my legs. I make long jumps through the water, not splashing too much.

Ref reaches down and pulls me up to the other side. As he does, he has a twinkle in his mismatched eyes. Like Eirik the Red, Ref has an amused respect for my determination.

"I was coming to get you, Gudrid, but you're too fast for me."

I return his smile, my lips cracking. It's been weeks since I've smiled. I pull my skirts back down, and we continue toward the camp.

On the way, I talk with God. The darkness covers me, making me comfortable. Freydis and Ref are in a world of their own, a world of love and pain, wrapped in marriage vows.

Finn is on my mind—every part of him. I can see the flecks of darker blue in his eyes, the tattoo moving on his arm sinews, and the way his hair curls over his small ears. I pray again for his health, and for success in his search. He's a trader, I tell myself. His very livelihood depends on finding a shipload of goods in Vinland. But what if he wants to settle there, instead of returning to Greenland? When I came to this new world, I chose my husband over my safety. Now that I have a child, would I do it again?

I've always been a loyal wife, going with my husbands wherever they wanted to travel. The Eastman took us from my Icelandic home to Greenland, finally wrecking our ship in his drunkenness. Thorstein the Red sailed for Vinland to avenge his brother's death, only to get so off-course we had to live in upper Greenland through the winter.

And now Finn follows his dreams of plundering Leif's Vinland, but already, we've had a near-mutiny, sickness, and an attack by the Skraelings. I didn't have to come here.

In fact, Finn never asked me to. I was stubborn and unwilling to be apart from him for so long.

The Eastman made a journey, then became ill and died. The same thing happened to Thorstein the Red. Somehow, my life was spared both times.

But I don't want to survive if Finn dies on this journey. Foolish thought for a woman with a baby boy to live for, but it's true. Since Finn left me, I have not been myself. Unlike my other husbands, my love for him grows stronger when he's away from me. True, I'm surrounded by men, not only here at camp, but in my own intrusive dreams every night. But I know these dreams are wrong, and I fight to keep my mind from wandering to Leif every time I feel abandoned.

There are men who love me, or at least think they do. Snorri Thorbrandsson. Leif. But here, in the darkness of my soul, I don't want either of them. It's Finn I want, and Finn I will need for the rest of my days. I've finally married a man I love so much that I can't stand to be without him.

I'm smiling as we reach the camp. The longhouse fires are still glowing, strange for this time of night. Perhaps the women work with Suka, or they're waiting up for Freydis.

I run forward, giving Ref's arm a light squeeze. "I'll stop here," I say. He nods and takes Freydis toward their hut, where he's probably set out food for her return.

I walk into the longhouse, but I'm not prepared for what I see.

Finn, holding our son in his lap.

Chapter Twenty-Four

The earth seems to rise and swallow my feet, preventing me from being in his arms fast enough. My Finn. The smell and feel of him overwhelms me as we embrace, our child between us. He smells like ocean salt and sweat from ship-work. The darkened circles under his eyes alarm me. His gaze reflects deep sadness, too, and I wonder if someone has told him about Freydis' child or Suka's attack.

It's been at least six weeks since Finn has held me. Already the trees are red and gold. I can think of no words to say.

He holds me closer. "We found the wheat. And a land teeming with fish and deer. We took logs that will make Ref cry, the burl on them is so beautiful. But it was time to come back."

"So you found Leif's Vinland?" I hold baby Snorri's leg, stilling his excited kicks.

"We did. We camped there for the month. It's a much larger camp than ours. Don't know why, since Leif didn't take as many men as we did."

Of course the camp was too large. Leif does everything on a grand scale, as befits the chieftain son of Eirik the Red.

"So Hallstein went the wrong direction." I wonder where he is now, if he gave up and sailed for Greenland with no goods for Leif. Or perhaps he might return to our camp....

Finn chuckles, and the sound warms me. "Old Bjarni was right, Vinland was south of us. And not so very far away, my love."

I look up, waiting for him to say we'll settle in the south, in that land full of choice goods. But he doesn't.

"I prayed for you." I lay my head on his shoulder, while the baby clutches at Finn's tunic.

"I know." Finn adjusts my sleeve, fingering my arm. "The men got sick. It spread like fire on the ship, but I didn't become ill. It was your prayers, Gudrid. I could almost feel them."

Nerienda comes into the longhouse, smiling through her crooked teeth at Finn. She turns to me. "Suka is alive. But he needs something to stop the bleeding. Do you have an herbal cure?"

I do, but I don't want to leave my family here. Finn sees this, and motions me toward the door. We need to save the warrior slave, no matter how disloyal he may be. I kiss Finn, reveling in the moist strength of his lips. Linnea stands nearby, waiting for me to kiss the baby and pass him to her. She has filled a bottle for the night so she can put him to sleep.

Outside, the starless sky darkens the camp like a heavy cloak. I light a fire in our hut for Linnea, then take the herb box and sneak out before she comes in with my boy. Nerienda, waiting outside, leads me to one of the men's huts. Suka is the only one inside. His groans are subdued, which either means Nerienda's given him something for pain or else he's growing weaker.

"*Bjorr*," she explains. It's the sweetest and most potent of our drinks. From the way Suka's eyes are half-closed, Nerienda must have given him plenty.

She has wrapped his arm tightly with fresh cloths, but the blood still seeps through. Once I pull back the cloths and examine the deep, ragged gash, I know what I'll have to do. In Iceland, I watched the monk sew large wounds together with a needle and thread. He used a simple stitch, then rubbed the wound with herbs.

I could use leeches to staunch the flow, but I don't like using that method, even though many Europeans swear by it. It seems to me the life is in the blood, and once the blood is gone, so is the life.

"Is this the deepest wound?" I ask. Nerienda nods. He'll have scars on his back and stomach, but nothing to match this arm wound. It's as if there's not enough flesh to cover it. Still, it's a wonder the wolf didn't tear the arm off when she shook it.

"I need a clean thread and a needle."

Nerienda nods, then shuffles off to her hut to retrieve them, taking longer than I'd like. I use hot water and a rag to clean the wound and slow the bleeding. When Nerienda returns, I apply fire to the needle, as the monk showed me. He said it makes it easier to pierce the flesh.

Suka seems unaware as I stitch the outside of his arm. I'm careful not to pull the skin too taut, so it won't pucker. I prop my elbow on Suka's bed, making pass after pass through the wound, until my fingers ache. Nerienda holds the lantern over me, mouth open. She's never seen this before.

As I finish, I instruct her to make a paste with thyme and garlic. As she gives it to me, I crush a few dried mushrooms from Europe in my hand, then mix them into the paste. I lightly rub the pungent salve over his stitches. The mushrooms will help keep the wound clean. Finally, we wrap fresh cloths around it.

I tell Nerienda how often to dress the wound before finally heading to our hut. Finn waits outside the door for me, sitting on the small stones. It's early morning now, and the sun already lights the edges of the sky.

He takes my arm, motioning toward the forest. "Linnea had to stay with Snorri last night. He was over-excited to have me back, I guess. So I just stayed outside till you came back." He smiles, his eyes crinkling at the corners.

I'm thankful he did, because I don't like the thought of Finn alone in our hut with the entrancing Linnea. Even though I trust him, what man wouldn't be tempted?

At the edge of the woods where the stockade ends, the waves crash against the rocky shoreline. It feels strange standing together after all Finn has missed. I wish I could explain to him how I've been brave in some ways, yet so needy in others.

I can't even look at the forest without holding my breath, as I did when we hid from the Skraelings, and later, from Suka. I see Freydis' dead child when I close my eyes. Finn has missed these experiences that will stay with me forever.

He knows my thoughts. "Snorri has told me much. You've been braver than any Viking woman should have to be, Gudrid. You truly are a chieftain's daughter."

Just hearing these words of high praise from Finn brings embarrassing tears into my eyes. I bury my face in his chest. He wraps his arms around me.

"I can't tell you how relieved I was to find Snorri so healthy. You have a gift for healing, my volva girl. I'll admit I feared the worst." His voice catches. "And Suka still lives this morning?"

"Yes." My voice is muffled by his chest.

"That Skraeling should have been left out to die...and he would have been, in Greenland." Bitterness sounds in his voice, because he had chosen this man to protect us.

"Is he a true Skraeling? Greenlandic?" I ask.

"Yes, Vikings that settled above Brattahlid raided his tribal land. Many Skraelings were killed, their women and children taken. I should have known he wouldn't be loyal to us, even though Leif owns him."

"He came to this land to be free." I'm startled to understand Suka's motivation.

Finn tightens his arms. "Well, he *will* be free to stay here, because we're leaving."

I pull back, meeting his eyes. Today, they're deep blue, like the lapis lazuli arm-band he gave me when we married.

So we're sailing for Vinland now, before winter.

He strokes my cheek, answering my questioning gaze. "Yes, we're leaving. I won't endanger our child any longer. Or you. I know you miss Brattahlid terribly."

Brattahlid? What does that have to do with settling in Vinland? Maybe he thinks I'll feel closer to Leif at his camp?

Finn looks to the sea, a faraway smile on his lips. "I miss sailing, Gudrid. I miss trading. I miss trips to Norway and into the mainland. I want to take you there with me, someday, when Snorri's older and stronger. You wouldn't believe the beauty of their palaces and churches."

"That is also my heart's desire, Finn. But how can we do this if we live in Vinland? Could you trade with the Skraelings there?"

"You misunderstand me. We're sailing for Greenland, back to Brattahlid. I've plundered enough of Vinland to fill both ships. Grape vines, wheat…Leif will be pleased. Maybe he'll make me a chieftain." Finn gives a short laugh, knowing Leif doesn't share power.

I grip his arms so tightly, he winces. He's said the words I've longed to hear, and yet, I don't want him to forfeit his dreams. Not because of me.

"*You* want this?" I ask.

I wonder if Suka woke and knocked me unconscious when I was stitching his arm. But no. Finn stands before me, smiling and happy. I reach into his sleeve, finding the tattoo. The serpent—representing the ocean—defeats Thor in the end. And the ocean always wins with my sailor husband. I wonder if baby Snorri will be a sailor, too. But for now, I'm content Finn wants to sail from this new land I loathe.

"Home…we finally return home." I've finally found a reason to smile. Finn snatches me into a hug and swirls me around.

A familiar form approaches from the camp. Features come into view: tight leather pants, sturdy chest, shining bald head, and rusty beard. As he draws near, it's plain to see his smile doesn't extend to his eyes. Perhaps he will miss being my defender.

"Thorfinn." Snorri inclines his head toward Finn. I remind myself that Snorri Thorbrandsson is my husband's closest friend, not mine. He only acknowledges me with a quick glance out of the corner of his eyes. "The men want to discuss our departure plans."

So he already knows we're sailing for home. Or maybe more than that—maybe Snorri pushed Finn this direction. Snorri alone knows all the trials I've been through in this land, and the bone-deep weariness I feel because of them. Not only that, he knows my homesickness for Brattahlid, and how close I am to Eirik's family.

Finn sighs. "Of course. We'll talk tomorrow. Today I must sleep, and my sailors should too. And so will my wife." My husband winks and gives me a meaningful grin.

Snorri squints, like he's keeping the sun out of his eyes, even though the sun's barely up yet. He acts like an animal that's been kicked. Finn doesn't notice, as he wraps an arm around my shoulder and walks me back to camp.

Part of me wants to run back to Snorri, to hug him and thank him for being there for me every time I've needed him. He's seen the deeper things in me, my weaknesses and my strengths, and he still seems to love me.

And I love him. But it's a brother-love. I feel sorry for his loneliness. I want to comfort him. I'm thankful he protected me when Finn sailed. But I don't share his feelings. He'll only be happy when he's married; when someone can return his love. And he can't marry me.

Chapter Twenty-Five

Days come and go, and Finn and I stay in our hut for the most part, snug against the dusting of snow and increasingly bitter winds. Finn does go out to talk with the men, and I keep up with my chores, which are minimal, now that Inger seems to have taken over my milking. She has a good touch with the cows. Rumors fly that she has a special power with animals. Vikings want spiritual explanations for any ability, linking it to the gods or trolls or valkyries or whatever seems to fit.

We all need something to believe in. Thor, Odin, and Freyja are fickle gods who revel in death and fighting. If I owned a book of Holy Writings, and if I could read it, I'd be able to tell others how different the Christian God is. Right now, all I can do is pray and try to be a good example. But I determine to get one of those books someday, perhaps when Finn is trading in the European mainland again.

Baby Snorri continues growing and changing, not even a baby anymore. His hair has grown in curly and thick, like Finn's. He walks around, climbing anything, whether stable or not.

Freydis recovers. She goes into the woods for long stretches of time. I think she sits on a tree limb overhanging her boy's grave.

Suka's arm has almost healed. The stitching wasn't perfect, and he'll have a large scar. But he's alive. He stays mostly in his hut, since he's forbidden to be anywhere near Freydis. This is enforced by Tyr, who's voluntarily assumed his bodyguard duty again, sticking to Suka like a shadow.

When I go into Suka's hut the next week to remove his stitches, he greets me warmly. I suppose saving his life counts for something. He's very thoughtful, and even asks me questions. He has combed his glossy black hair and his emerald-green tunic looks clean.

"You've been married how many times?" From his intense look, I know he's not being disrespectful with his question.

"Three. My first two husbands died. You knew Thorstein the Red, didn't you?"

"Yes." His slanted eyes are like pools of dark light as they fix on mine. "He was a proud one." He gives a dry cough.

"He was the most sought-after man on the island." For some reason, I still defend my selfish, dead husband.

"Of course. All Eirik's sons were. But at least Thorvald was kind to the slaves who worked for him. And Leif is, sometimes."

I notice his *sometimes,* but don't remark on it. Instead, I continue cutting and pulling out the stitches. I have small metal pincers that work perfectly for pulling the thread out.

"You know we're leaving?" I ask.

"Yes, and I'm not going. I can survive here on my own. Perhaps some others will want to stay, as well. I've been talking to that brute outside my door about it. He'd be good protection from the Skraelings, don't you think?" He says *Skraelings* disdainfully. He probably knows everyone in camp thinks of him as a Skraeling, too.

"Indeed." I continue working.

"I could have died, thanks to your wolf." He looks at the doorway.

"Or thanks to me, had I taken up my seax." I yank a bit too hard at a thread.

He smiles at me, his smooth, deeply tan skin striking. His face seems ageless. "Perhaps so."

The next stitch is partially embedded in his skin, so I have to tug on it. I suppose he realizes I was only joking about being able to kill him.

His eyes show pain, but he doesn't complain of my tugging. "You know, if I had died, I couldn't even get into your Valhalla."

"It's not mine." I hold his gaze. "And I wouldn't get in either. I'm a woman, remember? But there is a heaven, and it belongs to the God of the Christians. It's for everyone."

I tell him the story of Jesus Christ and his Father in heaven, and how we only need to believe and ask Him to forgive us. Then we can talk with a God who hears us, unlike Thor.

"So he died on a tree?" He sets his jaw, trying to understand. But his words hit me like arrows—I had never thought about the cross that way. Yes, He died on a tree.

The perfect sacrifice.

"Gudrid?" He reaches for me with his good arm. As soon as he touches me, Tyr appears in the doorframe, blocking all the light with his huge form.

"Problem?" He looks at me, hand on his axe.

"No—nothing, Tyr. Thank you. I'm fine."

My heart is full as I finally see why I'm drawn to the story of Jesus Christ. He died like my mother, on a tree, only He came to life. If only she could have done the same.

I finish pulling out the stitches in silence. I want Suka to understand my faith, but I don't know how to put it into words for him.

"I heard you were a volva?" He whispers, probably afraid of another appearance by Tyr.

"Yes, my foster-mother taught me the old ways. But I gave it up—wrong sort of power."

"Ah, but you do have powers! I remember how your wolf came—only too well." He groans deeply.

"She likes me, for some reason," I say. "And it's not my power that brings her. It's God's."

He leans closer as I take out the last stitch. "What will happen to Freydis?"

Why does Suka care, after he took advantage of her madness? So far, Ref hasn't asked me about their relationship. And I don't want to know anything about it. Maybe they just shared that leafy mat for warmth. Surely her uncleanness would have kept him from getting too close?

"Do you love her?" I rub salve over the closed wound.

"She is my fire." Suka clenches his fists. No wonder Freydis liked him. He's the exact opposite of her gentle, quiet Ref. But Ref has his own strength—more like a mountain, while Suka reminds me of the crushing ocean.

"If you love her at all, you must forget her." I fix my gaze on his. "Don't doubt that Leif will kill you if you ever return to Greenland. You threatened my life, and, in so doing, hers. Just as you'll always remember my wolf's attack, I'll always remember yours."

I don't add that if Ref and Finn discovered Suka had shared a bed with Freydis, they would put his head on a stick.

He sits straighter and looks to the door again. "I'll think on this." He frowns.

Much as I dislike Suka for what he's done, I see he longs for something more than a woman. Something like faith.

"Life everlasting is the one thing no one can take from you." I know how he chafes to be a slave. "So belief brings freedom."

He says nothing, his dark eyes cloaking his feelings as I pack up my herb box. He stays at the table as I leave, lost in his thoughts.

Out in the camp, preparations for the voyage are underway. Finn's men have mostly recovered from their journey. In fact, Bjarni is the only sick person in camp now, and I fear it's the effect of mushrooms. He ate far too many when he attacked the Skraelings with his unfettered violence.

We feel the loss of the ship Hallstein took. Finn will guide one of the remaining ships, but the other ship will have to be steered by Bjarni. He is the only one who's made this trip to the new lands before. If either ship goes off-course, it could be broken to bits, or come ashore in another land entirely. Of course, both ships could use Magnus on board, with his gift of direction, but I'm hoping Finn has found someone else who can help Bjarni. I selfishly want Deirdre and Magnus on our ship. And I want Snorri Thorbrandsson aboard, for reasons I can't fully understand.

Deirdre has worked like a busy bee this entire week. From grinding fresh grain all day to packing the cured bull meat, she hasn't sat down once.

We will only have room for a few sheep on board, so we'll butcher the rest and use our remaining salt to preserve the meat. Since the cows are still plump and healthy from the lush summer, we'll take them along. One will be calving soon, a final gift from the dead bull.

Deirdre, much as I love her, starts to bother me with her endless references to Inger's gift with animals. She even goes so far as to say I should train Inger as a volva. I bite my tongue. I know Deirdre admires me as a spiritual leader here, since I know the chants and rune songs. She knows I've believed in the Christian God of Leif and his mother, but she doesn't understand how the pagan ways clash with that belief.

Inger herself doesn't mention her talents with the animals. I suspect she sees nothing out of the ordinary in her abilities, as I see nothing strange in my friendship with my wolf. I think what sets us apart from the others is that we spend time with animals and try to understand their ways.

Perhaps this would also explain why some are better healers than others. Good healers watch people closely, ask questions, and try to understand how the body works, because it interests us.

Deirdre has her own gift of insight into human nature. Usually, she has a good eye for romantic entanglements of any kind in the camp.

One day as Deirdre slices the mutton for salting, I ask about Inger and her golden-haired Geisli.

"Planning to marry once we are in Greenland, I shouldn't wonder. Geisli comes from Norway, same as her, so they might go back there one day." She carefully presses salt into the thin slices, then packs them in a small keg.

"Isn't she Leif's slave, though?" How would a slave have the freedom to travel to Norway?

"Why—she is your slave!" Deirdre knocks the salt bowl over.

I jump from the bench. "She is not!"

"We *all* are." She rakes the salt to the edge of the table, then puts it back into the bowl.

What is she thinking?

"You're not!" My voice fills the longhouse.

"M'lady, we were all Leif's gifts to you, not only for the trip, but for life."

I clench my shift in both hands. "Don't call me 'm'lady' again, Deirdre. Do *not*. You're my friend."

"You thought we were Leif's?" She continues packing the meat, not looking at me.

"Of course. I don't have slaves."

"I am afraid you do. I thought perhaps that is why you concerned yourself with the girls' futures."

I sit down heavily on the bench, not caring that I'm doing nothing to help. Leif did this, without my consent. Years ago, when I moved to Brattahlid with my father, I told Leif I'd never have slaves. Now I'm saddled with plenty of them. It was one thing to think they obeyed me because of Leif's orders, but quite another to realize they're obliged to me as *thralls*.

Did Finn know of this arrangement? Did he help Leif pick the most skilled women from the farm? Or even the most beautiful?

Everything shifts. I don't know who to talk to about this. I want to understand my position here. Until today, I thought I was only the expedition leader's wife, not owner of all the women in the camp. Or do I own Suka, too? Magnus? And Tyr and Bjarni?

I'll talk to the one person who knows Leif as well as I do, if not better.

I'll go to Freydis.

Chapter Twenty-Six

Freydis has packed up most of her hut, including all her sumptuous goods from Leif. Eirik's helmet still hangs on the wall, though. It's some kind of protective talisman for her, I suspect. Eirik was one of the most comforting people I've ever known, so I understand her attachment to it.

She has lost too much weight. Ref is probably the only reason she's eaten anything. I feel such pity for this devoted man Freydis married, as he tries to keep up with her emotional swings.

Her freckles seem to have faded into her paleness, causing her hair to stand out even more. I sigh. Eirik would be furious if he could see how his daughter has become a shadow of her fearless, exuberant self.

She gets off her bed and comes close to me, shifting from one foot to the other, like an old woman. I know where her concern lies before she speaks.

"Suka?"

I can't believe she still thinks of him, even after he tried to kill us. "He will live, but he'll have a scar to remind him of his foolishness." I know Freydis used to relish shocking conversations, so I dive right in. "Freydis, did Leif give me the slaves here?"

Freydis laughs. It's a little wobbly and weak at first, but it turns into a belly laugh that reminds me of her father. I'm grateful to pull her out of her sadness, if only for a moment.

"So, Gudrid, who've you been talking to? No doubt that loose-lipped Scotswoman. She had her orders to be silent about it. I should hunt her down with a horsewhip."

I know these are idle threats, especially since we have no horses or whips here. "Who do I own here? And why did Leif do this to me?"

"You were with…child." She can barely say the word. "He wanted to make sure you had a healthy birth. I've wondered about his concern myself. But perhaps he cared so much because the child was his?" Her cat-eyes glow as she throws out the question.

I can't stop myself. I smack her face.

She sucks at her lower lip, which starts bleeding. "My, you are quite the Viking." She clasps my hand in her long fingers. "I meant nothing by it. I wish your Snorri was my blood-relation, my true nephew."

I hold her hand tighter. "You might as well be his auntie, Freydis. And my sister. That's why I want you to take care of yourself. If Leif was so concerned about me, how much more will he care if his own sister returns ill?"

"Perhaps you are right." She pulls her hand away. "Is Suka coming home with us?" Her mind is fixed on her lover.

Ref comes in, carrying a heaping platter of steamed fish and leeks. His smile for his wife melts me.

"Inger prepared this meal," he says. "You must have some, Gudrid."

I shake my head, knowing I can't talk freely now. "Come and see me soon, Freydis." It is not a request.

I stop outside the door, distracted by a beautiful stand of trees nearby. The trees have stark white bark and are covered with yellow leaves, unlike any I've seen in Greenland or Iceland. I have been trapped indoors lately. My wolf hasn't appeared for days, since her attack on Suka.

Although I know my boy is safe in our hut with Linnea, I want to check on him before I take a walk. A pretty picture meets my eyes when I pull back the door's deerskin.

Inside, a fire blazes to keep out the chill. Linnea sits near Snorri's cradle, humming. And Snorri Thorbrandsson picks up more kindling for the fire, his eyes on Linnea.

As the wind snatches at the deer hide, I see glimpses of a new relationship in the camp. Baby Snorri stirs, and Linnea quickly tucks the blanket tighter to him. Snorri Thorbrandsson's eyes, reflecting the firelight, stare unashamedly at her long, fair hair. It truly could be my hair. It's the same texture, color, and almost the same length. Linnea is hard to ignore, with those wide-set, mesmerizing eyes. Though she is shorter than I am, she is still curvy in a way men can't help but notice, even in her loose overdresses. She's also good with my child—a natural mother. Surprised by this new direction for Snorri's affections, I turn toward the forest, an unexpected emptiness filling me.

Finn is likely fitting Leif's ships for the journey. He won't notice if I slip into the forest to see my wolf again, or perhaps to gather some of Bjarni's mushrooms. I think we have to wean him off them, much as I weaned my baby. Nerienda thinks otherwise—that we should take them all away with no warning. It seems to me Bjarni needs to come back to himself slowly, after all these years of deliberately warping his mind and afflicting his body.

Doubtless, anyone would say that the sky is perfect today—deep blue with no clouds in it. A pang of longing hits me as I remember growing up in Iceland, with its dolphin and ice-colored skies that rushed to meet the rounded mountains.

The wind whips at my hair and I begin to twist it into a knot. Another hand touches my head and I turn, expecting Finn. It is not.

Snorri Thorbrandsson. Here, on the edge of the woods, where everyone can see.

"Golden." He smooths my hair, looking into my eyes. His hand goes down and traces my chin.

"Snorri!" I must wake him from this stupor. If Finn sees this...if *anyone* sees this....

The sun lights his beard and eyes aflame. "Were you going into the forest?"

If I say yes, he'll want to come with me. But I'm not a liar. "I was thinking of it, yes."

"Will you let me walk with you?" His hand, which was resting on my shoulder, drops to his side.

I've never in my life felt unsafe with Snorri. I know he wouldn't hurt or force me. But right now, I feel unsafe with myself. I've had many days to lie in Finn's arms since his return. But when Finn left me, Snorri Thorbrandsson was there. Not only for me, but for my son. This makes me weak when I'm around him. I doubt he knows this, though, and I don't want to offend him.

"Of course," I say.

His arm brushes mine as we step on fresh-fallen leaves. As we pass the baby's grave, I feel a chill. How long will I be tormented by visions of that little body? Snorri seems to have similar thoughts, and he reaches for my hand. I cross my arms.

"I must find more of Bjarni's mushrooms." Like a deer, I bolt forward.

He stops short. I go just a few steps farther before respect makes me stop.

"How long are you going to pretend, and deny yourself?" He stands astride a fallen log, his foot propped up on it.

"I don't pretend, for you or for anyone." I put my hands on my hips, challenging him.

Snorri's light blue tunic is dirty from the work he's been doing. A heavy silver cross hangs from a cord on his neck, though it could easily be mistaken for Thor's hammer. Snorri Thorbrandsson was another of the monk's Icelandic converts to Christianity.

He nods, thoughtful.

Memories of our recent battle flood me, and my simmering anger rises. "How many Skraelings did you kill in the attack?" What coward would let an expecting woman defend us?

"Bjarni himself killed five men, near the stockade. Then the Skraelings started hurling flaming balls of whale blubber over our walls. You saw it—we had to fall back to move the attack from their catapults' reach. It's a wonder the huts didn't burn to the ground."

Surely that was God's hand of protection. "But how many did you kill?" I want to be proud of him, not embarrassed by his retreat.

"Six." It is not his nature to brag, though he killed more than any other Viking did that day.

"Thank you." I step closer.

He takes his foot off the log, then catches my hand in his, looking into my eyes. His eyes shine bright as the volcanoes in Iceland.

"I can't stop thinking of you, Gudrid. Even as I watch Linnea, I see you. But you belong to another man—I'm not even sure which."

Those are the wrong words to say, since I'm already loaded with guilt over my feelings for Leif. It is time for Snorri Thorbrandsson to find another woman. "I belong to my husband. This has to be our goodbye, Snorri. Just think of me as your sister."

"What about Leif? Is he only a brother, too?" Jealousy charges his voice.

"Yes, he is. He has to be." I stare at the perfect blue sky, wishing it would open and take me anywhere but here. I'm weary of being pulled in all directions by these men who think they love me.

He cocks his head, his beard shining like copper, even in the darkness of the forest. "Very well."

He seems to mean it. But the emptiness rushes in immediately. Will we talk anymore? Will he smile at me again? And what of the next time Finn travels? Who will protect me? Part of me knows God will, but I need human arms around me, human eyes watching over me. Why do I have to be so weak?

I breathe in, then release a sigh that seems to take all the air in my body with it.

Snorri still watches me. "Will you let me stay with you now?"

My insides feel as if they've been ripped open. I'm out of strength to resist, so I tell him to stay. I worry about my wolf, because no one has seen her all week. A chill passes over me even in the warm breeze, and I know we need to look for her, not the mushrooms.

We walk in the damp sweetness of dying ferns, up to the deep creek bed. We must keep going, even as far as the caves, to find my wolf. As I tuck my skirts into my belt, I blush under Snorri's intent gaze. He hasn't seen my legs before. I try to pull away from him, to show his attentions don't bother me. If only he'd stop watching my every move.

He waits at the creek bed until I shin down the bank. "I'll carry you across. No need for you to drench yourself."

I shake my head.

"You don't have to do it yourself, and you know it. Come here, Gudrid."

I suppose he's right. Besides, he's only doing what a brother would do. I put an arm around his neck, and his hand slides under my legs as I jump into his arms. My blush deepens. He looks at me, chuckles, then plunges into the water.

Once on the other side of the creek bed, he tries to put me down, but my dress hooks over his sword hilt. We both struggle to pull it off, hands touching again. Finally he unhooks it and places me on the ground, as carefully as if I were a glass bead on a necklace.

Grabbing at the tree roots, I pull myself up the bank before Snorri has a chance to help. I've been embarrassed enough for one day. I plunge ahead, not waiting for him. The clean sea air will be a welcome relief. The trees seem to push me down into the ground, like the sides of one of those heavy European caskets in Finn's storehouse. These forests are too thick, not like our sparse forests in Greenland. I can't wait until we ship out for home.

Snorri Thorbrandsson walks several paces behind me, giving me space. His thoughtfulness of my feelings always disarms me.

When we reach the bowl of rocks, I walk around it, toward the sea on the opposite side. The air's growing colder. I should have worn my cape.

I start to run, jumping small felled trees. The overturned dirt for the mass Skraeling grave lies in a loose pile on the ground. Our men didn't even bother to tamp down the dirt. Snorri's footsteps are never far away, so I don't bother to look behind me. Finally, we reach the edge of the forest, with its small beach opening onto the sea. I stumble over the small rocks on the beach, finally reaching the dark sand near the shore. My wolf lies there, water lapping at her feet. Her wild golden eyes stare at me. She has a Skraeling arrow through her middle. My wolf is dead.

Chapter Twenty-Seven

Snorri's arms wrap around me before my knees hit the rocks. I huddle next to my wolf, feeling for the breath I know isn't there. The arrow has penetrated all the way through her thin body. My tears cover my hands as I stroke the soft fur, a pleasure I never had while she was alive. I close her eyes as best I can.

The ocean that barely touched her feet quickly drenches her stomach. I try with no success to pick her up or pull her back. Snorri reaches down and throws her over his shoulder, making sure the arrow points out. The sight of her hanging there reminds me of a fresh rabbit kill, but it's the only way to move her quickly.

Snorri carries her back into the forest, where he places her on the ground and waits. I realize I don't even know where her den is. But her home is with me.

Burying an animal in the camp isn't allowed. However, this wolf has saved our lives, several times over. I won't leave her out here to rot. But I can't think of what to do with her.

Snorri rubs his chin. "Thorfinn needs to see this arrow. You know this means the Skraelings have found this shoreline? We'd thought it was hidden."

He's right. All it takes is a long and determined walk through the woods, and then invading Skraelings could be in the camp. And we have no wolf to protect our borders now.

"She goes to the camp, then," I say. Snorri graciously picks her up again. I wonder, selfishly, if there's anything he wouldn't do for me.

It's getting dark when we finally get back. I didn't realize so much time had passed on the beach. Geisli's on guard, startling me, yet again, with his long, butter-colored hair. He meets us at the treeline with his lantern.

"Karlsefni's been worried," he says.

His words have a double meaning for me. Is Finn upset I went walking in the woods? Or that I was walking with Snorri Thorbrandsson?

Geisli stares at the wolf. "And just what is *that*?"

Snorri Thorbrandsson doesn't take kindly to disrespect, so he deflects that comment with a glare that could curdle milk.

"We're taking the wolf to Karlsefni." He fingers his own sword for good measure.

Geisli's eyes travel to Snorri's strong left hand, then back to his blazing eyes.

"I'll take you." He is like a small boy in the face of Snorri's power.

"Thank you," I whisper to Snorri. It is all I can say. It's enough to receive his familiar smile and nod in return. I won't let myself cry here. Viking women control when and where they cry, or they're weak forever. Halldis taught me this much.

Finn meets us at the door of the longhouse, a hot flatbread in one hand, and a candle in the other. He holds the candle over the wolf, then touches the arrow tip. He looks at me, eyes dark. "Skraelings?"

"Yes—on the outer shoreline." Snorri answers for me. When he looks to me for instructions, instead of Finn, he seals our friendship.

"Please put her in back of my hut, away from the heap." I can't bear for her to be anywhere else right now.

Finn gives Snorri a questioning look. But he says, "You two eat. I'll take her, Gudrid." He hands me the candle, then takes the wolf from Snorri.

When I go inside, I sit right on the bench at the long table, not caring that I'm surrounded by men. They stop talking about the plentiful wheat in Vinland and continue eating in silence.

Deirdre is soon next to me, offering beef and flatbread. Linnea has already served Snorri Thorbrandsson, and he sprawls at the end of the table, eating with his wide, left-handed sweeps.

The men watch me. They probably heard us talking about the Skraeling arrow, and are anxious for explanations. I don't plan to give any. Snorri knows this, so he begins describing where we found my wolf.

Once Snorri stops talking, men discuss laying traps along the whole shoreline. Volunteers offer to patrol it. They're out for blood, after the last attack took two of our own. But it's useless.

Finn's voice, warm and low, carries over the longhouse. "No traps. We leave tomorrow. This land is done for us."

He has made this decision without even asking me. I want the same thing, of course—to leave here as soon as we can, especially now my wolf is dead. But his haste reminds me of The Eastman and Thorstein the Red. Why don't my husbands realize I can offer advice and wisdom, having traveled far and wide myself?

I have lost two protectors in one night. Will Finn be there for me, like my wolf and Snorri Thorbrandsson?

I stand, ignoring the curious looks I'm given. I brush past Finn, frantic to be alone in our hut. Inside, Inger rocks Snorri in his cradle. But after one look at my face, she jumps up, dropping a curtsy. "Good night to you, m'lady. Your boy sleeps so soundly."

As she leaves, I collapse onto my bed, pulling blankets over me. Later, Finn pulls me to him, waking me from my dream that Leif was yelling at me for more carrot soup. It must be early morning.

Need—not friendship or love—drives our passions. Though we are married, two seen as one, a hollowness fills my heart, even in my husband's arms. Finn goes to sleep quickly, as he probably stayed up so late planning our hasty departure with his men.

"And so we leave today." My breath comes out in a cloud as I speak to myself. The fire has died. My boy stirs, barely awake. I stoke the fire, then wake him for nursing, so he can warm up and go back to sleep. I need to bury my wolf.

I put on my warmest woolen cloak and a pair of Finn's trousers. I don't expect to meet anyone at this hour, with the sun barely on the horizon.

The shovel is propped against the wall near the midden heap. I'll bury my wolf in the empty bull pasture. It's still green and surrounded by colorful trees. It will be a reminder of how she patrolled the fenceline, watching over our camp.

The arrow remains stuck in her side. I try to get it out, but it's a difficult process. The stiffness of her body, combined with the width of the arrowhead, make it nearly impossible without some kind of tool.

Someone walks up behind me, and I'm afraid it's Snorri Thorbrandsson again. Instead, I turn to see Finn standing shirtless, wearing only his trousers and slippers. He comes up to my wolf, easily removes the arrowhead, and pulls out the stick. Then he takes the shovel.

"Where?" he asks. Gratitude floods me.

I take him to the fence and show him the spot. He starts to dig. "What has changed between us?" He focuses on the shovel, not me. His tight muscles move dirt so quickly, he'll surely dig a deep hole in just a few moments.

"Nothing." I try to believe that. I can't put into words all the disappointment and sadness I went through when Finn left me. I have been abandoned three times before in my life. Once when Mother died and Father didn't want me, again when Father died and left me in Eirik's care with no decent inheritance, and yet again when Thorstein the Red died and left me alone with the farmer. I haven't talked with Finn about those things, because I hate thinking about them.

"I've had Ref work on a surprise for you, for our trip." He sounds excited, like a boy with a new wooden sword.

"What is it?" I try to mirror his happiness.

"You'll see." As he smiles, weak sunshine hits his face. I know every line of it, from the strength of his jaw to the way his nose slopes. I'm suddenly proud of my knowledge of this man, this brave leader, and the father of my child. He's leaving this land for me, I tell myself. He loves me.

He finishes the hole, picks up the wolf, and brings her to me. I run my fingers over her fur, placing my whole hand on her muzzle. It's my goodbye not only to her, but to Straumsfjord. Once we get to Greenland, I won't think of this sea, this camp, or this forest, any more than I have to. But I'll always remember her.

I press my other hand on her forehead, then turn my back. I can't watch. Finn lowers her into the grave and covers her with dirt.

"You should sleep; you were up late." I touch Finn's tattoo when he comes up next to me.

"The day has begun." He pushes his curls from his eyes.

I feel the heaviness of those words. Our last day has arrived, and his plundering of this land is done.

He touches my hair, even with dirt on his hands. He twists a piece. "How I've missed you."

It may not be what I longed to hear. But it's all he knows to say, and it is enough.

Chapter Twenty-Eight

And, just like that, we are leaving. The two ships are packed; the food divided between them. I wait to see how our men and women will be divided. I've told Finn the people I want with us, but I don't know if he listened.

I could take a last walk in the forest, but my wolf isn't there anymore, and I don't want to see the child's grave again. We asked Freydis if she wanted to bring the bones back to Brattahlid, perhaps in one of Ref's carved boxes, but she said her child belonged here. Then she declared she'd be returning here anyway. I imagine Ref may have something to say about that. Leif will, too.

When she discovers she's not on my ship, Inger bids me a teary farewell. She looks very Norwegian with her dark hair pulled back off her face, her eyes blue as the skies. Both she and Geisli are on Bjarni's ship, since Geisli will help determine directions, and Inger will care for the animals. Magnus will be directing our ship.

As we hug, I encourage Inger to watch not only animals, but people as well, so she can learn to be a healer. Nerienda is on her ship too, and can teach her about herbal cures.

"But I want to learn from you." Inger sobs, momentarily forgetting she's my slave. I hope she will always forget it.

"I'll teach you more once we're in Greenland, my child." But I know we might not meet again. It is risky, sailing in the fall, and Bjarni isn't as skilled a sailor as Finn. I pray we will all arrive safe in Greenland before winter.

Inger hugs the baby, then wipes her eyes as Geisli comes over, his arm around a barrel. His hair shines in the sunlight, and Snorri almost falls out of my arms, reaching for it. Geisli laughs and lets him touch it. What lovely children Inger will have with him.

Nerienda runs to join us, which is a sight to behold. She lifts her skirts, showing her worn reindeer-leather shoes, her thin knees knocking together. She drapes a small blanket over my arm.

"I made this for the child," she says.

The soft brown blanket is edged with complicated red embroidery. As Nerienda hugs me, I can't hold back my tears. I know how she hates handiwork of all kinds.

"Keep the men healthy." I pull out of her embrace, giving a command to regain some control.

She nods her gray head. "And you'll do the same." She gives me a knowing look which brings back all the darkness of the day Freydis' child was born dead. "You're a healer—don't doubt that."

Bjarni comes over and walks Nerienda to the small ship's boat. I found more mushrooms and hid them in a locked box for him, giving Nerienda the key to keep on her belt. He's gaining strength and eating better with our approach of taking the mushrooms away slowly, instead of all at once.

Ref walks up, carrying what looks like a large carved block with a leather strap on it. He hands it to me, smiling as if it's a rare treasure. I smile back, uncertain, until Finn sees us from the shore and runs to my side.

"It's a seat for our boy. I knew you would worry about him on the open sea. He'll be able to sit under the crossbeams in this seat, safe and sound."

Of course I'll worry anyway, because I'm his mother. But it will help to have a secure place to put our child. I hug both men and thank them. The carvings alone must have taken hours. I recognize the Midgard serpent and a dragon head, as well as roughly-carved Skraelings. The light, honey-colored wood must be pine from Straumsfjord. It will be a good reminder for Snorri when he's older, although I'd rather he never knew about the Skraelings.

I check through our herb box as more crew members board Bjarni's small ship, ready to be ferried over to the knarr. Suka hasn't appeared yet. As far as I've heard, he plans to stay here. Freydis needs to get on board before she realizes he's not coming.

I don't have to imagine the kind of fit Freydis could throw, because I've witnessed several at Brattahlid. She's prone to having them any time she's thwarted in getting her way. It's how she secured her place on our trip to this new land. She'd fumed and shouted and forced Eirik to let her sail with Finn, so she would be equal with her brothers. All three had sailed for Vinland before, Thorstein the Red being the only brother who never arrived in the new world.

Most of the animals have been loaded onto Finn's ship, because they belong to me. I've given one of my cows and two of our remaining sheep to Bjarni for their crew.

Deirdre walks up, wrapped in her clean, rosy smell. She smoothes my hair and kisses Snorri on his little curls.

"Are you ready?" She is calmer these days, now that Magnus has returned.

"Are you with our ship?" I hardly dare ask, fearing she might not be.

"Surely, did Karlsefni not tell you?" Her voice is full of scolding. Deirdre doesn't understand why Finn shares so little with me. Not that her Magnus talks much at all, since Deirdre does enough talking for both of them. "He would not separate Magnus and me."

"Who else is with us?" I can't stop myself from asking, like a curious child.

"Freydis and Ref, of course. Snorri Thorbrandsson and Linnea…." The way she links those two together, I know there must be something between them. Why do I care so much? I gave up any rights to Snorri Thorbrandsson's devotion, misplaced though it was.

Finn stands on the shore, deep in conversation with Bjarni and Geisli. Their crew has already boarded the ship. I wave to Inger, knowing her insecurity as the only young woman in the group. Women who sail with the Viking men have to be wary at all times. Geisli will protect her, though. Their time in Straumsfjord has drawn them together. And most of the men are too superstitious about her abilities with animals to lay a hand on her—at least, I hope so.

Baby Snorri runs around on the beach, picking up small rocks and throwing them into the air. A pebble falls on his head. He looks at me and scrunches up his face, ready to cry. I don't run to him, though. It's not the Viking way. To show I hurt for him is to make him weak. I watch to see if he'll cry or run to me, but he doesn't. He stoops to pick up more pebbles, only this time, he throws them away from himself.

Finally, everyone is loaded and Bjarni's ship slides into the gray water. I watch until Inger's dark head and Geisli's light one look small as specks. I go back in my mind, remembering the freshness of feeling I had when Thorir the Eastman and I shipped out. We were just married, and my head was still full of dreams.

At first, I had noticed his strong arms, his long, light hair, and his humorous ways. These were The Eastman's obvious features. But I came to discover he was very aware of his good looks, and his humor always came at someone else's expense.

I also discovered the cold hatred he had for the Vikings who'd left Norway. Vikings like Eirik the Red, and even my own father. It was actually better that The Eastman died only a few weeks after Leif rescued our ship. He wouldn't have survived the winter with Eirik and his sons. He would have mocked Thorvald's Sami wife and Thjodhild's faith and Eirik's temper.

I try to let these feelings pass. Perhaps Inger's young love is different. Besides, if I hadn't married The Eastman and Thorstein the Red, I wouldn't have known I wanted to marry Finn. He was the one husband I chose for myself, because I knew him. We had often played King's Table on Finn's walrus ivory board, talking until all the embers died in the longhouse. I never worried about him taking advantage of me. He was far too well-bred for that. And he was careful with me. He treated me with gentleness, like Orm and Eirik had. It was a gentleness born of respect.

Such are my thoughts as I watch my boy digging a hole in the sand with a little stick. Suka's black hair flashes by as

he runs up to our ship, making me hold my breath until he
returns. He must have run an errand for Finn.

He smiles as he runs up to me, skin glowing. He
unlaces the bottom of his sleeve, showing me how his arm
heals. He's been applying the paste, and the wound has
begun to scab over. I clap out loud, because the scar won't be
as terrible as I'd feared. We stand and beam at each other,
neither of us knowing what to say. Yes, we tried to kill each
other. But now, somehow, we're friends.

"Tyr's agreed to stay on," he says.

"Just the two of you? It's not enough, against the hordes
of Skraelings!"

"I must stay. I would rather die protecting myself than
live serving someone."

"But where will you hide if they return? The caves?"

He shrugs, looking toward the forest. "We'll guard the
camp, and we'll do whatever it takes to survive."

There are so many obstacles for him. They have no
boats. We're taking the animals. They have no women to
cook for them or make new clothes. I have to help him
somehow.

"Watch the boy." I walk to the shoreline and talk with
Finn. He does what I ask, though he doesn't approve,
because he'll never forgive Suka for attacking Freydis and
me. Finn and Magnus take a small boat over, and load one of
our calves and a barrel of dried mutton into it.

Once Suka sees what they bring to shore, he starts
shaking his head. But I run and grab the calf's rope, walking
her to him. "This is for you. A sign of my forgiveness."

"You have already healed my arm. Why are you being
so kind to me?"

"I think…" I struggle to put it into words. "Maybe because I'm God's daughter now, not just Thorbjorn's daughter or Eirik's daughter. God forgave me, so I want to forgive you."

Suka smiles, the widest part of his face. "Thank you, *Gottesdottir*. I'll take my calf and meat and stay away from Freydis, but please get her on the ship soon. I've spent this whole day avoiding her."

"Thank you for hiding." I clasp his hand. "I'll bring her to the ship. And I'll pray for you and Tyr."

Suka walks off, and just in time. Finn shouts to me, "Everyone needs to come aboard now. Could you get them together?"

"I will." I brush off Snorri's clothes, which are covered with dark sand. I think he has tried to eat some, given the dirt smeared all around his puckered mouth. I can't resist kissing his face, gritty as it is. We walk into our camp for the very last time.

I lean over as a wave of nausea hits me. Snorri runs ahead. I'd tell him to stop, but Linnea stands nearby, arms open for my boy. She gathers him up, then quickly comes to my side.

"Are you ill, m'lady?"

I can't answer as my stomach clenches again. Snorri Thorbrandsson follows Linnea, concern in his eyes. He doesn't know I'd noticed them talking together in the longhouse doorway. The answer to Linnea's question flies out before I can shut my mouth.

"No, Linnea, I'm not ill. I'm with child."

Chapter Twenty-Nine

I haven't told Finn about his baby yet, and I don't plan to until we're underway on the ship. I won't give him any reason to delay. I would rather vomit half the trip than stay here, dreading what the next day holds. The Skraelings put an arrow through my wolf, and if they decide to raid the forest, nothing could stop them.

I pray they won't come back, so that Suka and Tyr can stay here. But something tells me Tyr will go looking for revenge. I can't blame him. Maybe they'll take Skraeling wives for themselves.

When everything is finally loaded, including Freydis, I distract her with questions. "Did you remember Eirik's helmet? Have you seen my herb box? Can you strap Snorri into his new seat?" She rushes around to help me. Her sense of family runs deep. It's enough to keep her mind from Suka, until our knarr is finally out to sea.

I spend most of my first day enduring sea-sickness. Finn is always amused at my ability to feel the slightest shifts of the boat. "You have some mainlander blood in you, wife."

When I was younger, Orm would never take me on the fishing boats, because I always ended up with my head over the side, instead of helping with the nets.

Freydis stays quiet, watching the waves and prowling around the ship like a caged animal. She's as much a seaman as her father was, but she prefers forests and high trees. For this reason, Finn puts her in charge of the mast. She does any climbing involved in bringing the walrus-skin sail down or hoisting it up. As leader, Finn handles the steering-board, but he has to work closely with Freydis to keep the sail where he needs it. To my surprise, they work well together. Both Finn and Freydis have grown up around ships. The ocean rhythms fill their blood.

I tend to my cows, and Linnea and Deirdre see to the food for the crew. The men always have huge appetites from the fresh sea air. Magnus is in charge of the handful of sheep, because he loves looking after them.

Any time baby Snorri isn't strapped in his seat, I hold his hand or carry him. I won't risk having him fall over the side. From his post at the oars, Snorri Thorbrandsson keeps watch over him, as well.

Traveling along the coastline, sometimes we weigh anchor off the beaches. Finn hopes to find where Hallstein docked Leif's other ship. As yet, there have been no signs of our boorish mutineer. Finn follows a river farther inland, to a place so thick with forests, it must be the *Markland* Leif described to us.

We take our sleep-sacks ashore overnight, sleeping near the treeline. Evergreen branches give us cover, so we can see anyone who comes to the river bed before they notice us. My boy doesn't like having to breathe under the poky tree needles, but it is necessary for all of us. Snorri Thorbrandsson stands guard during the night.

As the pale morning light trickles through the needles, we hear a whoop. I push the branches aside, only to see Finn and Snorri chasing a man and two women up the shallow riverbed. Two children huddle together by the water. They have no swords or arrows, and they look harmless enough. One of our men gets up to approach them, none too gracefully. When the children see him, they run upstream, toward their parents. By this time, Finn and Snorri are returning, so they catch the children and pull them up to our group.

We have to leave quickly, in case the adult natives return with others. The children's hair and clothing are filthy. "What sort of parents are they, leaving these children behind?" I ask.

They must be boys, because they have nothing on their chests but bruises. I clasp my growing stomach and become nauseous again, wondering how parents could care so little for their children. They ran and left these boys to fend for themselves. Cowards.

I compose myself, stepping closer to them. They don't flinch. "They'll come with us—but not as slaves. They'll come as my own children."

Finn raises his eyebrows, ready to contest my decision. I fix him with a meaningful stare. "Very well," he says.

Snorri Thorbrandsson chuckles, struggling to be respectful. "I've never seen green eyes shoot fire before, Thorfinn, but I believe Gudrid's just did."

Finn smiles, a welcome gesture in the face of my open demand. "Yes, I'd hate to be the man standing in the way of those sparks."

Deirdre takes the older boy's arm and I put my arm around the younger, then we lead them onto our small ship's boat. Their eyes seem to drink in my light hair, as if they've never seen the like before. They follow my hand signals easily, showing they are quick-minded. If I could talk with them, we could learn more about this part of the land. I have to try to learn their language.

Finn announces our search for Hallstein is over. We have to make headway toward Greenland before winter storms hit.

Back on the knarr, baby Snorri chafes under my ceaseless watchcare. He longs to run and climb all over the cross-beams. I finally allow Freydis to walk him the length of the boat, but I regret it soon after. As I'm milking my cow, Freydis holds my son's small body over the prow, like a figurehead for the ship. Finn actually leaves the steering-board to pull them back. He scolds Freydis, shouting curses I've never heard him use before. Linnea takes hold of Snorri before I can make my way through the men. She cradles him all the way back to me, for which I kiss her cheek. Freydis' carelessness with my child won't be forgotten.

The past couple of days, Freydis has been more heedless in her actions. Not only has she been changing her clothing out in the open like a man, with no blanket to hide her, but Deirdre caught her trying to break the lock on my herb box. I wondered what would drive her to do this, and finally divined that she was looking for mushrooms. She was very accepting of Bjarni's dependence on them, almost *too* accepting.

Sea-travel brings out the best and worst in everyone. Freydis isn't bothered by the cramped quarters or limited food supplies, since she's grown up at sea. But something deeper torments her. I hope it is the loss of her son, and not Suka's absence.

Tonight, Finn pulls his sleep-sack near my own, joining them together so he can hold me before relieving Snorri Thorbrandsson at the steering-board. Snug in Finn's arms, I tell him we're having another child. He stays quiet, and I can't see his face under the dark, starless sky. Then I hear the smile in his voice. "I knew you looked pale, but I thought it was the sea-sickness."

Finn is not like many Viking husbands, who whoop and tell everyone when their wife is expecting. He's always quietly happy, waiting to see how things develop. He's probably already thinking it's a boy—a brother for Snorri. I hope he'll be as happy if it's a girl.

In Iceland, girls weren't always welcome, because of the old pagan superstitions. In fact, the only reason I was allowed to live was because three brothers before me died.

Part of the volva's work was to see that the Vikings had plenty of male heirs to continue managing farms and maintaining borders. Many baby girls were left out to die. I saw this happen once, when Halldis and I were called to a small sod hut in Iceland. The father had taken one look at the babe, a plump, red-headed girl, and he'd turned his back on her. It was such a small gesture, but one that declared the child must die. Her mother, a mistress and not a wife, screamed with all the pain of a woman who'd carried a healthy baby for nine months—a mother whose breasts ached for her newborn babe. Instead, she'd have to begin working and the child would be exposed in the cold.

Halldis, decked in her purple cape, hair shining like bronze, took that baby up in her arms. I was sure she wouldn't kill a girl, because a girl could become a volva.

Stern as she was, Halldis had a loving, protective streak in her. It was against her nature to doom a helpless child. This wasn't a sacrifice to the gods. It was a man, refusing to overcome his pride and claim his child. Surely Halldis saw that?

She did not. She placed the lovely white baby on a tall rock outside the house, where doubtless the child would roll off. The moment I saw that, I knew I would never be a volva. I didn't even wait until Halldis was on her horse to turn back, not caring if she tried to stop me. Before I reached the rock, I could see the babe was gone. She hadn't rolled off, she had just vanished. Perhaps the mother had a friend hiding outside, waiting to save the baby. If that was true, the mistress would no longer be a mistress, but an outlaw to the village, because she went against the father's will.

Or perhaps the father had gotten to the rock first. Exposure to the elements didn't slake the bloodlust of some Viking men. They were fed stories of selfish gods like Odin, who sacrificed himself only *for* himself on the *Yggdrasil* tree. Viking men followed Odin's example. He was a god who was willing to destroy both his own family and humans to get what he wanted—wisdom. The sad truth was that in sacrificing their families, these Viking men sacrificed any wisdom they had along with it.

But Finn will love a girl as much as a boy. True, in the eyes of his family, a girl would make him look smaller. I selfishly thank God that he has already given us a boy to carry on the family name.

As we sail into the open sea, Magnus stays awake almost continuously. His wrinkles seem to deepen every time I look at him. Even though he can't see the sun, or the World Spike star for night navigation, he knows unerringly which direction we came from. And he can smell land long before the birds alert us to it.

Anxiety makes our men row faster. They have heard the stories of ships that have been lost on this sea. I think most of the men don't believe the sea-serpent tales Bjarni spouted, considering his mushroom habit. But other dangers exist on the open ocean, like none we'd find on land.

One night, Magnus calls softly in the darkness, and Finn slowly unwraps himself from me. From the excitement in Magnus' voice, we're getting close.

I begin talking to God in my head. I need help. I can't believe we're so close to the place I've dreamed of relentlessly for these past two years. I imagine the welcome we will have at Brattahlid. No doubt there will be feasting such as my child has never experienced in the sparse land we left behind. Thjodhild will want to hold my boy for days. She'll be just as delighted as if he were hers by blood, so intertwined are we with Eirik's family.

Sometimes it seems I can feel Eirik smiling on me. If only he'd become a Christian, I'd have peace I would see him again in heaven. Sometimes I find myself searching Snorri's baby face for Eirik's features, then I remember he's not Eirik's true grandson.

I think again of Brattahlid, and I can almost see the small crook of Leif's nose and the thoughtful crease in his forehead. These memories fill me up, spilling into tears. I'm almost home.

After watching my parents' and my godparents' deaths, and after traveling the oceans with all three husbands, my soul longs to settle down and have a safe harbor for our family. Perhaps the child inside of me causes me to feel this way. Perhaps I'm getting foolish as I age. I brush my tears off Snorri's hair. My dark-haired boys lie nearby, blending into the night.

Long fingers wrap over my shoulder, and I know it's Freydis. The air is suddenly charged—exactly the way it feels before lightning is about to strike.

"Almost here," she says.

I can't tell if it's deep love or deep regret that makes her voice so low. She squeezes my shoulder a little tighter. "And all my brother's goods have arrived safely."

PART TWO

Brattahlid
(Greenland),
Circa AD1000

Chapter Thirty

I keep forgetting I have three boys now. The two Skraelings, thick black hair falling over their haunted eyes, stand by my sleep sack every morning. They seem to be waiting for commands, but I have none to give them. I just want to teach them to talk.

The crew has started calling the boys *Hol* and *Hellir*, for the holes and caves they sketched with charcoal on one of our tanned deer hides. They also drew people in the holes and caves, so we guessed their people must have lived in them. After pointing at the pictures repeatedly, saying our words for holes and caves, the older one earned his name by saying *Hellir*. Then his brother shyly whispered *Hol*.

Their brown, glistening skin looks so different from ours. We washed the boys when they came aboard. Deirdre scrubbed them so hard, I think she made their bruises worse. They did have bugs in their hair, so we washed it in vinegar, then used our combs to pick them all out. Then I put rosemary oil on their heads and wrapped them with linen, hoping I wouldn't have to cut all their hair off. Two days later, my treatments had worked, and I thanked God.

GOD'S DAUGHTER | 229

Lice plagues are more common among Greenlandic slaves who live with animals. But since we carry animals on the ship, we've been combing our hair every day to avoid the bugs.

The boys eat heartily enough, favoring Linnea's porridge over all else. I think she must add precious honey to hers, giving it a sweet taste that sets it apart. When she isn't cooking or watching over Snorri for me, I often find her deep in talks with Snorri Thorbrandsson. This still gives me a peculiar feeling, like he's somehow my possession, but since I care deeply for both of them, I try to be happy.

This morning, Hol reaches for Snorri, pulling up his now-chubby hands. Hellir bends down, helping me up from my sleep sack. I find this so moving, I almost cry. Two serious little boys, trying to act like men.

"Many thanks." I say it two times, hoping my smile helps them understand.

I've never seen the boys smile, but their black eyes shine back at me. Hol immediately places Snorri's hand in mine. They've noticed I hold his hand all the time. These boys are more observant than Freydis, who dangled my son over the ship just to amuse herself.

We take the mid-morning meal early today, though everyone's too excited to eat. We can see the coastline now. No one has to ask if it's Greenland, because no one doubts Magnus.

The women whirl around the ship, packing up food and rolling sleep sacks. They're hoping we won't have to use them tonight. I know it's overly hopeful to think Magnus brought us straight to Eiriksfjord, right next to Brattahlid. Chances are, we'll dock somewhere north of it, on Greenland's wide coast.

The brilliant blue sky almost convinces me things are improving after our long period of death and sadness at Straumsfjord. Finn will be rich once we arrive in Greenland, given all the goods he's fit in the ships. I will be well-respected as Eirik's daughter-in-law and Thorfinn Karlsefni's wife.

Ref's chair has been a wonder, helping me so much when my body tires of holding my son's hand, or carrying him all over the ship. I thank Finn and Ref repeatedly for their thoughtfulness.

Finn looks more like a seaman every day, with his salt-blown curls and his reddish-tan skin. He has let his beard grow in, and it makes him look a bit wild. I find myself brushing my hair for long periods at night, because he likes to watch me. I also make an extra effort to bathe, even though it means using a rag and freezing salt water.

Sometimes I ask myself if I'm trying to look good for Finn, or if I'm preparing to see Leif. I pray God will take these thoughts from me, because it's wrong to love another man. When Thorstein the Red and I were married, we lived at Brattahlid. I had to pray almost daily that I wouldn't fall into Leif's ever-open arms. Torture is being married to a proud, insensitive man, while an attentive, supportive man lives under the same roof. Leif's wife Gunna, though brash and hateful, was the answer to my prayers. A married man is a preoccupied man.

The sail is unfurled to the favorable wind, and the ship slides easily between the hills. We weigh anchor mid-fjord, since the ship is too heavy to go closer to shore. It seems impossible, but the rounded hills surrounding the water look exactly like Eiriksfjord. Up on the land, a young shepherd stands near the sheepcote. Staff in hand, he seems to be deciding whether he should stay or run back to camp. The boy looks almost exactly like Leif. His hair is the same light shade, with just a bit more red in it. He's tall and lanky.

Finn recognizes this as well, and gives a whoop. We've arrived, exactly where we wanted to. No one thought we would be this lucky, even with Magnus. The confused boy who's almost my nephew calls out to us.

"Who goes there?" When he shouts, his voice cracks, making it obvious he's a boy on the edge of manhood.

Finn walks to the edge of the ship to answer, but Freydis gets there before he does, gesturing wildly.

"You're Leif's son! You're my nephew, boy!" Her shout is filled with an excitement I'm thankful to see again. "Do you know me? I'm Freydis Eiriksdottir!"

Pride fills her voice as she announces her name, the name Eirik chose for her. Eirik was never like those Viking men who discarded their mistress' babies. He loved every child he fathered, and even some he hadn't—like me.

The boy comes to the shoreline, gazing at the size of the boat. "Is this my father's ship?"

Finn leans over the side. "Yes, it is. I'm Thorfinn Karlsefni, my boy. Please run and tell your father we've returned from Vinland."

The boy's face twists into a scowl. He's not used to taking commands. But finally he nods half-heartedly and runs up the hill.

Soaking in the familiar views of Eiriksfjord, I almost forget to watch over my baby. I turn quickly, but thankfully, Hellir sits with him in the ribs of the ship, making funny faces behind his hands. These boys are like brothers already.

The sheep bleat near the shore, their timid flock splitting as people top the hill. I can picture Brattahlid, snug in its high green divot, hugged by the sky. I can envision its fires burning, the noisy animals, and slaves and family working side by side.

Freydis, determined to get to her brother first, unlashes the small ship's boat. Finn and Magnus lower it into the fjord. Finn gets in first, then helps Magnus and Freydis in before rowing to shore.

I stand frozen to the deck. Deirdre comes closer to me, putting her hand on my arm as if she understands my connection to this place. With her intuitive ways, I wonder if she knows my feelings for Leif.

Deirdre watches as Magnus carefully climbs out of the small boat. "That man will always be a shepherd before a sailor."

Sure enough, Magnus goes straight to calm Leif's sheep, and they nudge at his trousers and hands as if they remember him.

A group of men come down the hill, the boy among them. Leif's hair is longer now; his smile unmistakable as he takes the lead.

"Karlsefni!" His booming voice echoes off the rocks. His flame-haired sister runs up, throwing herself on him. This isn't the best way to approach a Viking, but Leif has been working and he carries no sword. Freydis barely stops to talk before running up the hill to see the rest of the family. Ref stands near me, beaming like the sun. We share the hope that Freydis will return to normal here, in her homeland.

When Finn finally makes his way to Leif, he's rewarded with a gigantic bear hug. Both men are muscled, but Leif stands a full head taller, and his muscles are bulky and noticeable. Finn has the compact, sinewy body of a sailor.

I feel eyes on the back of my head, and I know, without turning, that Snorri Thorbrandsson watches me. Even though his constant scrutiny is wearisome, part of me longs for the affirmation it brings. I pick up baby Snorri to distract my mind. I feel trapped in a web of men.

Deirdre looks at me, helpless without a command. I ask her to bring Hol and Hellir over, so we can take them ashore and show Thjodhild her new grandchildren. She'll either accept all three, or none at all. I won't let her dote on Snorri and ignore the other two. And she won't call them Skraelings. All this I resolve right now, even if I have to demand this from her myself. Finn has no real say in Eirik's family.

One of Leif's men brings our boat back, and Deirdre holds onto the ropes, slowly lowering herself into it. I pass baby Snorri down to her, but Hol and Hellir are afraid to leave the ship. I leave them no choice, lowering myself down by the ropes, then holding my arms wide to them. As understanding dawns, they both scramble to get to me first.

Once we are ashore, Leif falls silent, staring at me. My eyes meet his as I go by, but I won't stop, since I don't know how to handle myself. There's too much emotion in his gray eyes, with those long, light lashes.

But he doesn't let me pass. He's next to me in two long strides. He folds his arms around the baby and me, like a father with his child.

"Is this all the welcome I get from one of my favorite sisters?" He beams. "You have children now! Look at this little man! You've seen my boy already. But mostly—" He looks me up and down. "Mostly I need to know you're fine and healthy. You were gone too long."

He turns back to Finn. "I hope it was worth it?"

It's not clear if he's talking about plunder from the journey, or Finn's decision to take me along.

Finn glances at me. I'm pinned firmly to Leif's side by one of his long arms. He meets Leif's gaze.

"Very profitable, for all of us. I found your wheat and grapes in Vinland. And Gudrid is with child again." The proud, challenging note in his voice is unmistakeable.

Leif's arm moves only slightly as he turns to face me. "I never knew how jealous your Thorfinn is. We'll have to put his mind at ease."

He throws both hands in the air and winks at me. "You must go see Mother. She's been praying for you daily and has declared she'll go down to the grave within the month if she can't meet her grandchild. And even though she said that five months ago, she's still here."

The children and I start walking up the hill. Leif didn't ask about the native boys, who were holding Deirdre's hands. We'll have to discuss them soon. But if Thjodhild accepts them, he'll have to. Even the huge Eiriksson brothers would never cross their mother.

The blue sky reflects the ocean, making for a wide, uninterrupted view. As we top the hill, a small, black-haired woman runs to me. It's only when I see her children run up behind her that I recognize her. Stena! She must have returned to Brattahlid, despite Thjodhild's behavior. As she embraces me, she smells warm and golden, like rare cedar wood.

We smile at each other, not saying anything. Stena is the only person I've met who's as comfortable with silence as I am. I touch the faces of her two daughters and two sons, still speechless in my happiness.

I'll never forget helping with the birth of her youngest daughter. It was four years ago now, when sailors returning from Vinland brought reports of Thorvald's death by that Skraeling arrow. Stena gave birth the very next day.

Her daughter clasps my free hand, pointing at my hair. I pick her up, Snorri in my other arm. She's light as a feather, with Stena's small bones. Snorri watches her, wide-eyed, as she grasps a handful of my hair.

Stena bats her daughter's hand away, scolding her in her Sami language. She points to Hellir and Hol, who sit on the ground, encircled by her other children.

"Sons," I say. She doesn't ask more, just nods with an understanding look. "They had bad parents," I explain.

Deirdre looks impatiently at the longhouse, waiting. I know she's anxious to reunite with her friends as well. She'll tell them all the news of Straumsfjord, good and bad. Meanwhile, I just want to forget all about it.

A tall, slightly stooping woman with flowing hair the color of buttermilk stands in the doorframe. She squints as if she can't see us well.

"Thjodhild awaits," Stena says.

I walk toward Eirik's wife, alone and unprepared. Thjodhild is one of the most intimidating women I know. She always gets her way. But this time, I determine that I will have mine.

Chapter Thirty-One

Although not as well-born as I am, Thjodhild might as well be royalty in Greenland. Her husband is the one who brought everyone here. And the fact she stayed with Eirik the Red is reason enough to respect her.

Right after Thjodhild married Eirik, they were outlawed to the south of Iceland because of Eirik's knack for finding conflict. Maybe he didn't start the fights, but, as he told me often, "By Odin's ugly face, I always finished them."

After getting into several feuds in south Iceland, Eirik proceeded to move himself and his disappointed wife to an island off the coast. He made friends quickly, with his outgoing personality and his seemingly boundless generosity. Unfortunately, Eirik made the mistake of loaning his favorite maple headboards to a man named Knut. When he finally asked for them back, Knut refused. Eirik took a group over, killing several of Knut's slaves and two of his sons.

My father, Thorbjorn, had met Eirik around this time. They immediately liked one another, each assuming the other wealthier than himself. Eirik stayed around long enough to be condemned as an outlaw at the Althing meeting. At that point, he set out for the land he later returned to tell everyone about—the Green Land.

The place attracted outlaws and rabble-rousers from all over Iceland. In the absence of the heavy hand of the volva, the wild settlers of Greenland created their own rituals, often involving women. This resulted in countless forest children, many of whom were left to die. The pagan practices in Greenland grieved Thjodhild. Her grandmother, a Christian from Norway, had taught her to pray.

Thjodhild put a stop to this madness when she showed up at Eirik's mistress' hut, right as the poor woman was giving birth. It was Thjodhild's hands that brought Freydis into the world. It was her hands that placed the red-haired babe in her husband's arms. Eirik told me later that his wife's icy eyes froze his blood, and he swore right then never to be with another woman. Thjodhild had won his respect, and that of every woman on the island. The men had no choice but to follow their leader's example.

Eirik and Thjodhild agreed to disagree, but fighting somehow kept their marriage alive. He felt he'd earned her disrespect. She felt a religious obligation to bring him to repentance.

When I arrived at Brattahlid, claiming Christianity and not paganism, Eirik was immediately suspicious of me. He liked my father, but didn't trust him. But the first time he looked curiously into my eyes, I believe he saw me as I was—a girl who needed protection.

Thjodhild wasn't jealous of our friendship. In fact, she welcomed more time to herself. Since she'd learned more about Leif's Christianity, she preferred to live like a nun, giving up worldly pleasures. Her constant refusal of Eirik's desire only fanned the flames of his ever-present temper.

And so Thjodhild had tamed the red-headed plunderer, in her own way. I didn't approve or disapprove. I might have done the same thing in her place.

I walk toward this determined woman now, sorry to see how the years have aged her. Her back used to be straight as a rod. Now it seems to have lost all its strength. And yet, her face is still beautiful in its very lack of color. Her lashes are light as her hair, instead of light brown, like mine. She seems unworldly, even angelic.

She reaches out for an embrace, and I know Leif spoke the truth. She missed having us here.

"Gudrid! My daughter! I must see your child! And the others?"

"They're coming—talking with Leif, Mother. They'll be here soon."

"No, I mean these other children. Whose are these? I can see enough to know they're not your blood."

The coldness is still there, then.

"Native children from the new land. They are now my children."

So she brings it into the open first thing. Very well, if I must explain it to her now, I will.

Stena's warm presence beside me gives me strength. Thjodhild must have decided that having Thorvald's children around, even with their Sami mother, was better than having no grandchildren nearby.

Instead of resting against the doorframe again, Thjodhild stands completely still. Nothing moves, not even the air. We wait. Hellir and Hol are oblivious, playing chase with Stena's children.

Thjodhild is not going to move, no matter how uncomfortable she is. I hold Snorri out to her. She takes him, her stooped back straightening. Her pale eyes look deep into his. He must see something he likes, because he smiles and starts saying "Mmmaa."

Leif, Finn, and the others top the hill, ready to join us. I wonder how much information Finn has given Leif about the boys. I suspect it's precious little.

"Well, Mother, how about a meal for our conquering sailors?" Leif asks.

Now, as Eirik's widow, Thjodhild must decide whether she will make a show of hospitality or not. Leif may run Brattahlid, but it belongs to her.

Her eyes meet mine, even as my child jabbers, then buries his face in her shoulder. I hold her gaze.

"Ja, of course! Saldis, Dalla, set out our meal."

Two slaves peep from the door before scurrying about in the longhouse. Most likely, they were listening the entire time, awaiting their command.

I motion for Hellir and Hol to come to my side, and we all walk in to the table. Leif outpaces Finn to sit beside me. Snorri Thorbrandsson and Linnea come in behind us. There will be room for everyone to eat here, because one of the first things Eirik did in Greenland was to build the biggest longhouse anyone had ever seen.

As Finn sits, his men surround him at the table. Leif sits alone at the head, with me on one side and his mother on the other. I want to know where his wife is, but I can't think of a tactful way to ask. Leif's son, Gils, watches unhappily as his father gives me delighted looks. I don't want to be *that* woman. I try talking with Stena, on my other side, but she's very quiet. Leif pretends Stena doesn't exist and keeps asking me questions.

"Your man told me of the haul you brought back. But two of my ships have gone missing, you know." Soup drips from his spoon onto his embroidered mustard-colored tunic as he waits for my response.

"Did he also tell you about Hallstein and his dishonorable behavior? He's the one who took your larger ship and left. His big, yellow-haired man—"

"Yes, I know the one. Built like a tree. Vani."

"He tried to attack Linnea. Although he might have been looking for me—" Leif interrupts me again. "She does look like you...funny, isn't it? I thought that might come in handy over there." His slanted grin is endearing, but he doesn't understand.

"Listen to me!" I get closer to his ear. "That fool was determined to go north. And we didn't stop him, since he was splitting up the camp. There would have been mutiny."

"Of course. Calm down, Gudrid. I won't hold that against Thorfinn. I can spare that ship, I suppose. And I do hope someone turned Vani into a corpse."

I have missed Leif's forthright way of saying things. Freydis has a similar way of talking, though her words often bite.

"Yes, someone did."

"Hm." Leif's gaze travels around the table, as he guesses which man it was. He doesn't know the murderer could be his own sister, and I pray no one tells him. It would bring dishonor on the family name, as yet unscalded by vengeance killings in Greenland.

We drink from Thjodhild's good Rhine glasses. Every glass has a different swirling color. Leif's glass is golden amber, like the perfect wheat we brought back. Mine is green, like the sea today, or like my son's eyes.

After the surprisingly sparse meal, Thjodhild rushes off to her own little chapel that Leif built for her. Leif tells me she spends most of her time there. "She's probably praying God will forgive her for the many times she refused Father." He watches for my smile, but it's slow in coming.

He studies me a moment. Though he tries to drop his voice, it's still rich and clear. "Something has changed over there. Didn't I provide enough help for you?"

Feeling someone else's eyes on me, I turn slightly. Both Snorri Thorbrandsson and Finn watch our conversation. Finn's men are laughing and eating more than they should, and the women are moving off to the cooking area, sharing gossip and playing with the children.

"Too much has happened. Sometimes I wish I never went along." There, I've spoken the truth that's tortured me into silence with Finn. And I don't care if the others are watching. At Straumsfjord, Finn never noticed when men talked and flirted with me openly. Why should he care now?

Leif's observes me under light lashes, same as his mother's. I'm pulled into his gray-blue eyes, deep as the fjords. His freckles stand out a bit, sprinkled over sunburned cheeks. His gaze doesn't waver, pulling my emotions to the surface easily. I look over at my children to compose myself.

"And so, it's nice to be home." I can't think of anything important to say.

"I've been waiting for you," he says. Then he stands, hooking his smallest finger over the back of his chair before tossing it aside. "We're glad to have your crew home, Thorfinn Karlsefni."

Finn's lips are tight, but he smiles to acknowledge Leif. Once he smiles, his men shout, "Hear, hear!"

After the meal, Leif takes Finn and me to a house on the farm. Its thatched roof is well-kept, its boards tight against the winds. I would expect no less, since Leif is attentive to details, unlike his father, who traveled most of the time.

"Here's our house!" Leif gestures grandly, ignoring Finn's angry glare at the back of his head. "Don't know if anyone told you we have to share houses at Brattahlid now? Mother's latest idea of charitable living. You'll be with Gunna and me."

Chapter Thirty-Two

Most of the men at Brattahlid don't appreciate Leif's humor, and Finn is no exception. This little joke about us sharing a house with him rouses the sleeping anger in my gentle sailor husband. Finn's hand drops to his knife. I quickly step between the men, covering Finn's hand with my own.

"Ha, ha—very funny, Leif. I know your mother better than that," I say. Finn relaxes his grip. If he decided to kill Leif, I couldn't stop him.

"And I'm sure you know Gunna wouldn't share her house, either!" Leif turns back toward us with a grin, unaware of Finn's reaction. "That woman is proud as a queen, I'll tell you that!"

Finn won't respond to that remark, since insulting one's wife is generally looked on as cowardly unless she's done a great wrong. He turns toward the hill and mutters something about getting our cargo from the ship.

When Finn's out of sight, I scold Leif heartily. "You can't joke with Thorfinn that way—you know this!"

"Well, I can't help it if your husband's overly touchy about his fair wife, can I?"

Gunna approaches us, her face hidden under her fluffy cloud of red-blonde hair. Her stride is deliberately slow and she carries herself stiffly.

"Your son needs help with the sheep." She looks from Leif to me, flipping her hair out of her eyes. "Why, Gudrid! You're back already?"

Unlike Leif, Gunna never jokes. Her words are almost always hurtful. I think it has something to do with the way she's stuck in Greenland, far from the Hebrides, where her father's wealth and her family's land opened every door.

I force a smile. Halldis always told me *Smiles carry more power than hateful looks.* "Yes, it's so good to be back at Brattahlid. I can't tell you how much I've looked forward to it."

Leif still stands, solid as a rooted tree, at the door of our hut, wearing the stubborn look he only gets with his wife. He won't go help his son, because it would mean giving in to Gunna's command.

"Well, thank you so much for showing us the house, Leif," I say. "Don't let me keep you from helping Gils." I turn back to Gunna. "My, how that boy has grown. Have you had other children, too?"

She shoves her hair out of her face, exposing slanting hazel eyes focused on me like a forest cat. "No more children." She acts as if I'm strange to think she would want more.

Leif is tired of being ignored, and in two strides he takes Gunna's arm. "Let's go find Magnus, since *he's* the shepherd around here." They walk away and he sharply rebukes her. Things are still rough between them, even after all these years.

I stand alone on the hill. The sun slants in a way I've only seen in Greenlandic skies. I'm here, I try to convince myself. I'm surrounded by the trees and fields and rocks I've longed for. I've seen the man who's haunted my dreams for years, and he still cares for me.

However, all I can think of is Skraeling skinboats, sliding up in the water. I see the small blue head of Freydis' son as she kisses him. I see my wolf, her yellow eyes staring, no longer able to protect me. And I feel Snorri Thorbrandsson's hand on mine at the bonfire.

Can I ever be happy where I am, with my own husband? What is wrong with me? And why do I always search for a protector? Freydis, the wolf, Snorri, Leif…even Finn. He brought us all back to Greenland, where he knew we would be safe. And now that we're here, he acts hostile toward Leif, complicating everything.

We only had one winter at Brattahlid as a married couple, before leaving for Vinland. When everyone eats under the same roof and shares chores, men can't help but notice the women, and Leif and Snorri Thorbrandsson watched me tirelessly. But Finn was excited about our trip, and he didn't notice it then.

Men often compare the wives on the farm. Who's the best cook? Who has the best figure? The best face? Who gets along best with the parents?

Women spend time comparing, as well. Who's the bravest? The tallest? Who fathers the most children? Who can kill fastest?

Some avoided these kinds of talks, like Stena and Eirik. But talking is the best way to get through the long winters in Greenland. Talking and drinking. I don't imbibe in either one, since I've seen the destructive results of both gossip and mead.

My mother-in-law and Gunna used to pass the time talking about once-wealthy families who'd lost land or status. It gave them a sense of power, because Eirik's farm was doing well and probably always would be, with Leif managing it. He was born to fight and farm. But such talk never sat well with me, because my own father had lost his position when his farm failed.

Freydis wakes me from my thoughts, spinning up to me with her arms outstretched, hair flying in the breeze. She has dark circles under her eyes, but other than that, she seems happier.

"Well, I caught up to my brother," she says. "I told Leif about being accused of murder and losing my boy, and…that is all."

Of course she didn't tell him about Suka and his attempt to kill us at the caves. Leif would probably ship a man over to hunt him down, if he knew of it.

"I'm planning a return trip, maybe next summer," she continues. I can't believe she thinks of leaving so soon. Did Leif make her feel guilty over the murder?

"You need time." As a healer, I know this. She's not well yet.

"I'll over-winter here, and that will be enough. I'm sure Leif would let me take a ship, and Ref could find more wheat and wood, maybe grapes…."

Her eyes are somewhat glazed, her energy almost unnatural. My mushrooms should be sitting in my locked box, but it'd be just like her to figure out a way to sneak into it. I'm disloyal to think this way. But I worry about Eirik's strong-headed forest child.

"I need to find my husband." She cuts our talk short, then belies her words by flitting away from the ship where Ref unloads. She's trouble waiting to happen, I fear.

I take a last look at the sky and go into our hut, noticing the lock on the dark wood door. The extra security pleases me, as does the house itself. It is very cozy, with tapestries on the wall and gold cups and ceramic vases sitting on trunks and tables. I laugh when I notice our bed is framed by the very maple headboards Eirik feuded over. Leif probably put those here on purpose, just to amuse me.

After reveling in the rich details of the room, from the alabaster statues to the feather-stuffed pillows, I go to find my boys. Though Hol and Hellir are nowhere to be seen, I find baby Snorri in longhouse. He stands in one of Thjodhild's copper pots on the floor, clapping and dancing around for her. The unreserved look on her face tells me he's melted her hardness. I sneak out, determined to find my older boys.

Linnea talks with Snorri Thorbrandsson near the longhouse. He turns to look at me. I ignore the intensity of those amber eyes, smiling at both of them before walking down the hill.

I hear the shouting long before I reach the sheepcote— the deep, heated voices of Finn and Leif. My throat feels dry. Surely they're not fighting over me?

But Finn stands in front of my boys, Leif in front of his son. All three boys are bruised and bloody, but Leif's Gils looks like he got the worse end of it. And Gils doubtless attacked first, from the look of hatred on his face.

Finn shouts, "We won't stay or share goods if this is the welcome we receive!"

Leif moves too close to Finn's face. "Why are these Skraelings here? Their kind killed my brother! Why'd you even let them live?"

I step in, trying to speak reason into their thoughts. "Leif, it was my idea. They're just children—my children now. They will be helpful for the next journey."

Leif kicks his black leather boot against the heel of the other, as if trying to restrain a kick to Finn's leg. "There may not *be* a next journey," he says. "I'm missing two boats and many of my men. I can't afford such a costly risk again."

"What? Thorfinn brought back more goods than you did! And we've avenged your brother's death. Fifteen Skraelings are buried outside our camp in Straumsfjord."

"Thanks mostly to my sister." The way he half-grins at me makes me want to stamp on his big feet.

"You weren't there; you don't know the whole—"

Finn interrupts me. "Either the boys live with us, as our children, or we leave."

Once Finn determines something is right, no one can argue against his reasoning. It's obvious that Leif's dislike for these young boys is pointless, having nothing to do with Thorvald's death. The men who have been unloading the ship must have seen Gils' attack, and they're quick to step up and join Finn. Magnus even leaves the sheep and sidles over closer to him.

Leif, even with all his physical strength, doesn't hold the loyalty of his men like Finn does. He's often careless with their preferences. I remember how Suka told me Leif was *sometimes* good to his slaves. But not good enough for Suka to return.

Gunna comes running down the hill, hair flying back so we can see her furious looks.

"Gils! Your face!" She glares at Leif, who happens to be the only one trying to defend her son. She grabs Gils' arm and pulls him up the hill with her, even though he's taller than she is.

Leif reacts to her disrespect by giving in to Finn's demand. "Very well. We'll consider them your children. I'll talk with Gunna and make her understand."

Rage flickers across his face. I'm afraid *make her understand* might mean *beat her senseless*. But surely Leif wouldn't do that?

Finn turns to the boys, hugging them briefly before sending them to me. His eyes meet mine for a moment, and they're dark as obsidian. I'm thankful the two most powerful men in Brattahlid didn't start warring today, forcing a departure the same day we arrived.

The boys look like they will only have bruising from the fight. Hol's fist bleeds a bit, but he's had the good sense to stop the flow with his tunic. Both boys smile at me for the first time. Maybe now they understand I care for them.

Later that night, after wrapping Hol's fist and putting cold cloths on the bruises, we return to the longhouse for the evening meal. A golden bell rings for mealtimes here. In Thjodhild's house, during evening meals, men, women, and children sit at their own tables. Thjodhild's eyes widen as Hol and Hellir take their place with Stena's children, but she says nothing.

Gunna prepares a plate for her son. I walk to her side slowly, like I'm approaching a wild animal. She probably waits to pounce on my first misspoken word.

"Is he badly hurt?" I ask, summoning up more boldness than I feel.

"What do you think? Your Skraeling brats attacked him like the dogs they are."

My face flames, betraying that her darts have hit. But I won't give her what she wants.

"I'm a healer, you know. I'll help, if you need me."

"We have our own healer here, with more powers than you, *volva*." She tosses her plume of hair.

As my face burns even hotter, Snorri Thorbrandsson takes my arm, walking me to the back of the room before I can react. "Step lightly." He grits his teeth, probably wishing he could hit Gunna himself. He's trying to help me.

"I understand," I whisper.

Snorri makes a big show of motioning a slave over for a second platter of fish for the men. "We can't get enough of these Greenlandic fish of yours, Leif!" He shouts down the table. "How do you cure them? You must have loads of salt!"

The mood of the room lifts, all eyes shifting to Leif at the men's table. Stena puts her arm in mine, walking me back to our bench. At least I have one woman friend I can trust here, besides Deirdre, and she's supposed to be my slave. I look for her, suddenly realizing she and Linnea probably eat in the slave's longhouse now.

Suddenly, the fish tastes rancid in my mouth, and it seems I can smell berserker mushrooms everywhere. My stomach heaves. I bash my leg into the corner of the table before running out the back door, where I stand and vomit out all the sourness of my first day back at Brattahlid.

Chapter Thirty-Three

Even snug in the new linen bedclothes Stena laid out for me, I am unable to calm myself for bed. Finn pretends to be asleep, his breathing taking a long time to drift into its regular rhythms.

Snorri sleeps in a little wooden bed that might have belonged to Gils. I tucked him in so tightly, he didn't wiggle at all before going to sleep.

Hol and Hellir sleep like animals, as close to the floor as possible. Hol's little dark arms and legs stick out in all directions. Hellir sleeps curled into an impossibly tight ball, as if warding off any possible beatings. Stena brought them reindeer hides and pillows stuffed with lavender before bed, using her special talent for comforting others.

Finn and I talked about renaming the boys—something honorable, like Eirik or Thorvald—but we couldn't agree on anything. They don't have Eirik's blood, making it more offensive than complimentary to name them after family here.

My nausea keeps me awake, along with the creeping feeling someone watches me. I know it's impossible for anyone to see into our house, which only has tiny square windows near the roofline. No one could climb up to look in without making noise, which I'd surely hear in my alert state. Sensing unfriendly spirits in this house, hours pass until I finally toss into a weary sleep.

Sure enough, in the middle of the night, I'm trapped in a horrifying dream. Little Snorri walks toward a tree surrounded by dancing pagan girls. They chant something, and I feel the words, rather than hear them—words about a need for blood. An evil, moldy smell hangs in the air, reminding me of the midden heap. As I run toward the tree, it grows until its branches scrape the gray sky. The volva chant changes into the Yggdrasil chant for the world-tree. The limbs droop down toward the earth, grabbing at us. Branches wrap around my boy's chubby little arms, jerking him up into the air, and I wake myself up crying.

Finn rolls over, groggy, but aware of my cries. "What is it?"

I feel smothered, as if I can't even speak. Finn seems far away, on the other side of the room. I don't want to faint, so I say the only thing I can think of.

"Christ is God!"

The powers release, and Finn is next to me again. He rests his hand on my forehead, like a mother comforting a child. Although I can't put my fears into words, he seems to understand.

"Brattahlid's not what it used to be, is it?" He jokes, trying to stop my tears.

I give him a weak smile. No, it certainly isn't. And something tells me that the root of unrest lies with Gunna. She's brought her pagan spirits and ways here, with no fear of God or man. Only one thought flashes through my mind. I can't let Freydis be around the *eitr*—the poison—that is

Gunna. Freydis is unstable enough without evil spirits tormenting her.

Dawn comes to Greenland exactly how I remembered, with yellow light dancing on the dust and roosters crowing proudly. I half-expect Eirik to bawl into my doorway, "Get up, woman; feed those chickens!" He loved to tease me about my eagerness to care for his cows and chickens. I did it because I knew it pleased him.

Thjodhild meets me in the grass between houses, taking my arm and turning us toward her chapel. "I want to show you what Leif made for me." She gives me one of her rare smiles.

Inside the stone fence, we walk through a light wood entryway draped with a purple flowering vine. The church itself is small, with hardly any carvings on the doorposts. Inside, the floor is cool with flat stones that Leif has laid down. A large cross is the only ornament. It sits on a table in the center of the room, made of dark stone that could be marble. The back door directly overlooks the sea. We each sit on one of the benches.

"Leif brought back something else, a gift from the King of Norway himself." Thjodhild pulls up a heavy object from the end of her bench. I look at the black leather binding, trying to read the Latin letters the monk taught me long ago.

The Holy Writings!

Thjodhild's smile now matches my own. It is what I've needed, a book to tell me of this God I love, and of the Christian heaven that even women can go to. But I must learn more Latin words first. I take it from her, fingering the gold lettering on the outside. Looking over the first page, I only know two words. I'll find a way to change this.

Thjodhild examines my face intently. "You're even more beautiful now than when you sailed for Vinland, dear. Eirik couldn't speak highly enough of you." She leans toward me. "Gudrid, you know I don't like Skraelings—they killed my firstborn—but I do respect you for taking in those children."

I search her pale violet eyes, looking for clues that she's joking. She's never called me *dear* before. What happened to Eirik's cold, bitter wife?

"We all changed, after my husband's death." It's as if she knows my thoughts. "When Stena left, I finally saw how she'd always treated me kindly, even in my harshness. And her children are dear to me. They're all I have left of Thorvald. I was alone here with only Leif and that woman and her child. She hates being in Greenland, even more than I hated it when we came here so many years ago."

I keep quiet, not willing to get involved in family conflicts with Thjodhild. I don't know how much my mother-in-law has truly changed. What I say could find its way back to Gunna's ears.

"I am sick." She grips the bench. "It is not a sickness that will pass. There's a constant aching in my bones. I don't think I have long to be on earth."

My face mirrors hers now—lips downturned and eyebrows tight. "Have any healers seen you?"

She nods. "Many. They all agree, even the ones from Norway."

I look over her pale hair, crumpling back, and wrinkled hands and neck. Yes, she's aged too quickly. My tears spill over. She's the last parent I have left, no matter how she's acted in the past.

"Don't cry for me, my daughter." She surprises me again with her endearing names. "We both know where I'll go. I've spoken with a nun from Norway. She came to try to convert everyone at Brattahlid. She didn't have much luck, but I did ask many questions about heaven before she left. No need to bury treasures with me, as we did for Eirik."

The Vikings still foolishly bury all their wealth, often leaving their families practically penniless, just like the Egyptians. The Eastman used to read me Egyptian stories, knowing how angry they made me. I told him gods who demanded those kinds of sacrifices have no mercy for the living. He just laughed and said I was dreaming if I believed women would do anything besides sweep for all eternity. He said we were lucky Odin remembered us at all, since we're so unpredictable and curvy and weepy, and of no use whatever in battles. I wish he could have seen Freydis that day in the forest.

I hug Thjodhild, wiping my eyes on my sleeve. I have to be strong for her. "Does anyone know?"

"Leif does, and Stena. That's all."

We both fall into silence, looking at the cross while balancing our duties and our feelings. No one else needs to know of Thjodhild's illness. But many preparations need to be made. The power of Brattahlid will transfer to Leif soon. And, if there's any mercy, none of it will pass to his hateful wife.

"What happened to Leif's other ships?" she asks.

"Bjarni should arrive someday with the smaller knarr, but Hallstein took the larger one and went north. We couldn't find him."

"Hideous fool." She spits out the words. "He tried to take advantage of me when I first came here. I never told

Eirik, but I should have. He would have cut him down then and spared the world his poison."

This is shocking news. Hallstein acted as if he'd been Eirik's closest friend. I hope he returns soon, to be exposed to Leif as the liar he is.

A light knock sounds on the door, and Deirdre enters, bowing toward the cross before turning to me.

"A slave came from the town east of us. They are needing a midwife for a young girl, hardly fourteen."

I touch my mother-in-law's arm before following Deirdre out. "Thank you, Thjodhild, for everything."

Outside, Deirdre's voice is thick with her accent. She points. "A white horse waits for you just there, in that fence."

The slave, a young girl herself, waits on her own horse. I mount the white mare. She must often have different riders, because she doesn't shy away or startle. We gallop swiftly along a path I've never seen to a newly built town. As we approach a large, two-floor house, the heavy, moist air can't muffle the sharp screams drifting out to us. A male slave immediately takes our horses to the stable.

I step into the well-lit long hall. An older house slave rushes over, leading me up carved wooden stairs to a private bedroom. An oversized bed dwarfs the small girl lying in it, her dark brown hair tumbling around her. I'm reminded of Inger, and pray for her ship even as I'm praying for this child.

The house slave is ominous. "There's no husband. She was used by the men before the master's funeral."

"And she wasn't killed with him, to follow custom?"

"Too beautiful to kill, the master said." She looks fondly over at the girl.

Perhaps she was then, but not now. Her face, though small, is unnaturally puffy, as well as her feet and hands. She screams like one who sees Death itself coming for her.

After much manipulation, which only brings louder screaming, I'm able to get the baby into a place where it can descend. Slaves hold the girl by the arms so she can squat over the blankets. Only the rich use blankets for births, and throw them away afterward. Her master left her a very wealthy girl.

"Is there a wife?" I shout over one particularly loud push.

"No'm, she died years ago. This girl stayed with the master in his loneliness."

I'll just bet she did, because she didn't have a choice. It's a good thing the kindly master is dead, or I might just go kill him myself. How dare he allow her to be used by his men, with no word of protection before he died? She's just a child!

It is pagan tradition that one family slave volunteers her body for the men's parties before the funeral. She's washed and dressed, then enters the tents of every free man in the household. Finally, she is sacrificed, a gift for her master in the afterlife.

The poor girl cries like a baby on my shoulder, recounting horrors the men did to her. These things should never have to be spoken, by anyone. Maybe I could tell Leif to hunt down each of those men and kill them. But he might not want to. They were only obeying pagan laws, and having the time of their lives doing it. Once again I stand helpless, looking at the mess Thor has made.

Chapter Thirty-Four

The baby is born, looking remarkably handsome for a child with any possible number of fathers. The slave takes the baby to clean and swaddle him. The new mother is so beside herself, she can't string words together anymore.

I ask if there's dandelion root available. In a house so wealthy, it's possible they have this European remedy. Another slave brings the herb box, and I dig until I find it.

"Make a tea for her three times a day with this," I say. This will reduce some of her swelling. I also order the slave to let the girl nurse the child herself. Usually a nursemaid is called in for times like these. But she needs to bond with this child quickly, or she may grow to hate him for the pain he represents. She also needs to realize she is no longer a child herself, but a mother.

I ride home alone, lost in thought. What a country Eirik has founded—filled with criminals and exiles. *This* is where the king of Norway needs to send his monks and nuns, not to Iceland. Much of Iceland embraces Christianity now, from what the women say at mealtimes. The king has outlawed the long-standing pagan practice of eating horseflesh. If that tradition can be overturned, how many others will soon topple?

My white mare trots along slowly, as if sensing my distraction. I love a good-natured horse. And of course she is, because Leif trains his horses from their first wobbly steps. Too bad he doesn't have the same gentle hand with his disrespectful wife.

I breathe in the heavy smell of fallen leaves. Leif. That straw-colored hair and beard that make my breath stop. A largeness of frame that matches his large laugh. But his strength is in his stubbornness, and it's unyielding. I've seen that here. He refuses to honor Gunna. Truly, she may not deserve any honor, but she is still his wife. Perhaps if he would appreciate her, or do her bidding, only once....

But it's not his way. He is contrary, like his father. If you tell him he can't settle somewhere, that is the very place he'll go. If you tell him not to love you, he'll just love you all the more.

I feel for young Gils. He has a hateful mother and a father who wouldn't have married her, had she not used her child as bait.

I rein in the mare, listening to the distant, consoling lapping of the ocean. A low-flying hawk swoops over the forest, beautiful in its cruelty as it hunts the small birds. I wish I could fly like that hawk, rising and falling with the still spaces in the air, far above all this sickness and death and evil. And yet, God created me for a reason. Maybe just to save lives, like that young mother and her baby. Or Hol and Hellir. Or maybe I'm here to heal others, like when I weaned Bjarni off the mushrooms or stitched Suka's arm. Right now, I wish I knew how to heal Freydis' damaged mind.

A horse rushes up behind me, so I move my mare off the path. Snorri Thorbrandsson charges along at full-speed, trying to stop when he sees me. He's not a natural horseman, so the black stallion continues down the path for some way. Snorri yanks at the reins and finally gets the horse to trot back to me.

"Looking for you." He's breathless, shooting murderous glares at his willful stallion.

"It was a safe birth," I say. He gives me a confused look. He doesn't even know what I'm talking about.

"What is it, Snorri?"

He swings his sturdy body off the horse's wide back. "Nothing horrible." He smiles, but not convincingly. "Come down here and walk with me a bit, will you?"

We walk along in silence, his horse huffing, while mine contentedly munches any bits of green along the path. He's been my friend for so long, and he knows so much about me. After all we've seen in Straumsfjord, I feel I could tell him anything.

"Snorri, you were going too fast. That stallion could have thrown you."

"Leif's been friendly enough with you." His smile fades as he speaks what he's really thinking about.

"Well, of course, you hairy outlaw." I punch his arm lightly. "I *am* part of the family, you know."

"What—because of Thorstein the Red? He's dead!"

How can he be so thoughtless?

"Well, Thjodhild and I have been talking together, believe it or not. She's the only mother I have left." Snorri knows how piercing my own mother's loss was.

His eyes soften, and so does his voice. "I understand that. But Leif puts you next to himself at the table, talking with you as his own wife. We all notice this, even your husband."

And now he dares to talk to me about Finn?

"Now *you're* the one who should tread lightly, Snorri Thorbrandsson." My arms shake.

"Why? I speak the truth. You shouldn't be alone with Leif."

"But I can be alone with you? You, who declared your love for me? Who once asked me to marry you? What makes you any different?"

Snorri stops pacing. He turns to me, taking my shoulders in his large, strong hands. "Perhaps there isn't any difference." His light eyes flash. I can't tear my gaze away.

I put my hand on his. "I don't want to talk about this. Why did you come all the way out here? Just to scold me for Leif's kindness?"

He continues pacing, making short turns in front of me. "I'm leaving Greenland."

I'd half-expected this. Finn gave Snorri a portion of the Vinland goods to sell, since they're partners.

"And Linnea?" I ask.

"What? Oh…the slave?"

"*My* slave, you mean? I'll give her freedom. Not only does she have good child-bearing hips, she looks at you like a cow at a fresh pasture."

He chuckles, a relief to me. Perhaps he has thought of marrying her.

"I'm going to Iceland." He looks skyward. "Would you ever think of returning there?"

"Me? How could I? I have a husband, and now three children, Snorri. One of them is your namesake. Please release yourself from whatever obligation you feel for me."

His wounded look swiftly changes into something flaming and alive. His rough fingers wrap gently around my cheeks. A kiss, volcanic as his eyes, presses into the middle of my lips.

Inexpressible yearning fills the kiss. Many images fly through my mind, but I vividly remember how earnestly this red-beard asked for my hand in marriage. He is hungrier for me now than he ever was before—even willing to cross Thorfinn to have me. And I can no longer think of him as a brother.

His hands move to my waist, eyes searching mine. The warrior's soft touch threatens to melt my doubts. "Could you not see us together, as we should have been? I would do anything, just to buy one of your smiles."

My lips tingle, full of heat, like my flushed cheeks. Wicked thoughts swirl into my mind. Snorri knows me better than any man. He wants me for who I am. He would make time to protect me, as Finn has been unable to do.

He bows his bare head, awaiting my sentence. If I open the door to him, he will never leave me. Isn't this what every woman wants?

And yet a power stronger than my own, stronger than Snorri's fierce kiss and longing words, pulls me. The power of doing what is right.

I unwrap his hands, still resting possessively on my waist. His eyes flicker with defeat. I can't hold back my urge to comfort him. "Please understand...you helped me survive at Straumsfjord. You have always meant so much to me. But I can't."

Snorri reaches over and wipes a stray tear from my face. He squeezes my hand once, then yanks the unwilling stallion toward him. He mounts it, kicking it several times before galloping away toward Brattahlid.

The heavy air presses on my scattered thoughts. What if I had married Snorri, years ago? Where would we be now? And how can I think like this? I have children with Finn!

I feel displaced, body and soul. After all those months dreaming at Straumsfjord, practically tasting Brattahlid, I don't even fit here. I'll stay while Thjodhild's sick, because I may be able to ease her final pains. But after that? What do I want with my life? I've never asked this of myself, because I always follow my husband's lead. And truly, I've been happy to follow Finn anywhere. But perhaps I should help determine which direction we go.

Overgrowth spills into the path, thick berry brambles grabbing at my mare's legs as I head for home. The evenly spaced Greenlandic trees seem naked and exposed against the gray sky.

Once again, unbidden, I see the red-haired boy, prepared to come to my aid at my mother's hanging. My tears flow, releasing the storm inside me. Has Finn ever loved me like Snorri Thorbrandsson has?

As Brattahlid comes into view, a churned patch of brambles by the path draws my eye. I slow my mare and dismount. Following the trail of crushed branches, I push my way into the forest. The sky's dark shadows cloak the trees. A gust of rain-kissed wind sweeps over me, as if invisible hands tug at my soul.

I stumble near one thick, outstretched limb. The black stallion stands just beyond it, not even tied up. The mist of rain turns into drops, large and heavy. I force myself to turn, my chilled body warning me before my heart can.

Close by, Snorri's bald head shines on a wide rock, leather-clad legs sprawled at strange angles. Blood trickles from his ears and pools on the gray stone.

I drop to his side, feeling his neck for a heartbeat. None. His beautiful eyes are closed; his lips that so recently touched my own, open. I trace his strong arm, down to those wide hands that carried my wolf through the forest and cradled my face. Something deep inside me flutters, perhaps the first kicks of my child.

I am frozen beside him, unable to think what to do next. All my healing powers are useless. The black sky continues its torrent, but I can't bring myself to drag him anywhere. I lie down on the bloody rock, forcing my own hand into his stiff, curled fingers. He must wake to comfort me again. The darkness surrounds me now, and I don't run from it.

Chapter Thirty-Five

You killed him. The voice in my head pounds, louder and louder, until I finally open my eyes.

I lie on the bed in our own house, dark except for a lantern's dim light in the back of the room. Someone sits in the rocking chair next to it.

For a long while, I watch the chair go back and forth. *You killed him* beats in time with the chair's motions. Long hair spills over the chair's back, like a river of spun gold. Linnea.

Everything seems too silent, even with her steady rocking. My head spins. I see Snorri Thorbrandsson, blood trickling over his ear. How can I explain it to Linnea? Maybe I won't have to. Maybe it was a nightmare, and I was here, asleep the whole time.

Linnea doesn't turn, but she stares at my boy's empty little bed. I lie still, pretending to sleep. My fear and dread of her grows, with the words unspoken between us. Does she know about Snorri Thorbrandsson's love for me? Does she know he's dead?

Finally, after what seems like endless hours, the door opens. Stena comes in, the white light of morning behind her. She takes a quick look at Linnea, then walks over to my bed. I've been watching with my eyes slitted, but now I close them, trying to breathe deeply and evenly.

Stena sits lightly on the bed for a few moments, observing in her silent way. She does what I'd hoped she would, turning to Linnea. "You may leave now. I'll watch over her."

The rocking stops, but not the voice in my head. Linnea's steps slowly move past my bed, then out the door. I wonder if she lives in the house with the other slave women. I should have asked her to make a room with us. She's all alone at Brattahlid, with Inger still at sea. Doubtless, Bjarni doesn't have the sense of direction he did earlier in his life. What if that whole crew died, as well? I can't take one more death.

My rejection pushed Snorri into such a passion that he couldn't control his willful horse. I'm the only one who knows he wasn't planning to marry Linnea, as everyone thought. I'll make sure that no one else ever knows, for Linnea's sake.

"You can sit up now, since you're not really asleep." Stena smiles in a knowing way. I oblige her, feeling foolish.

"She knows about him—we all do." Stena's voice cracks as she hugs me, her glossy, thick black hair smelling of rosemary. "Your boys stayed with Deirdre last night."

"How did you find me?" I look down at my dry clothing. Someone must have changed my shift and overdress. I don't remember travelling back.

She misunderstands my question. "Well, Leif said he found you with your hand in Snorri's. Of course, he just said this to make Finn jealous. We can all see their rivalry."

I could strangle that brute! What's he trying to do to me? He's overly harsh to everyone. Everything he says is designed to make Finn furious. And a furious Finn is something I've never seen. Why didn't I notice these flaws in Leif before? Or has Gunna changed him so much?

Stena sits quietly, her presence calming me. She's waiting for me to talk. I don't trust myself to tell the story, though. She squeezes my hand, bringing fresh tears to my eyes. I remember my baby's flutters in the woods, when I found Snorri. My hand flies to my stomach.

"My baby?" I ask. She understands I'm not talking about baby Snorri.

"You're both fine." Stena's helped with births before. She would have checked to see if I'd miscarried because of the shock. Someday, I'll thank the God in heaven for protecting my unborn child when I found Snorri dead. But not today.

"Could you eat something?" Stena stands, smoothing the blankets. "The mid-morning meal will be soon, but Finn waits for you in the longhouse."

The tide of nausea rises in me again, but I swallow to push it down. Yes, I will go to my husband. I need his arms around me.

Unfortunately, he's not alone in the longhouse. Leif and Gunna sit at one end of the table; Finn at the other end. Thjodhild, standing near the fire, gives me a desperate look. Given the way the men glare at each other, I should have stayed in our house. But I've done nothing wrong. I have *not*.

I gather new strength. "Where are my boys?"

Thjodhild looks relieved for something else to think about. "Your Snorri's with Deirdre. That woman may be pale as a banshee, but she loves your boy as much as I do. And the other two ate early—they're helping Magnus. He says they're gentle with the sheep." Her hand flies to her mouth as she realizes her words may offend. Gils has probably been shepherding for years.

It's unusual for such a fearsome, elegant woman as Thjodhild to worry about what others think of her opinions, especially since she's the matriarch of Brattahlid. But she can't afford to offend Leif.

Gunna scowls. "His corpse is laid out in his house." She jerks her thumb toward the door. "In case you need to say a *personal* goodbye."

She doesn't look directly at me as she says this, but I know it's meant for me and no one else. She can't even respect Snorri Thorbrandsson by saying his name.

"Shut your mouth." Finn's voice fills the room, before I can even speak. I look back at him and see the lion has wakened. His chin is iron; his eyes dark.

Gunna looks at Leif for the support he'll never give. She slams her glass down so hard, it breaks.

Thjodhild's face hardens as she takes control of the longhouse. Rhine glass is not easily replaced. "Get out, thankless wench!"

Gunna gets up and strides out slowly, swinging her full hips as if she has all the time in the world.

Leif watches everything, but does not intervene. In fact, I get the feeling he's enjoying this. Eirik would take a strap to him, were he alive. Gunna may be horrible, but she'll always be the mother of Leif's child, and at one point, he found her irresistible.

The slaves hesitantly place steaming bowls on the table. I suppose they've decided we're taking our meal early.

Linnea is among them, her beautiful hair pinned up with a folded linen cap over it, making her look like any other slave on the farm. This infuriates me even further. "I release this slave," I say. "Linnea, you are free."

Leif's brows draw together and he jumps up. So I can drive him to action. Finn also jumps to his feet.

I match Leif's glare. "Well, isn't she my slave, Leif? If you don't know, ask your sister. She knows better than I do which slaves I own."

He looks from Finn to me, then slowly sits down.

"You know my sister." He waves his hand around like a bird's wing. "Crazy. She wants to go back to Vinland this very winter. I think she wants to be as wealthy as your man there."

The room is charged, and we're all shooting lightning bolts at each other. Stena walks up behind me.

"Please eat something, Gudrid." Her black eyes scold me as she lightly pushes my shoulder. Then she goes to Finn, her whisper reaching my ears. "You'll need to oversee the burning. Snorri was your partner. It's how he would want it."

As Finn rises to leave, Linnea's eyes trail after him. "Go with him, please." I request this, instead of ordering it. Linnea wants to help prepare Snorri's body. Her eyes fill with tears, but she nods and follows Finn. The next Althing meeting will buzz with news of her freedom.

Leif leans forward, looking at me. "And will you release them all? Deirdre, Magnus, Nerienda, and the others?" His eyes dare me to do just that.

Where is the Leif I dreamed of? The one whose feelings were as soft as his beard?

Well, he's not the only one who has changed. I've seen enough in these two years to make me hard and angry, if I chose to be. I do not. I won't become a cold woman, spiteful and irritable, like Gunna, or like Thjodhild used to be. I ignore Leif instead, drinking the cabbage soup before me and enjoying hunks of fresh wheat bread.

As a slave girl picks up shards of Gunna's broken glass, Thjodhild finally sits to eat. Stena positions herself right next to me. Leif sighs, still waiting for my response.

He finally groans and jumps up. "Too many women. Where are all my men?" He stalks out of the longhouse, leaving his half-eaten meal in his bowl.

We don't even look at one another, knowing the slaves are already gossipping about Gunna's behavior. Instead, we eat our food and ask for more. Thjodhild drinks at least four glasses of beer. I can't grudge her that—Snorri Thorbrandsson's death is a harsh reminder of how quickly life can end.

Stena draws us both into conversation with her clever questions. She's so easy to talk to; never hostile. I used to have the ability to unify people, as well. But here at Brattahlid, it seems my only ability is stirring up conflict with men.

I don't know how Leif feels about me now, though I really shouldn't care. He needs to change his habits to heal his marriage, and I can only hinder and distract him.

And Snorri Thorbrandsson. It was my fault he charged off on that skittish stallion. I was too harsh, too blunt with him.

What would Finn think of my story? How much would he understand? I haven't had two moments to speak with him, much less enjoy his body here, with all the boys sleeping in our room. I need to find a way to put up a deer hide curtain, since it's a larger house and the older boys are so quick to comfort Snorri. That would give us some privacy.

Something pricks the back of my thoughts, like a briar I can't locate. When Stena mentions Freydis' thinness, I realize what it is: Leif said Freydis wants to sail to Vinland this winter. No reasonable person would dare ship out from Greenland then.

I stand. "I need to go talk with Freydis."

Stena gives me a look of disapproval, but she doesn't try to stop me. Thjodhild seems too tired to respond, blankly watching the fire and the bustling slaves.

Before searching for Freydis, I check in on Snorri. I haven't seen enough of my boys here. I remember how Snorri Thorbrandsson stayed up all night with my son when I was too exhausted to continue. My boy will never see his namesake again. Uncontrolled tears stream down my cheeks and I furiously swipe them away.

Deirdre spins wool in her house. It's not as large as mine, but decorated beautifully, with ceramic vases and dyed linens on the bed. She also has plenty of toys for Snorri, who pushes around rolling wooden horses. The minute he sees me, he drops them and runs into my arms. I hold him tightly, marveling at his good health.

Deirdre whispers, as if Snorri could understand her. "I've been hearing some things."

"And what are they?" I ask.

"Gunna's healer woman—well, really just an old witch, if you ask me—says her mistress will be going back to her homeland in a of couple days." Deirdre shakes her head. "It's an ill wind that blows, given what's happened to…."

She goes silent, patting my boy's plump cheek. She knows I don't want prophecies of doom based on Snorri's accident.

I say nothing, so she finally speaks again. "Magnus says your boys are wonderful with the sheep, instinctive as if they were blind, too." She has all the pride of a doting grandmother, reminding me of the news I want to share.

"Deirdre, I want you and Magnus to be free. You are no longer my slaves. Do you want to leave Brattahlid?

"No longer your slaves? Leave Brattahlid? What's this about? We'll go nowhere!" She grips her silver necklace. Someday she's going to break it, handling it so often. "We stay with you and your children, slaves or not."

"But don't you miss Scotland?" Snorri wraps his fingers in my hair. Fresh tears fill my eyes at Deirdre's loyalty to our family.

"Only on misty days. Or when the grass smells fresh and new. Yes, I do miss it, and I imagine my Magnus does, too. But your God brought us to you."

I put Snorri on the floor and hug her. Yes, my God brought her to me. Deirdre and Magnus have always sought the best for my family.

She pulls me back and looks at my face and eyes, still reddened from crying over Snorri Thorbrandsson. "I know what you need, dearie. A warm bath in one of Leif's fancy washtubs, then you can snug up in your own bed. You must take care of your unborn baby, too."

She is right. Even though I need to talk with Freydis, I feel tired and useless after Snorri Thorbrandsson's death. I had almost forgotten I'm expecting.

Deirdre knows my question before I ask. "I'll watch the boys. Snorri loves playing here, and we have extra beds for

Hol and Hellir. They could even learn to play King's Table with Magnus."

How a blind man plays board games, I can't imagine. But Magnus doesn't ever seem limited in anything he does.

"But I need to talk with Freydis, and Linnea..." Who am I to sleep at such a time of unrest on the farm?

Deirdre's concerned blue eyes focus on me. "You must not worry yourself so much over the others. Think only of your own babe. You are too good at mothering."

The truth in Deirdre's observation strikes me. It explains why I feel guilty for rejecting Snorri; my continual worry for Inger, Geisli, and Suka; my burden to help Thjodhild, who's not even my mother-in-law anymore; and why I can't let Freydis return to Straumsfjord. I mother everyone except my husband.

Finn enters the house, his face gray. He has seen Snorri Thorbrandsson. I hope someone wrapped Snorri's head, so Finn couldn't see the gaping wound that killed him.

He takes little Snorri from my arms, into his tight embrace. His eyes swim with unshed tears. It is my fault his best friend lies dead.

When Finn finally returns Snorri to Deirdre's arms, he takes my hand, leading me out of the house without a word. We walk across the farmyard to our house. As we pass Leif and Gunna's door, their angry shouts make their way to our ears.

Finn is acting strangely. This husband of mine can be overly secretive when he wants to be. He doesn't say why he's taking me into our house. He might want to ask me about Snorri's death, or scold me for releasing slaves, or....

He shuts our door, turning to face me. "Gudrid, we have to talk."

Chapter Thirty-Six

Thorfinn Karlsefni has never been a man of words. He acts. I used to believe he had given all those goods and food to Eirik so he could have decent housing in Greenland that winter. But later, I realized he'd planned it that way. When he and his men stayed longer, it depleted Eirik's supply, making him reliant on his merchant boarder. And, when Eirik had to ask for food, Finn had the advantage. It gave him the powerful position of being able to ask for my hand without any reason for rejection.

I'm sure Snorri Thorbrandsson knew Finn planned to marry me. It's probably why he asked for my hand first, earlier that winter. But it was already too late. Eirik respected wealth and title. Snorri had some wealth, but not as much as Finn, and he had no title. Eirik never truly considered Snorri worthy of my hand.

Men instinctively recognize Finn's determination and loyalty. He makes friends for life. And not many fathers would have accepted two Skraelings as their own children. But, as a husband, I feel I know him less now than when we first married.

And now he wants to talk. The light from the window hits his cheekbones, and his face looks thinner to me. The circles under his eyes have darkened. Why have I not *seen* my husband lately?

But he seems calm enough. "First of all, are you well?" He sits down on our bed and motions for me to join him.

I sit, straightening my soft brown skirts around me. "Don't worry about me. I'll sleep soon. And you?"

He doesn't answer, looking at the floor. "Are those new boots?"

Why does he talk so seriously about boots? "Yes, Stena gave them to me, because my others got ruined by the mud at Straumsfjord—"

He speaks quickly. "I know many things happened when I was away from Straumsfjord. Snorri told me much of it, but not all. I figured out what he wasn't telling me. The man was transparent as glass. I knew he loved you, from the time he was young. He couldn't stop talking about you, telling me about your family in Iceland and your godparents, Halldis and Orm. He also spoke often of your hair and your figure and your eyes—things other men would never have mentioned to me. But I thought he was only like a friend to you, and I couldn't pick a better protector while I was gone."

"And so he was," I say.

Finn's foot taps on the floor in a regular rhythm. "But lately he was distracted by you—so distracted, he neglected his work. You're a distracting woman, Gudrid—I wonder if you even know it? Leif, too, watches you openly, like a hungry wolf. He'll regret this if he continues." His foot rests on the floor. "So I talked with Snorri this morning. I told him to marry Linnea or take his goods and go back to Iceland."

I breathe slowly, but inside I'm in turmoil. My husband has seen all the things I thought were hidden. I nod at him slightly, so he'll continue. He has never talked this openly with me before.

"He was upset, Gudrid. He tore off on that stallion, the one Leif couldn't tame. Any other man would've had sense to pick a better horse. You haven't seen Snorri in a rage. I did once in Iceland—the time he got an arrow run through his thick neck."

He sighs deeply, looking at the unicorns dancing on the tapestry.

"I've done wrong. I've been living with this guilt," he says.

What? He didn't cause Snorri's death. I did.

"Do you remember that night? When Hallstein was leering at you, and his men were doing the same?" Finn focuses on the small window, as if looking back in time. "I knew he was drunk when he was in the longhouse. I knew they were stupid and desperate for women. And then Snorri told me about Hallstein's remarks to you. I left early, and hid behind our hut...I was going to jump out and kill Hallstein if he came anywhere near you."

He had been aware of the danger that night. He *knew.*

"I waited...then I heard Vani's steps and saw his huge shadow. I let him scratch around at the midden heap, looking for an entrance to the house."

Why? Why would you do this? *Your wife and child were inside.*

"I needed to know, in my mind, that I was justified in what I had to do. I knew you would protect the main door, and I knew you'd kill anyone who came in. You're quite a fearsome woman when it comes to your children. But I'd posted Snorri in front of the hut, so I wasn't worried about anyone coming in that way."

If only I had known that night! Instead of fearing for my life, gripping my seax until my hands were numb, I could have rested secure, knowing I was protected.

Finn's eyes finally fix on me, dark blue and bright. "So I let him dig in the waste, pig that he was. He started hacking at the wood frame, and then would you believe he started pulling his trousers off? That was enough for me. I took my knife and cut into his throat—not very cleanly, I'm afraid. I would never let him hurt you."

His foot starts tapping again. "Soon after this, Freydis came behind the huts. She carried her knife. I stood behind her when she tripped over the body. I put my hand over her mouth and wrenched the knife from her, then shoved her out of the way, in case anyone else came. She was smart enough to run the other way, toward the forest. She never realized who I was."

His eyes search my face, waiting for a response. I can't move, and my face feels frozen. Finn was there all along. He risked everything to protect me—if Hallstein had found out, the men would have demanded punishment. Finn would have lost his position as leader. And, if they'd followed Althing rules, he would have lost his life. Now I know why he got to Linnea so quickly—he was already positioned outside, listening for trouble.

He puts a hand on my shoulder, rubbing it, as if to wake me. "Hallstein wanted to blame Freydis, since she liked to threaten him. I tried to protect her when she returned with you. I told the women Vani was sick, so we could burn him quickly, before any of the men looked closely at his neck. Of course, Snorri Thorbrandsson knew

I'd killed him, but he wouldn't tell anyone about me. He would have killed that troll himself, given half the chance."

His eyes search mine. "And now you know why I've felt so guilty. Freydis was with child. What if I killed that baby, when I scared her behind the hut? Or when she was accused of murder? I should have stepped up, but the men were on the verge of mutiny and I wanted to keep as many loyal to me as I could, so I could be there for you. Hallstein's men wouldn't have had mercy on me."

Everything falls into place so neatly in my mind. Snorri's talk of men who needed killing, his eyes travelling to the back of the longhouse. Freydis' knife, knocked into the bush. The mark on the neck not matching her knife. Finn's lie about Vani being sick.

And his feelings of guilt could be grounded. It is possible for shock to kill babies.

All this time, I never really believed Freydis when she denied killing Vani. But all she had done was try to protect me, prowling behind my hut with her knife.

Finn leans closer. He chews on cloves, and his spicy scent warms me. He loves me enough to risk his position, his wealth, and even his life for me.

I take his bearded chin between my hands, pulling him toward me on the bed. He will know of my forgiveness, and that will be forgiveness enough. No one else will ever know what happened that night—least of all, Freydis.

Chapter Thirty-Seven

Along with the bright reds and yellows of sunrise comes a clearness I haven't felt for years. It's as if God has taken all the lies I've believed about Finn's carelessness and burnt them on a funeral pyre.

Morning also brings news. Deirdre wakens us with her insistent knocking. When Finn opens the door to her, I fear for my boys. Wearing only my shift, I slide from the bed, racing to her side.

She sees my worry and stops it, holding up her hand. "The boys are fine. Gunna left, in the middle of the night. She took her son and her witch. One of Leif's men left with her. Those two had been *close* for some time...but now Leif is throwing things around and shouting. Thjodhild is afraid he'll make his way to her chapel or even to her house, and break all her valuables."

Finn pulls on his boots. But if he walks into this, both men will get killed.

"I'll talk with him," I say.

Finn sighs heavily, as if this family's problems weigh on him. "You don't have to fix this. I can do it."

"He won't hurt me, because I'm family." I hope I'm right.

Deirdre gives Finn a look, but nods. "Truly, Gudrid may be the only one he'll see."

I throw on my red shawl, another gift from Stena. I'm surprised Leif even misses Gunna. Perhaps he's angry she took Gils with her.

Glass crashes against Leif's door as we approach. Deirdre sucks in her breath. "Do not let him get behind you," she whispers. I wonder what she means, until I remember that he once strangled a man for his father, walking up behind him and wrapping one arm around his neck.

I murmur a quick prayer, asking God to bring Leif to his senses and calm him for me. Then I push the carved, honey-colored door open.

Leif holds a box in one hand, a vase in the other. He throws the vase toward me, but I duck.

"Sorry...sorry! I thought it was someone else," he says.

His eyes are dazed and his hair tumbles over his shoulders. He wears only his trousers, seemingly unaware of his lack of a tunic.

He turns the dark box over, and its little drawers crash to the floor. "She took it all, that wench. She took every bit. *There* was a wife who had no business having my keys."

Viking women still keep the keyrings, a tradition since the days when their men went out plundering. It shows the transfer of power. Keys can be for anything, from barns to storehouses to treasure boxes. This last is what Gunna has raided, I'm sure. She would have needed gold and silver for the trip. She probably also traded her huge emerald brooches that were gifts from her father.

"I'm sorry." I lean against the wall to protect my back. I can't be too careful, although I'm almost sure Leif wouldn't hurt me. But Snorri Thorbrandsson's last words about Leif echo in my head. "You can't be alone with Leif," he'd said. What did he mean? Did he know something I don't know?

To my dismay, I start shaking, revealing no small measure of doubt.

Leif comes over to me, and instead of meeting his gaze, I notice how the golden hair on his chest matches his beard. He takes my arms in his hands, and I look into his eyes, more gray than blue today. He towers over me, making me feel small as a child again. His lips crook halfway up and his eyebrow raises. He's waiting for me to say something.

"She was an ill-tempered woman; we all saw that, Leif." I hope this is what he wants to hear. I don't mention that his own behavior toward her was far from honorable.

"And you came here to tell me that, shivering in your thin shift?" He smiles as if we are conspirators. "Yes, you're right. She never wanted to be here, and she poisoned Gils against me, always making me out to be some kind of fool. Still, he could have had this farm someday."

His eyes wander across the room, taking in the damage for the first time. "What've I done? Probably broken half my mother's trinkets. Many thanks for coming over when you did." He pulls me to him in a sudden hug. I try to pretend it's what a brother would do. But the way his hand trails down my back isn't so brotherly. I need to leave, now.

"Tonight will be the burning for Snorri Thorbrandsson." I try to distract Leif while I slip away from his wandering hand.

He blocks my forward movement, catching a stray piece of my hair and twisting it in his fingers. "Won't you stay for awhile, my beautiful sister?" His hand slides to my shoulder, as his other hand smoothly moves to my waist.

A little laugh sounds from the doorway, and Stena's youngest daughter comes running straight toward me. Her little round face scrunches in a smile, and she extends her arms. Thankful for the interruption, I pick her up. Her brown eyes smile downward, just like Stena's.

I don't even know her name yet. "What are you called?" I point to her chest.

She grins shyly. "Gudrid," she whispers.

"No, I'm Gudrid...who are *you*?"

It's Leif's turn to laugh. "She was named after the woman who brought her into the world." He points to me.

Stena named her daughter for me...my thoughts fly to my sister-in-law, remembering the way she clung to me after Thorvald's death. She needed someone with her all the time; to feed, bathe, and dress her child. It was as if all her willpower had been taken away when her husband died. Even when we had to leave for Vinland, three months after she'd given birth, Stena still hadn't named her baby.

But now, I have my own namesake—this radiant, loving girl in my arms.

Leif watches my face, not even looking at the girl. I carefully put little Gudrid down, trying not to cry. "There are funeral preparations to make," I say. "I'll send a slave here to clean for you."

"Many thanks." Leif's eyes hold my own a moment too long, breathing new life into my nearly-forgotten dreams of him. Fresh guilt floods me. Was I truly thankful little Gudrid interrupted Leif's enticement? Or does some part of me feel privileged to hold sway over such an esteemed, powerful man?

I follow little Gudrid outside, pulling the heavy door shut. Deirdre and Stena wait nearby. Stena's eyes are on mine, and we both know she sent her daughter in for a reason. "You didn't tell me she's my namesake!" I try to scold her, but she sees my proud smile. "And thank you, for...distracting Leif."

"Of course," she says. "Thjodhild was worried sick. She's taken to her bed—she didn't even go to the chapel today. Her health is failing." Stena's deep eyes tell me she understands how ill Thjodhild is; perhaps better than I do. She was a reindeer herder, after all. They always had to watch for sickness or disease among their animals.

"I'll go to her." I turn to Deirdre. "Do you need help preparing the body?" I cannot put feeling into my words.

"No, indeed." Deirdre looks at my stomach. "You've seen enough. Go, help the mistress."

Thjodhild has always been the mistress of Brattahlid, from the time Eirik established it. I find myself wondering again who'll replace her, now that Gunna is gone.

Fights, sickness, and death follow me everywhere. Why do I spend all my time running from one disaster to another? I must talk with Freydis about this journey she plans. And I must speak with Linnea about her plans for the future.

I miss seeing my own children here at Brattahlid. I had looked forward to teaching Hol and Hellir our language. Instead, I have more responsibility here than at Straumsfjord, between my daughter-in-law duties and the never-ending burdens of family struggles on the farm. I'm sure Finn feels my absence, as well.

Thjodhild's in a state, walking back and forth in her house, cursing Gunna with pagan curses I haven't heard since my childhood in Iceland. I don't stop her rant, since she isn't cursing with the real God's name.

"She took Gils! He was the heir of Brattahlid, and my grandson!" Her pale eyes are frantic. "I told Leif not to marry her. She trapped him with that baby. She would've liked to take Leif away from Brattahlid and put him under her father's heavy thumb. At least he had the sense to make her come here instead."

"True, true." I try to calm her.

"And now she's run back to papa! Weak and hateful hag! I'll disinherit her boy!"

I ignore the fact that she has no power to disinherit. "Thjodhild, I have some herbs that might help you."

"I don't want to be calm! I'm angry! I'll say what I want!"

"Of course you will. Maybe you'd like to visit the chapel?"

"I'm too upset." She still paces the room.

"People will expect to see the woman of the farm at the funeral tonight." I know she won't refuse her duty.

She stands straighter. Thjodhild is a woman who always wants to appear strong in her position as owner of Brattahlid.

"Yes...perhaps I *should* rest for a while. Are there enough hands to help with preparations?"

"More than enough—Brattahlid has plenty of slaves." I know she'll take this as a compliment.

"Yes." She sighs. "I suppose I could have one of your herbal teas."

I take my leave and retrieve my herb box. In the longhouse, I instruct the slaves how to make a calming tea for Thjodhild with dried chamomile and lemon balm. Stena meets me there to discuss our mother-in-law.

"She's not so unreasonable as she was when I married Thorvald, but she still forgets herself sometimes." Stena looks at me. "Did you rest last night?"

At some point in the night, I suppose I did, despite Finn's revelations swirling in my head. I nod. "Where's Freydis? I haven't seen her for so long."

Stena's eyes darken. "She's plotting. Ref isn't able to talk sense to her."

"Plotting what?"

"Plotting a return voyage to Vinland, so Leif avoids her. She talks of nothing but how she's going to be as wealthy as Finn someday and make everyone respect her position as Eirik's daughter. I heard she rode up the coast to meet some sailors visiting from Iceland."

"When did she leave?" I ask.

"Two days ago."

So Freydis doesn't even know about Snorri Thorbrandsson. She will probably return in time to see the flames of his pyre. Another death, which could push her further out of her mind.

At least I can do one thing now—talk with Linnea. Stena tells me she is washing clothes at the waterfall. Past the field, there's a waterfall that gushes down the high rocks, into a deep green lake. I went there often after Thorstein the Red married me. We would sun ourselves on its banks and chase each other through the deep grasses. Even though he was proud, when we first married, he loved me as much as he loved himself.

It is the same field Leif and I walked through years ago. He knew I was loyal in marriage, even then. Now he seems to ignore my married state, goading Finn with his remarks and touching me every chance he gets.

He picked the wrong husband to joke with. I remember when he'd argue with Thorstein, but they were brothers, so things were usually resolved with a wrestling match. Sometimes, Thorvald would jump in to smooth things over, reasoning with them both. Neither brother could argue with Thorvald's orderly mind, but they'd always try to outsmart him anyway. Pranks were common among those three men, but they never involved their wives.

One mid-morning meal, Thorstein the Red raged into the longhouse. Someone had shattered the glass in his three mirrors. He thought some slave wanted to bring him extremely bad luck. Of course, I knew it was just Leif, trying to show how attached Thorstein was to his own good looks. Leif never admitted his guilt, but I noticed when he returned from Norway, he brought back a few mirrors for his younger brother.

Now two of those brothers are dead. Death lurks everywhere, for Vikings. I let the sunlight blind me and murmur my question toward the sky. "What's the point of living if you lose everyone?"

My eye travels to the top of the waterfall, and I freeze in shock. Linnea stands on the ledge, poised to jump onto the jutting rock pile below.

Chapter Thirty-Eight

I race to the edge of the lake, my legs finally functioning. "Stop!"

To my surprise, Linnea straightens up, looking down at me.

"You?" She leans forward slightly.

I breathe slowly, trying to calm down. "I need to talk with you about Snorri."

Her hair flows freely around her body, like a cloud. She wears only her white shift, making her look unearthly. She nods, but stretches her arms to her sides. She jumps.

My scream roars into my ears and I close my eyes.

Moments later, I hear a splashing, then a voice next to me. "Gudrid? M'lady?"

I open my eyes. Linnea stands next to me, dripping wet and looking at me strangely. Then realization hits her, and her hand flies to her mouth. "You didn't know about the dive spot? I thought everyone knew. Snorri showed me— you must have thought—oh, I'm so sorry, m'lady."

"*Stop* calling me that, Linnea. No, I didn't know of it." My body trembles and there's a light, fluttery kicking in my stomach.

"You wanted to talk?" She walks to a pile of rocks nearby and pulls out a large drying cloth and her overdress. As she squeezes out her hair, I note our similarities again. We're the same in almost every way, yet our faces differ slightly.

Her large green eyes focus on me, and she bites at her full lips. If Leif can't tear his eyes off me, poor Linnea will be in his line of vision very soon. Now that he has no wife around, he will watch every woman who lives at Brattahlid. Just as I'm a woman who needs a man, he's a man who needs a woman at all times.

"Linnea, what are your plans now? I know Snorri Thorbrandsson was special to you."

"Oh, yes'm. We've shared so many laughs together. He told me of all his adventures in Iceland. He gave me so much advice. He thought—"

"Yes?"

"He thought I could go home to Sweden, when you and Karlsefni travel to the mainland for trading. If you released me, I could do it, he said. And now you have!"

She smiles, talking about him as an older brother or a friend. Why would he want her in Sweden, when he was traveling to Iceland? Did I imagine their closeness? She isn't acting like a bereaved lover.

"I'm sorry you found him that way." She speaks softly. "He told me things about you. Mostly about what a strong woman you are, but he still liked protecting you at Straumsfjord. In the end, he planned to go home to Iceland, you know. He told me he wished he could have fathered children with you, because you're such a good mother...but I don't want to speak evil of the dead. He respected your marriage. Even though he loved you, he pretended to like me, so you wouldn't be upset."

I stare into those wide green eyes, not finding any words. She continues talking, without noticing.

"He kept a little book, full of charcoal pictures he drew. He showed it to me once. It had the same black binding as his leather pants. From that old bull, he said to me. They were lovely pictures, m'lady—Gudrid. Of you and the boy and our time in Straumsfjord."

My hand rests on my stomach as I try to hold in my sadness. I feel ill, knowing how deeply Snorri Thorbrandsson loved me. He knew I couldn't return that kind of love, and it made him desperate.

Linnea notices my hand and concern fills her voice. "Are you well? Did you need to speak to me of something?"

"No, Linnea, you've answered all my questions. Please know you are welcome to travel back to Sweden with us, when we go. You're so good with my boys."

She beams, sunshine lighting her hair and eyes. "You honor me."

I should respond, but there's nothing left to say. I turn abruptly and walk through the dead grass, lost in thought.

Finn meets me, which is unusual during the day. Perhaps something has happened.

Watching his confident, familiar stride, I feel a surge of pride. I picture his strong arm, where his tattoo is, and a blush creeps up my cheeks. When he gets close enough, he notices it.

"And what makes my wife blush so deeply?" His eyes are as light as the ocean today.

"You, my man. We never have enough time together."

"Agreed." He wraps his arms around me. I rest my head on his chest, listening to his steady heartbeats. I don't want to think of the funeral tonight. Please, don't let him talk about Snorri.

"We have guests today." He moves a hand to the small of my back, gently rubbing it. "Freydis has been busy. She found some sailors from Iceland. I haven't heard of them before, but they've been in Norway, trading. Helgi and Finnbogi. They bring news of our home."

Sometimes I forget Iceland was Finn's home, as well. He grew up far from where I did, on his family farm in Reynines. Even though it no longer feels like home, Iceland does come to me at the strangest times, in dreams and smells and bits of memories.

"And why has Freydis been hunting them down?"

"Big plans. I heard from the ever-present Deirdre that Leif might loan her a ship to find more grapes and wheat. He's feeling like a poor man, since his thieving wife ran off."

I giggle, feeling a bit treacherous. Finn has no high regard for Leif—that much is clear.

"And Ref?" I wonder how Freydis' mild husband responds to her planning.

"You know him—he can't say no to her. And it's a pity he won't. I love Freydis like my own family, but she's so headstrong. She needs a man who loves her enough to stop her. Ref never pushes back."

My husband talks with me so often, it's like a geyser has burst open inside him. Maybe he has to confide in me, now that Snorri Thorbrandsson is dead. Yet I wonder how much he truly confided in Snorri, knowing he was in love with me?

Doubtless, Suka is what drives Freydis to return to the new world. She hopes for a renewed relationship with him. I picture him there at Straumsfjord, with no one but the hulking Tyr for support. I hope these Icelandic sailors can't retrace the journey to that inlet. Ref and Suka would surely have a fight to the death, with Freydis in the middle.

Finn shields his eyes, looking to the lake. "Who's that lying on the bank?"

"Linnea. She'd like to travel with us if we go to trade in Sweden." I wonder when that will be. Our baby should be born in early summer. "Finn, do you think Linnea looks like me?"

"She does...everyone's seen that. She could be your sister. Perhaps that's why Snorri liked her."

I don't answer. He doesn't need to know Snorri spent time with Linnea only to hide his desire for me.

Finn leans in to kiss me, fingers entwined in mine. "Tonight." He speaks in a low tone, laced with desire.

"Yes." I pull him close and kiss him again. His sweet, yet salty taste stirs all my senses.

As we walk back, he holds me loosely, yet there is possession in his touch. His other hand rests on his sword, and he watches the woods. Why didn't I see how closely my own husband guards me? Or has he just started acting this way in Greenland?

Freydis interrupts our comfortable silence, running toward us from the longhouse. Finn gives a small sigh, dropping his arm.

"Gudrid! You'll never believe it! I found a couple of sailors from your homeland! They're going to sail me back to Straums—to Vinland!"

Her eyes have that distracted, far-off look, but then she focuses on me. Her excitement dies. "Deirdre told me about Snorri Thorbrandsson."

Her eyes flick guiltily to Finn, as if she's said too much. She remembers Snorri's hand on mine that night at the campfire. But Finn is distracted by the horses kicking in the pasture.

"I'm so sorry you found him." She pulls at her loose overdress.

"Yes."

Her excitement returns. "Today was the only day Helgi and Finnbogi could come. Then they have to travel back to Lysufjord. I wanted Leif to talk with them and see what good sailors they are. Then he'll support me."

"Does he even have resources for this trip? And why do you want to go back this winter, of all times?" I ask.

Her blue eyes sharpen. "Because we need more goods, of course. That witch Gunna stole Leif's gold and jewels—all the things he got from the king of Norway...besides, Helgi and Finnbogi bring many stories about Christianity in Iceland, which I'm sure you'll want to hear." She's trying to divert my attention.

Though Freydis herself has no interest in Christianity, I would like to hear from the Icelanders. And I don't want to stoke the fires of her determination by arguing with her. "Yes, I will enjoy talking with them. I'm sure Finn would, too, as they're fellow traders." I nudge his arm gently, and he swings back around.

"Looking forward to it." He excuses himself to oversee the men, busy transferring his goods into Leif's storehouses for winter.

Knowing Freydis' contrary nature, I don't even mention Suka. I try a different approach.

"I wish you would stay long enough to help me with the birth. Nerienda isn't back yet, and I'll only have Stena to help." Freydis should feel the obligation of returning my favor, when I helped with her birth.

Her face twists into her half-grin. "I'm no good at it; you know that. Nerienda should be back by summer, surely, unless…where *is* Bjarni, anyway? I thought he'd made this trip so many times."

She speaks my own thoughts. If Bjarni docked elsewhere in Greenland, we should have heard of it by now. I remember how Inger helped me during the sickness. I pray she and Geisli will live to marry someday.

"Well, I'm determined about this." Freydis smiles. "I think you worry too much."

"I worry about *you*, sister."

She sets her chin and tosses her head, much like an unruly horse.

I continue. "And don't tell me you can take care of yourself, because I clearly remember you cannot."

I visualize Freydis—keening outside the caves, unable to accept her baby's death. She looks thoughtful for a moment, but dislikes the truth in my words. "Come and meet the sailors, Gudrid. I'm sure they have news of your family."

What family? Most of my family is dead. I was the only child of my parents. My foster parents had no children, either. The only thing I want to hear about Iceland is that Christianity is replacing paganism—and the volva.

Freydis takes my hand, pulling me toward the longhouse. There's lively talk inside, mingled with the smells of smoked pork—Leif's favorite.

"I need to check on my boys." I pull my hand from hers, my appetite vanishing.

"But—" Though Freydis calls to me, I continue striding toward our house.

Inside, Hol and Hellir are eating their meals at our small table. "Why aren't you in the longhouse?" I ask before I remember that they don't speak our language.

Hol shakes his head and points. "No longhouse." The words are clear.

They're learning to speak without me!

"Where's Snorri?" I wonder how many words they know.

This time Hellir stretches his long, brown finger and points at the door. "Deirdre."

Magnus must have been teaching them, or Deirdre. They have been spending the most time with them. I must remember to give the older couple my thanks. But why aren't my boys eating in the longhouse? I kiss their heads. So help me, if Leif kicked them out, Finn is going to know about it.

Chapter Thirty-Nine

Men fill the longhouse, from Brattahlid and other towns. There are hardly any women here besides farm slaves and Freydis. The children's table is empty, so Leif must have ordered them all to dine elsewhere.

My stomach heaves at the smell of the meat. With this child, I feel I could live on cabbage and celery, not the heavy smoked meats often served here at Brattahlid.

Leif notices me and calls me over. To show respect for him as the head of the farm, I walk to his chair. Ignoring him would get us all thrown out, family or not. I'm glad Finn is not in the longhouse yet.

Leif throws his long arm around me, fingering my belt. "This is my father's ward, Gudrid, famed for her beauty. Well, she's mine now, I suppose!" He laughs too heartily and too long—he has already drunk too much of the good wine. "She made the trip to the new world—can you believe it? Her husband brought back my ship, loaded with goodies. Now, have any of you heard tale of Bjarni? Where's that old man and my other ship?"

One man with carrot-colored hair speaks up. "No word of Bjarni, but we do know of your third ship, the one

Hallstein used. It's docked off the coast of my hometown in Ireland."

I pull away from Leif's fingers, which have been tracing the embroidery on my belt. Hallstein, alive? He probably didn't find treasure, then sailed around Greenland's coastline to avoid Leif. But now he has even more reason to fear, because he took Leif's property.

Leif slams his fist into the table. "Ireland, is it? That fiend! That demon! He'll regret this!"

The Irishman speaks up again. "He's telling everyone he was blown off-course. He says he plans to return your ship, but there are men who wish to purchase it from him."

Leif's light eyebrows tighten, and he frowns. Hallstein has a price on his head now. Plenty of men in Ireland would love to gain favor with Eirik's powerful son by capturing Hallstein for him.

I start to sneak away, but Leif remembers me again and grabs my skirt. The men chuckle. But I'm not his slave. I yank my skirt back, smacking his hand away.

"I'm going to find my *husband*." I move toward the door.

"Wait, Gudrid! Meet the men Freydis has brought us." He gestures to two men, obviously Icelandic. Their hair is almost white; their skin and eyes light. They could be twins.

The man on the left stands in respect. "Good day, Gudrid Thorbjarnardottir." It's the first time my full name has been spoken for years.

The other man stands and bows shortly. They obviously have good manners, treating me as a chieftain's daughter. And so I was, once.

"Finnbogi and Helgi." Leif gestures from right to left. "Or maybe it's Helgi and Finnbogi." He laughs. "I can't rightly tell them apart!"

The one on the left raises his sleeve. A scar runs up the length of his arm. "I am Helgi. My brother has no scar."

Eirik's men look impressed. One man pulls up his trouser leg to reveal his discolored, jagged scar. Several others adjust clothing to point out their own. Typical Vikings—comparing whose scar is the biggest.

Freydis rolls her eyes at the corner of the table. "I was telling Leif that these men have sailed around the coasts of Iceland and Greenland. They'll doubtless be able to make the trip to Vinland with me." Her eyes slant a bit, suddenly intense. "And they're *honest* men, so everyone says." Why does their honesty concern Freydis so much?

Ref sits silently on a bench, apart from his wife. I wish he would say what he thinks of her crazy idea. No one should be putting out to sea at this time of year. Instead, he watches the Icelanders and chews his food.

"We bring news of your cousin." Helgi speaks to me.

My cousin! I have wondered about her. The last time I saw her was at Mother's hanging.

His speech is practiced, its familiar Icelandic inflections soothing. "Yngvild is married and has four children now. She owns your mother's farm, Laugarbrekka. She's married to Einar Thorgeirsson. They're very prosperous."

Einar. The trader's son who wanted to marry me so long ago.

"I am happy to hear that." It is good that my cousin prospers, and that Einar maintained his wealth, despite what my father thought of him.

Both brothers smile with their tidings of good news. They'll have no other word of my family, because the rest are dead.

But Finnbogi speaks up. "Christianity has swept into Iceland. There have been many miracles—the volva fight to maintain control."

I lean against the wall, their news finally overwhelming me. When I was last there, the volva held the entire island in their stranglehold. No one dared contest them. If only Christianity had come years earlier, my mother would still be alive.

Like a pebble tossed into a pond, Finn strides into the longhouse. The men ripple around to make room for him. Benches are pulled out; hands extended. Every man wants to sit by my husband, the trader who's returned victorious from Vinland.

He sits next to Ref. No longer does Snorri sit by him, a source of advice and unquestioning loyalty. I can't look at Finn's face, knowing we're feeling the same loss.

But my husband notices I stand near Leif. "Gudrid?" His smile invites me closer.

I willingly leave my post to stand behind Finn, resting my hands on his strong shoulders. In one of his possessive public gestures, he covers my hands with his own. The warmth and strength of his grip flows into me like heat from a fire.

The men's chatter doesn't break my newfound peace. Iceland is changing for the better. I close my eyes, remembering...the earth, alive with the blood of volcanoes and geysers coursing through it. The rocks, jutting over the ocean, covered with gulls. The yellow poppies I'd pick in bunches for Mother, the same color as her hair.

Stena suddenly appears by my side. She whispers in Finn's ear, then guides me out of the longhouse. She takes my hands in hers, steadying me for her news. "Thjodhild isn't well. She was playing with your Snorri, and she fell to the ground. Deirdre is with her."

We rush to Thjodhild's house, where Snorri toddles over, grabbing my skirts. I whisk him up. Thjodhild lies wrapped in blankets on Eirik's gigantic bed.

She tries to smile up at me. "Your son is a delight. He has all the charm of my Thorstein."

She does not think clearly, so I don't remind her that Snorri isn't Thorstein's son. I feel her forehead. There's no fever, but she's wet and cool. The heartbeat in her wrist is irregular.

I take Stena aside. "What did the healers say of her condition? Or the doctors from Norway?"

"She only saw one doctor. He was from the king's court, sent by King Tryggvason himself. The doctor said it was a disease he sees sometimes, a mass that eats the body from inside."

I've seen this disease only once, in Iceland. The man had a peculiar smell before dying. Thjodhild has the same smell now.

"Did he leave medicines? Herbs?"

"Yes, an Arabic cure Leif paid for dearly. It has done nothing."

"We must make her comfortable, then, at all costs."

Stena nods. "I will bring your herb box."

I shift Snorri to the floor, where Deirdre sits in silence on the bearskin rug.

"Thjodhild." I gently move the white hair off her face. Her light eyes don't focus on me, and she groans.

She is closer to death than we thought. She must have been pushing herself just to walk around. I admire her strength, that of a true lady.

I lean in closer. "God is with you."

She smiles slightly, then closes her eyes, quickly drifting into sleep. Every death pulls my own strength from me. It takes all my will to stand by when I know cures are impossible. Thjodhild will need someone to sit with her for days.

Deirdre observes me from her corner without a word, rocking Snorri in her lap. She knows I appreciate her watchcare of my children. In fact, it's been her primary occupation since we've been at Brattahlid. There are plenty of slaves to take care of the kitchen work and the spinning.

Stena carries my box in, bringing with her a sense of peace. She, too, has believed in the Christian God, but not in a showy way, like Thjodhild and Leif.

I have talked with Stena of her nomadic upbringing and the *noaidi*, the Sami men and women who go into trances with their drums. Because the reindeer herders embrace the spiritual side of life, when Stena heard the story of Christ and his spirit sent to those who believe, she was quick to accept it. Sometimes I feel she is closer to God than I will ever be, with her instincts for comfort and kindness.

I take the key off my belt for the herb box, but the lock springs open without my turning it. As I open it, I'm not surprised to find several mushrooms are missing. Freydis won't get away with this. I will tell Leif, before she heads off on her doomed trip. Ref also needs to know. Perhaps this news will wake him from his submissive stupor.

I find the dried meadowsweet, known to lessen pain. When Thjodhild wakes, we'll brew it into a honey tea.

The heaviness in my heart seems to spread throughout my body, and I drop into a chair. Snorri runs to me and climbs all over my lap, jabbing my stomach and legs with his little knees and elbows. I don't mind, since I've missed the feel of him near me now that he's stopped nursing.

"How's my boy today?" I kiss his face repeatedly.

"Norri, norri?" he asks.

"Yes, how's my baby Snorri?"

"Norri?" This time he points to the door.

I understand now. He asks for Snorri Thorbrandsson.

"No, my baby, he isn't coming." My eyes flood with tears and I grip his tiny hand. I stare at the door, as if the weight of my wishing would bring Snorri Thorbrandsson walking back into our lives.

My son seems to sense my sadness, and curls into a ball on my lap. The babe inside me kicks, as if enjoying the attention. Snorri's gold-touched curls shine beautifully against his red tunic. I vow to spend more time with all my children. With little Snorri, I've been too busy, unable to tend to him, except while nursing. And Finn has been gone for so much of his life. My son probably knew Snorri Thorbrandsson better than his own father.

Leif clunks on the door and charges in, obviously drunk. I quickly send Snorri back to Deirdre. Leif is the same as his father, drinking heavily when he's frustrated. And now he is under pressure from his sister to provide more ships and resources, so she can hire the Icelanders for her trip. Perhaps I can convince him to stop her.

"My mother...." Leif lumbers to her bed, not bothering to take his boots off first.

"Don't shake the bed." I order him away before he sits next to her. His weight alone would make her thin body bounce.

He gives me a questioning, desperate look. I nod.

"That worthless doctor!" He starts to curse. I go to his side, trying to calm him down so he doesn't wake Thjodhild.

"Leif, not only is there a child in this room, but you are a Christian now."

Leif looks over, noticing Snorri for the first time. "Oh...yes...so sorry."

"There is no cure for this disease," I say. "But your medicine may have kept her alive so she could see us return."

He yanks out a chair and slumps in it. "Perhaps, but who can tell? I've no wealth to spare now."

I sit next to him, lowering my voice. "All the more reason to keep your ships from Freydis. She has had too much pain at Straumsfjord—you didn't see her baby, Leif. And I am sure she hasn't told you everything about her time there. It has dimmed her ability to make wise decisions."

He looks at me, gray eyes clouded, his hair still wild. He wears his favorite brown leather tunic, the one his father gave him. Because he looks up like a guileless, injured child, all my instincts are to comfort him.

"Yes, we all see how my sister has changed. But my men say Finnbogi and Helgi are the best. And Ref wouldn't let me down." He stretches his legs, then leans toward me. The closeness of his long, tan fingers pulls at me. I try to forget how perfectly they wove into mine years ago.

"There is more going on here than you know." I wonder how much I should reveal about Suka.

His gaze sharpens. "Tell me."

"Your sister is one of the bravest women I have ever met." I compliment her, and thus his family. "But there was a man there, a Skraeling slave of yours, who took advantage of her weakness after her poor child's birth."

"Suka! That son of a..." Leif mutters, fighting to stay quiet. "Someone told me that coward stayed behind, keeping one of my best men with him. No doubt to protect his sorry hide!"

I won't tell him how Suka tried to kill us. It's pointless, and Leif might organize his own trip to Straumsfjord. "I do think Suka will leave her alone now, Leif. But it is unwise to let her go back. The babe's grave is in that forest, and it would only serve to cloud her thinking even further. She is already stealing my mushrooms."

"What?!" He roars in my face. "Wherever did she get that idea?"

I push his knee, hoping to quiet him. His eyes widen.

"Well, your old berserker, Bjarni, surely didn't help. Freydis admired that man like she did your father. You know she likes power."

His eyes close and he begins to sob. Leif's emotions are easy to understand, always in the open for all to see. I used to admire this about him. In contrast with Finn, though, I can see that the deepest feelings are in the quietest man.

He swipes at his eyes with his sleeve. "I've failed her. My father would know what to do."

"Your father is part of her problem." This stops his sobs. "He gave Freydis too much, and he didn't listen to Thjodhild when she told him to stop spoiling her. Now it's your turn to do what is right. Ref isn't brave enough to stand up to her."

"Yes, she can be a regular flaming devil, can't she?" Leif is proud again, for all the wrong reasons. He takes my hand, sending an unwanted charge through me. Deirdre picks Snorri up and moves closer behind us. "Things are so changed. Why do things have to change? I can't bear to lose my mother."

Leif needs to wake from his stupor. Life is full of change and loss. "At least you'll see her again in heaven," I say.

He looks doubtful. "Perhaps."

I push his hand off. "'Perhaps?' Don't you dare talk like that, Leif Eiriksson. You've believed in God, just as your mother and I have. You must have heard more of the Holy Writings than us, given your time in the king's court. And I believe Snorri Thorbrandsson is with the only true God even now."

Leif stands, towering over me. I fully expect him to slap me, given the intense look in his eyes. Stena walks over to the bed, pretending to check on Thjodhild.

Instead, Leif gives me an appreciative clap on the shoulder. "You don't know how much I needed you here. Gunna did nothing but speak against me, without reason. You only say what needs saying. I'll talk with Freydis, but don't hope for much. You know how stubborn she is."

He nods at Deirdre and Stena, then stomps out. I hadn't realized how much his presence filled the room, until it is empty of it.

"That man is like one of the white ice bears." Deirdre walks up beside me and puts her hand on my arm. "And you are the only one I've ever seen tame him."

Chapter Forty

Orange and red flames light the sky tonight, like streams from a volcano. The very sunset hints at the funeral fires, which are ready to be lit. I've decided that I can't go. I'm not sure where I *will* go, but I can't be at Brattahlid.

Because Snorri believed in Christ, I've helped Stena practice some words about God to say over him. There will be no chanting tonight. Finnbogi and Helgi have agreed to stay and sing Icelandic songs for the funeral.

Everything is prepared, even a small plot for the bones near Thjodhild's church yard. Thorstein and Eirik were also buried there.

Deirdre has agreed to stay with my children tonight. I wonder if she knows of Snorri Thorbrandsson's love for me, but she's never spoken of it.

Finn will lead the ceremony, not only as Snorri's best friend, but as his trading partner. All Snorri's wealth will pass to him tonight, making Finn the wealthiest man in all Greenland, and perhaps Iceland as well.

I take my lamp, walking up the path where I last saw Snorri. The woods breathe his name, reminding me of walks with my wolf in Straumsfjord. All too clearly, I remember the recent feel of his lips, desperate for my own. I had to reject him. But perhaps I was too harsh?

I close my eyes, and I can almost see him walking toward me, tight leather pants, bald head, rusty beard. I can feel his rough, square hand on my own. I hear him say *golden* as he touches my hair.

When my feet ache from walking, I find an uprooted tree and sit. I don't light the lamp, even in the dim twilight. The leaves have all fallen in Greenland, leaving nothing but limbs. Deadly limbs.

Trees surround every desolate event in my life—my mother's hanging, Freydis' childbirth, the fight with Suka, the search for my dead wolf. And now, Snorri's death.

I spent all my nights at Straumsfjord dreaming of Brattahlid and Leif. Yet I had to return to finally see things clearly. Leif was never meant to be my love, because he was never mine to enjoy. I always belonged to someone else, be it Thorir the Eastman, Thorstein the Red, or Thorfinn Karlsefni. And, for the short time I didn't belong to someone else, Leif did. Even though he doesn't love Gunna, they are married, and bound with vows. We aren't pagans anymore, free to take whomever we please and spread our love around.

And Snorri Thorbrandsson, my protector since childhood, is dead. I have always thought of him that way, as *my* Snorri. My possessiveness probably hindered him from considering Linnea. Will I feel guilty for his death until my own? Finn laid all the blame on Snorri, saying he had been reckless and thoughtless for loving me. He even blamed him for choosing the wrong horse that day. But Finn didn't realize how needy I was when he left me at

Straumsfjord, and how easily Snorri comforted me, like family.

Flames and smoke hang in the sky above Brattahlid, but the air around me is unusually crisp and fresh. This will be a new beginning. I must move forward. There is no use looking back at my constant weaknesses with men. Perhaps they will still watch me and wait for their chance with me, but I can't get close to them. Nor can I regret the days I spent at Straumsfjord, using all my energy to keep the camp healthy and protected, instead of playing with my child. Responsibilities fall heaviest on those willing to take the load. Snorri Thorbrandsson and I took it.

And here at Brattahlid, who will take the load? Who has the strength for it? Leif will probably lose his self-control quickly, with no wife and no wealth. Freydis plans to leave as soon as she can, to lose herself in another land. Thjodhild's life is short; I'm certain of it. So that leaves only Stena and me.

A loud, united whoop fills the air near the farm. Snorri's funeral is over. How long have I been here? I strike a flint stone against my seax to light the lamp wick. I don't fear walking home at night. It fits my mood, to be swallowed up by the darkness of the trees. There are no stars, but the moon is low and almost full. It will be light enough for me to see the path.

Footsteps approach—a large man. I grip my seax closer, backing into the brush. Leif comes into view. He raises a lamp, lighting his hair and face like the sun. "Gudrid?" He searches blindly for my face.

I step into the circle of my lamplight. "Here, you loud brute. What are you doing, wandering around the woods tonight?"

"I could ask you the same thing." He sits on the fallen tree, watching me expectantly until I sit next to him. "I understand why you couldn't stay, after the shock…but it was an honorable Christian funeral. I wanted to apologize for that stallion. Granted, I still can't figure why Snorri chose that fool animal. I was planning on selling it. Well, now it's dead."

"What happened to it?"

Leif looks at me strangely. "Don't you know? Your husband killed it. 'Curse you, beast!' is what he shouted, before running Snorri's sword through it. I have to say, Thorfinn has more…well, he's a fearsome man. I don't see many like him."

We sit in silence, listening to the night-birds. Peace seems to embrace us. The smell of smoke drifts toward us on the misty air, and moonlight filters through the tree limbs.

Words come to me from nowhere. "So many have died…so many who shouldn't have. Your brothers. Freydis' child. Snorri Thorbrandsson. Even your father. Eirik would have lived a fuller life than any of us."

Leif sighs like a dying animal. "And now my mother lies on her death-bed. My son is gone from me. Who can say if I'll ever see him again?"

Leif's self-centered emotions weary me tonight. "You will—if you follow them to the Hebrides," I say. "But you will *not* if you just sit here at Brattahlid, complaining about it."

"You advise me well." He slides closer, loosening chunks of bark from the dead tree. "I did talk to Freydis, like you wanted. I told her she couldn't have my ships. But she says she'll raise the funds and borrow someone else's ship.

Of course, no one in miles would loan her one, knowing I won't. But she will do it, eventually—you know her."

Too many things in Freydis' life have been explained away with those words, *But you know Freydis.* Leif is right when he says there's no way to stop her. And perhaps I am making a huge fuss over nothing. Maybe I wrongly suspect her, as I did with Vani's murder. If Freydis returns to the new world, she could search out her own treasure and grieve over her dead child.

We look at each other, both of us glowing in the lamplight. His smile turns into a mischievous smirk. "I guess I wasn't the only one who wanted to keep you for myself. I found you with Snorri Thorbrandsson that day, your hand in his."

I try not to give him the reaction he wants. "Snorri was like my brother. He has known me since I was a child in Iceland."

"Well, he never looked at you as a brother would." Leif continues prodding.

"No, and neither do you, Leif." I fix him with a steady gaze, daring him to defend himself.

He laughs. "You know, I've never met a woman like you, soft and hard at the same time. You're a healer and children love you; yet your words hit me like icicles sometimes."

"And so they should. Sometimes you need a good cooling off." But even as I laugh, I see that he watches my lips far too closely. I have done it again—drawn attention to myself when I didn't intend to.

His arm reaches out and I instantly pull away.

"What?" His voice is rough.

"Don't try anything with me tonight, Leif, or you will regret it. You've drunk far too much of your father's old wine today."

"Then we'll talk...I have something to say." He moves so close our legs touch. "I have loved you far too long. From the moment you left until the day you came back, I prayed for you. I dreamt of your hair and your face and your...it was like you were with me, on my bed. Do you know how long I've wanted you? Since I saw you on your father's wrecked ship, with that huge oaf of an Eastman by your side."

Not so long ago, I felt the same. I dreamed of the day I could be alone with this massive Viking, enjoying his light beard, his wrinkled brow, and his sideways smile. At one point, just the sight of his chest would have knocked the breath out of me.

Yet now I only want the familiar arms of my husband. I want to trace his tattoo, symbol of the ocean and the death of Thor. I want to feel his blue eyes on me, growing dark with desire. He fathered this babe, and he loves my children as he loves me.

I blush, thinking of Finn's gentleness. But Leif misunderstands and reaches to stroke my flaming cheek. Snorri Thorbrandsson warned me against being alone with Leif. In these woods with no one to interrupt, he's free to do something foolish. The sheer bulk of the man beside me heightens all my senses. I am like a twig next to him.

I stand, brushing off my skirts and trying to look calm. "I must get back. People will wonder where I am."

With one easy move, he pulls me gently onto his lap. "You're even lovelier when you're expecting, did you know that? Does your husband ever tell you things like that,

Gudrid? Has he mentioned your full hips and tiny waist can drive a man right out of his mind with lust? Or that your smile brings out the best in a man?"

"I'm seeing the worst right now." I grope for my seax. "Let me go, Leif. Right now."

He pins my arms with his own, leaning in toward my face. Suddenly, there is a knife between us, against his throat.

"My wife told you to let her go." Finn's deep, calm voice fills the air.

Leif shoves me forward. He leans back, grabbing his own knife.

"Go!" Finn shouts, and I run. I stumble along the path in the moonlight until I reach Brattahlid. In our empty house, I sink to the floor, exhausted. All night, I beg God for one thing: that He will let both men survive.

Chapter Forty-One

Morning finally comes, rays of light slanting into our upper window like any other day. Finn lies next to me on our bed. He isn't harmed and there's not a scratch on him. Finn, my true protector, who killed Vani by ripping his throat open.

But Leif has killed many men. What happened to Leif?

I stand, almost tripping over Hellir. All three boys sleep on the floor, Hol's arm draped over Snorri. Deirdre must have returned the boys late in the night.

A steady, persistent knocking on our door grows louder. I get up, dreading to see who is on the other side. Probably one of the slaves, come to tell me Leif's body was found in the path. Finn sleeps like a dead man.

I open the door, not to dreaded tidings, but to a miracle. Inger. Sunburned and filthy, she says nothing. I pull her inside and hold her. She finally asks for tea. I prepare the hot water over our fire and dig into my herb box for something to restore her.

"Where is Geisli?" I fear her answer. There have been so many deaths; it's all I expect now.

"Good...he is good. He's here." Her smile wavers. "But Bjarni isn't. And most of the men. And Nerienda..." She focuses on the fire, seeing something that isn't there. So Nerienda is gone from us, too.

Inger continues, her voice hoarse from days onboard the ship. "We couldn't get out of the Sea of Worms. The shipworms were destroying Leif's ship. There was only one escape boat, smeared with the whale blubber worms won't eat. Bjarni wanted to draw lots. Bjarni and I drew long straws, so we got into the escape boat. Nerienda drew a short straw, so she had to stay on the ship. She didn't care. She told me she was an old woman, and ready to meet her Maker."

Inger pauses, drinking the tea and watching the slow smolder of the fire. "Then Geisli drew a short straw. He told Bjarni he hadn't gone all the way to the new lands and back, only to die at the end. Bjarni asked him what he wanted to do about it."

She hugs her tattered cape closer. "Geisli suggested trading places. Bjarni thought about it for some time, then said, 'We might as well, since it seems you value life far more than I ever have.' So Geisli came with us. We rowed into Eiriksfjord late last night."

She takes a deep breath. "Gudrid, you wouldn't believe the things I saw on that ship. I thought our time at Straumsfjord was bad, but the men lived like animals. If not for Geisli, I would be with child even now."

I had feared as much. No women should have traveled to the new world in the first place. But Freydis and I had been so determined.

I look deep into her eyes, puffy from too much sun. "You need rest."

"I have already seen Deirdre. She wanted me to visit you first." Inger puts her hand on my arm. "I'll stay in their house for now."

"Of course." I let her finish her tea, then we walk back to Deirdre's. Magnus comes out stretching, preparing to go to the sheepcote.

As he passes by me, Magnus slows, sensing who I am. "Leif lives." His words are low and quiet, but they hit true, like one of Freydis' arrows.

I clutch my chest. Neither man was killed. How Magnus knew what was in my heart, I can't understand. His blindness is his strength.

"What's this about Leif?" Inger asks.

"It is nothing." I cannot say more, but Inger understands my need for silence.

Deirdre steps outside, promising to make sure Inger bathes and eats. I tell her I plan to watch Snorri today, so she doesn't have to worry about him.

Stena closes Thjodhild's door, joining us. "She still sleeps. I used all the meadowsweet yesterday, so she could go out to Snorri's funeral. She wanted to."

"We'll find more for her." I point to Inger as she stumbles into Deirdre's house. "Inger is also a healer. She will help once she has rested."

Stena nods, her dark eyes welling with tears. "It was a good funeral. But I am not ready for another one."

Affection for this compassionate woman fills me. I pat her arm. "Nor am I, sister. But together, we'll make Thjodhild's passing easy."

As Stena turns back to Thjodhild's house, I stand in the middle of the farm, wondering which way to turn. Left, to Leif's house, or right, and back to ours? Snorri's cries pierce the air. I go to my children, rousing the older boys with a light touch.

"Good morning," Hellir says. I hesitantly give him a light kiss on the cheek, which brings a fleeting smile to both boys' faces. They pull on clothing, then leave for the longhouse and sheepcote.

I change Snorri's clothes, then put him in bed next to Finn, hoping he'll go back to sleep. Instead, he flails around and wakes Finn by hitting him right in the face. Finn looks at me, curls tumbling over his half-opened blue eyes.

"What happened?" I ask.

"What? Oh, that." He shoves his hair aside. Snorri grabs at his father's fingers. "When Leif tried to pull his knife on me, I knocked it out of his hand and took him by the throat. He begged for mercy—said he was drunk, had been all day. That was nothing new to me. Men like him don't think before they act. That's how I knew where he was going after the funeral. He's drawn to you like…like a seal to water."

He yawns and lies back, strong arms above his head. Snorri slides off the bed and starts running around the house.

"So, that was it?" I hold my breath.

"Were you hoping we'd killed each other, woman?" He laughs. "When he started talking about how perfect you were, I sliced his cheek—not deep—just to scare some humility into him. He seemed shocked I actually drew blood. And to make my point, I told him he'd have none of my goods if he couldn't keep his eyes and hands off my wife. I think he'll leave you alone now."

I laugh, the first real laugh I've had in years. "Thorfinn Karlsefni, you're the only man I know who could make Leif Eiriksson shake in his big boots."

When we walk to the longhouse for our mid-morning meal, we go together. I place Snorri next to me at the table, and Finn sits on his other side. Leif stalks in, trying to look proud, but he covers his cheek with his hand and shoots hidden glances at Finn.

Inger isn't awake, but Geisli is. He sits at the other end of the table, the men circling him. Between his huge bites of food and his quick talking, no one can understand what he says. Bjarni did the right thing, letting this young leader take his place and live. Geisli and Inger are needed at Brattahlid.

Throughout the entire meal, Stena remains silent, her eyes shadowed. I know she misses her own children, tired of caring for her mother-in-law. I picture her little round-faced Gudrid, with her dark eyes and sweet ways. May God grant her peace, and not the sort of trials I have had. I want to be a good auntie to her, like Stena has been for my boys. Tonight, I will sit with Thjodhild to relieve Stena.

Freydis and Ref don't come to eat. Maybe they traveled with Finnbogi and Helgi back up the coastline today.

After a rich meal of mutton, peas, and milk, I take Snorri with me, hoping to find some eggs in the chicken house. But Freydis finds me first. Her hand shakes as she puts it on my arm, all her fingernails bitten down. She doesn't bring good news.

"Did Stena say anything to you?" Her words, like her movements, are abrupt.

"No, but I have a feeling you want to tell me something."

Her voice bounces like choppy waves. "I'm leaving— I've borrowed a ship. It's a small one, but it will do. I'm getting a crew together. Don't look at me that way. I will take some of Leif's slaves with me. They want freedom, just like Suka did. I am going to find him and pile my ship with grapevines and wood. Then I can come back and have my own farm, away from my drunk, unreasonable brother."

"You sail with Finnbogi and Helgi?" I ask.

"Oh, those two. Yes, I have to. It's their friend who loaned the ships, so we have to go together. Of course, they took the biggest ship. We're supposed to take equal numbers on the crews. I didn't want another mutiny, like Hallstein's, so I'm bringing a few extra men."

When she says *mutiny*, she sets her chin and her blue eyes turn icy. She is planning for one, then. After all, if she's willing to take Leif's slaves out from under his nose, what more is she capable of? Where is the Freydis who prowled behind huts to protect me from Hallstein's man? Where is the pregnant warrior who dropped from the trees, ready to risk two lives for ours? Where is the helpless girl I led like a lamb back to camp, after fighting Suka at the caves?

There is much I need to say to her. She is so lost. It's like her baby carved a hole into her soul when he was born. She can't believe God could love her and still take her child. But how many women in Iceland and Greenland have lost children—perfectly healthy children—to the hand of Thor? Yet now those women are ready to accept the love of the Christian God, because he offers healing...and perhaps because his son died, as well.

Snorri pulls on my hand. "Chickie, chickie!"

This is not the time or place to talk, because Freydis won't listen. I hug her, stroking her long red hair one more time. Who knows when I will see her again? Her blue eyes sparkle like her hair in the soft morning sun.

I manage a whisper. "I love you, sister. Come back soon."

Her lip turns downward as she struggles not to cry. Snorri tugs at me again, and Freydis pats his head, one rogue tear falling on his curls. Her wet eyes barely meet mine before she turns and runs to the horses.

If she tries to steal more mushrooms, she won't find them. I have burned the rest. Bjarni doesn't need them anymore.

The gold and blue light of day slowly turns to night, and at our evening meal, everyone speaks at once. Freydis and Ref have gone, taking half the slaves. News has it that Finnbogi and Helgi have borrowed ships to sail to Vinland. Leif shouts and rants like a child. But when Linnea joins us at the table, he crosses his arms and sulks quietly.

This day is a turning point for us. I must stay here, with my family, and help Thjodhild to the end. It is my duty as Thorstein's wife; Eirik's daughter. But after that, God can raise up another woman to run the farm, even though I have always felt I'd be the next matriarch of Brattahlid.

Leif won't understand this. He will stay at Brattahlid for the rest of his life. He hoped I would, too.

But there is a tree, on a hill in Iceland, that beckons to me endlessly. I have felt its pull my whole life, even when I traveled across the ocean. I can't escape it. Even now, I can almost see a young, carrot-haired boy standing under it, watching me, waiting for me to say goodbye. I will live to tell my children about this tree and its story.

And here ends this saga.

AUTHOR'S NOTE

I'll never pretend to be an expert on Viking history. However, I have spent quite a lot of time poring over *The Sagas of Icelanders,* and that's what I've based *God's Daughter* upon. I operated on the assumption that the sagas were not mere fairy tales, since archeology and dendrology consistently line up to support the truth in the Viking stories.

I also operated under the assumption that the climate was different in AD 1000. *Global warming* wasn't a theory then—it was a reality, and it allowed the Vikings to settle in Greenland in the first place. In fact, global cooling is why they had to leave, around AD 1350.

Thus, we find self-sown wheat in Vinland (North America), long before regular history books tell us it was there. But the Vikings saw it, and took some with them. The warmer climate would also explain the grapes they found, as well as a nine-day ship's journey from Greenland to the North American coastline.

I've also changed the names of many of the lesser characters in this story, due to confusion over all the recorded *Thor* names. You will notice I did keep the two Snorris. I felt this was significant—Finn and Gudrid named their child the same name as Finn's business partner. And baby Snorri was the first European baby to be born in the new world. I also kept Eirik the Red's sons' names—Leif, Thorvald, and Thorstein. This is purely sentimental, since I'm supposedly related to Thorvald Eiriksson. The central women—Gudrid, Freydis, and Thjodhild, also kept their names.

In the sagas, characters and timelines overlap strangely, so I melded the facts in a way that seemed logical to me. But if you study them, you will see that the bare bones of this story are there. Gudrid was lovely and kind and wise. She was also a Christian, in a time when pagan volva ruled Iceland and Greenland. The pagan rituals (hanging, exposure of babies, eating horse meat, the Prophetess' ceremony) have also been documented.

As far as the map, experts don't agree on where Vinland was located. I placed it south of Straumsfjord (which was also an educated guess), since according to the sagas, Thorfinn went south and Hallstein (Thorhall) went north to find it. Hopefully, it helps you picture what I envisioned as I wrote this novel. I also have a glossary of Norse terms used in *God's Daughter* here: http://heatherdaygilbert.com/gods-daughter-glossary/.

To lend authenticity to the writing, I researched nouns, adjectives, and adverbs that would've been used around that time. I frequently consulted the Old Norse dictionary. However, I did insert occasional words that may have developed later—only because I assumed Vikings would have had similar descriptors we aren't aware of. That's the same reason I incorporated contractions. I'm sure they shortened things as they spoke, just as we do today.

I would love it if you, too, got the Viking "bug" and did further reading on the subject. To that end, I'm happy to share my list of resources I consulted every step of the way.

The Sagas of Icelanders, forward by Jane Smiley, Penguin Classics, 1997. Particularly, I used the chapters *Eirik the Red's Saga* and *The Saga of the Greenlanders.*

Http://www.vikinganswerlady.com. This resource was critical to me, for immediate answers on foods, customs and clothing of Vikings.

The Far Traveler, by Nancy Marie Brown, Harcourt Books, 2007. Nonfiction story of Gudrid.

An Illustrated Viking Voyage, by W. Hodding Carter, Pocket Books/Simon & Schuster, 2000. Photos of a Viking knarr.

English-Old Norse Dictionary, compiled by Ross G. Arthur, In Parentheses Publications, Linguistics Series, 2002. (http://www.yorku.ca/inpar/language/English-Old_Norse.pdf) Online resource to which I constantly referred, to keep my wording authentic to the period.

The Vikings, forward by Magnus Magnusson, Osprey Publishing, 2006.

Viking, by Susan M. Margeson, DK Publishing, 1994. Great visuals.

Norse Mythology, by John Lindow, Oxford University Press, 2001.

Women in Old Norse Society, by Jenny Jochens, Cornell University Press, 1995.

And one of my favorite films, *Vikings: Journey to new Worlds,* by Sky High Entertainment. I've watched it several times, and it just never gets old.

Finally, I want to thank anyone who's helped with *God's Daughter.* My husband, who believed in this novel, even though he'd never read it. Thanks for picking up countless last-minute frozen meals and groceries for us, and for listening to my writerly rants.

And more thanks...to my family, for putting up with my erratic writing hours. The agent/editor I had for this novel, Andy Scheer, who believed it had great potential, and who also informed me that sweet potatoes would *not* be part of a Viking meal circa AD 1000 (what was I thinking!?). My *Married...with Fiction* cohorts—Jennifer Major and Becky Doughty—you were there for me through the unpredictable highs and lows of getting this (and all my novels) published.

Thanks always to my parents, Stan and Betty Day, and my second parents, Ed and Jane Gilbert, and siblings on both sides who never let me give up. My brothers—Jon, who designed my cover, and Stefan, who provided all kinds of techie support. Grandparents who have supported me in my writing dreams—in particular, Grandma Wilcox, Grandma Day, and Grandma Gilbert. My great-Aunt Jenny Lee, a writer through and through, who is one of the best storytellers I know.

Thank you to my special friends who are always willing to pray for me as I hit writerly hurdles and who've anxiously awaited my first published novel—I have four in particular (you know who you are!) but I could list pages of loving friends who've prayed me through things. One of my earliest supporters, Diane Austin, who begged to read my first completed novel and helped me find my first agent. My historical crit group—I wasn't in it long, but it shaped this story. My blog and FB author page followers, who've cheered me every step of the way. My current agent, Ruth Samsel, a tireless advocate for my writing, who encouraged me to go ahead and self-publish *God's Daughter*. My formatting/critique partner guru, Becky Doughty, who helped me polish this story and manuscript, not to mention made sure the right emotional tones shone through my words. Much love to every one of you.

And the One true I AM, Who was, and is, and is to come. Thank you for bringing Gudrid into my life. She didn't have much moral support in her Christianity, yet she went down in history for her integrity and wisdom. Someday I hope I'll meet her, in the same heaven she had hope of.

CONTACT THE AUTHOR

I would love to hear your thoughts on Gudrid and the Vikings in *God's Daughter*. You can find me all over the web. Here are the links:

Blog: http://www.heatherdaygilbert.com
E-mail: heatherdaygilbert@gmail.com
Facebook author page:
https://www.facebook.com/heatherdaygilbert
Pinterest:
http://pinterest.com/heatherdgilbert/boards/
Twitter: https://twitter.com/heatherdgilbert
YouTube:
https://www.youtube.com/heatherdaygilbert

ABOUT THE AUTHOR:

Heather Day Gilbert writes character-driven novels that go beyond the vows, capturing the triumphs and heartaches unique to married couples. Both she and her husband graduated from Bob Jones University, and she's a staunch supporter of homeschooling, having taught her own children for ten years. Born and raised in the West Virginia mountains, she believes that bittersweet, generational stories are in her blood.

Made in the USA
Charleston, SC
26 December 2013